G000254826

Best Wishes

Carol M Creasey

2024,

NOBODY'S PERFECT

Also by Carol M. Creasey:

Biography:
My Life is Worth Living!
Candidly Carol

Fiction:
Fatal Obsession
Not Just an Affair
Evil Woman
Evil Woman...Takes Revenge
The Power of Love
One Moment of Madness

Nobody's Perfect

Carol M. Creasey

UNITED WRITERS
Cornwall

UNITED WRITERS PUBLICATIONS LTD
Ailsa, Castle Gate, Penzance, Cornwall.
www.unitedwriters.co.uk

British Library Cataloguing in Publication Data:
A catalogue record for this book is
available from the British Library.

ISBN 9781852001988

Printed and bound in Great Britain by
United Writers Publications Ltd.,
Cornwall.

To my dear friend Debs,
thanks for everything.
Also Genevieve for
your continued support.

Chapter One

"Eleanor, I need to freshen your make-up before you go on," said Lyn Cartwright, observing the slight shine on the otherwise perfect nose which Eleanor possessed. It was turned up and in proportion to the rest of her face. Her small features were doll-like; a perfect mouth, and eyes so turquoise blue and large that they gave her an air of innocence. Her skin was like delicate porcelain, with only a very slight tan, and her golden hair was worn in a mass of curls which reached to her shoulders and bounced enthusiastically when she walked.

Lyn had been her make-up artist for many years now, ever since the golden haired little girl of eight had been put into show business by her ambitious mother. Although still only thirty-five, and looking much younger than that, Eleanor's journey had been a long one. She had been an actress now for twenty-seven years, and a very good one. She was adored by the public and always in demand.

Putting make-up on Eleanor had never been a chore for Lyn. With such a natural beauty, and expressive eyes, she always looked fabulous. Her skin was still as perfect as it had been when she was a teenager, in contrast to some of the other older actresses who had resisted having Botox or any cosmetic surgery but still expected Lyn to achieve a miracle.

Eleanor smiled, revealing her very white teeth. To Lyn's knowledge it was natural, she had not had them whitened. A slight feeling of jealousy coursed through her, which she squashed down guiltily. At the age of fifty now, with greying hair,

7

and carrying more weight than she should, Lyn wished she could look like that, but she had never been a beauty. She knew how to make the best of herself with make-up, and she could always colour her hair, but she could never look like Eleanor.

She felt ashamed of herself for feeling this way. She had a devoted husband George, and they had two beautiful children, now grown up, who had provided her with lovely grandchildren.

In contrast to that, Eleanor was divorced and alone. Whether it was her choice or not, no one really knew. Her private life was kept very private. She hadn't even announced the break up of her marriage. But, of course, the newspapers had got hold of it when her ex-husband Alfie had been spotted with another woman, and so Eleanor had been forced to announce that they were now divorced. Whether she was upset was difficult to tell, as she said it with a smile on her face, and never mentioned it again; not even when a few months later the new couple had a baby son. Being an actress, Eleanor was used to playing a part and hiding her emotions. It was then that Lyn realised, even though she had known her for twenty-seven years, she didn't really know her at all, as Eleanor was well versed in playing a role.

Lyn hastily applied a light touch of lipstick and finished off with a dust of powder. It would be unthinkable for Eleanor to go on stage with a shiny nose. There was a knock at the door, and a voice called:

"On stage for act two, Miss Harrison."

Eleanor jumped up from the chair and opened the dressing room door, and her face broke out again into the smile that all her fans loved, and one which could melt the stoniest of hearts.

"Thanks Joe, I am ready," she said, gathering up the skirt of the crinoline she was wearing for this period production and following after him, but not before she had turned towards Lyn and thanked her. Lyn watched her go, and she wondered for the umpteenth time why Eleanor's marriage hadn't worked out. Eleanor was the most loved and talked about actress that ever graced the stage. Her beauty was not in doubt, her charisma was clear for all to see, and yet she was alone. He must have been mad to leave her, because from what Lyn could see, Eleanor didn't have a mean bone in her body.

Not that Eleanor complained about being alone. She had a smile and a kind word for everyone, and as she didn't share that much about her private life, maybe she was dating but wanted to keep him a secret and see where it all went. Lyn could only guess, and her naturally curious nature found the whole thing intriguing.

Eleanor was enjoying the swish that her crinoline made as she walked; it was great for theatre, but she was thankful she hadn't been born in those times. Not only were women considered only suited to sitting around doing crochet and sipping tea, unless of course they were a poor girl in service, but with those sort of voluminous skirts and tight bodices, women must have been really restricted. She was glad she could strut her stuff on stage, playing lady of the manor, and enjoy the escapism that acting allowed her.

Ever since she was a small child, her mother had set sights on Eleanor achieving what she had failed to. Jean Harris had been a model. She had an hourglass figure, with long slim legs, and her hair had been worn in a pageboy style, as was in keeping at the time, and she had experimented with different hair colours, finally becoming blonde. But Jean lacked the charisma that Eleanor had, and when her modelling days were over, she had to settle for working as a saleswoman in a high class department store. It helped to pay the bills, and she managed to persuade her long suffering husband Richard, that they should send their beautiful and talented Eleanor to drama lessons.

Richard knew his wife was a strong woman, with her own mind, and he was also aware that Eleanor would flourish in an artistic environment. Her face was obviously going to be her fortune. She loved to perform, and being the centre of attention really pleased her. So between them they scrimped and scraped to give her the best chance. She had drama classes, and at the tender age of eight, Eleanor had a part in a film playing a child who ran away from home when her father dies suddenly, and although she was not the main star, the performance she gave captured many hearts. She seemed to know how much emotion to portray to win her audience, and she became the youngest supporting actress to win an award ever. Jean didn't think the surname Harris sounded quite right, so she became Eleanor Harrison, which had a much better ring to it.

But so much had happened in the last twenty-seven years. Eleanor had been devastated when her father Richard had died prematurely of a massive stroke when she was only ten years old.

9

Two years later, Jean had remarried, and it was a time that Eleanor had strived to banish from her mind. She had not got on with her new stepfather, and as soon as she was able to, she had left home and for a while lived with her elder sister Isabel, and Isabel's husband Sam. When she was seventeen, she left her sister's to share a flat with another actress friend. She had left school by then and, unlike some other actresses, the work kept coming in. She played a teenager in a family soap, and the public watched her growing up before their eyes. She was a typical English rose, with a ready smile, and an empathy that shone out of her.

It was well documented that she supported many charities, and had been to Africa to visit underprivileged children. Seeing Eleanor with tears in her eyes, hugging disadvantaged tots, and begging for financial help in providing them with basic requirements such as clean water, made such a difference. The money came pouring in, as having watched her blossom from eight years old to a caring young woman, Eleanor had now become a National Treasure.

As she took her curtain call at the end of the performance, the smile fixed on her face, hiding the feeling of weariness which would soon envelop her when she was away from the bright lights, she saw him. He was sitting in the middle of the front row, leaning forward, and then he stood up to give her a standing ovation, and others then copied him.

A standing ovation was a compliment, it meant the performance had been exceptional, and as she took her bow with her male stage partner, she made sure she didn't meet the man's eyes. He was obsessive, his behaviour showed this, and she had no wish to encourage him. He was always at the stage door and she had posed for endless selfies with him, always trying to keep that smile on her face no matter how she felt inside; she never let that mask slip. But she no longer went home by tube, as he had stalked her, and then given her love notes. Such was the force of his obsession that she had found it a bit frightening.

It was part of her job, the facade she showed to the public, and people really believed that smile she showed to everyone meant that all was well. If only they knew about all her insecurities. Her life had been a troubled one, and still was, but the public had taken her to their hearts since she was eight years old in such a way that they well might forgive her anything, but she wasn't about to test that, her private life was exactly that.

Back in her dressing room, it was a relief to Eleanor to finally rid herself of the cumbersome skirts and tight bodice. It had been hot under the lights of the theatre, and she couldn't wait to get home and take a shower.

It would have been easier to go out of another exit, to avoid the man with the piercing eyes, but she would still have to walk round to the back street where the stage door was, as her taxi was waiting there.

She had told Lyn not to worry about helping her to remove her heavy make-up, so her dressing room was empty. She cleaned her face, and then added just a light touch of lipstick, thankful that her skin was youthful enough not to need foundation and bright eye make-up.

When she exited the stage door there was a crowd of fans. Some women were clearly there to see her co-star, Greg. He was a heart-throb with his dark sleek hair and limpid brown eyes, and most actresses would have died to be his co-star. Eleanor was paired with him in many productions, but she had seen a vain and arrogant side to him off stage, so although she might act on stage as though she adored him, and the chemistry between them was clear for all to see, privately Greg had not managed to touch her heart, and she thought he was rather shallow.

When she spotted the lady in the wheelchair, she was glad she had come out, even though she was aware of the man with the penetrating stare. He was clicking away with his phone; even the amount of pictures he took was obsessive.

Eleanor went to the wheelchair lady first; there was another lady pushing it, and both their faces broke into a smile when they saw Eleanor approaching them. Inside Eleanor was sad for her, she was thin and pale, and her hair was very sparse, and she had clearly been very ill. Her companion broke enthusiastically into conversation.

"Miss Harrison, your performance was incredible, you touched our hearts. Could you oblige us with a photo for Janet, she's your biggest fan?"

"You don't need to speak for me Alice, but she's right, I have followed your career ever since you were in Family Ties."

"Of course, with pleasure, and I am so glad you liked the

production," smiled Eleanor, pleased to see that although Janet looked frail, she still had spirit. She felt a great rush of empathy towards her. To be confined to a wheelchair, unable to have your independence, must be the worst fate ever. She had met many poor souls with illnesses and difficulties who were brought to meet her at the stage door, and knowing that her performance gave them pleasure felt uplifting. It made Eleanor grateful for her own good health.

She posed for pictures with both of them, and avoiding Mr Obsessive for as long as she could, worked her way through the throng of fans who wanted selfies and signed programmes, and a few words with their favourite actress. She could see the taxi waiting out of the corner of her eye, but she didn't want to disappoint anyone, so she would just have to pay him extra waiting time.

Mr Obsessive didn't mind being last, as he could study his idol from all directions. Peter Grant lived his life and existed solely for this woman. He had always been a loner at school, without many friends but with obsessions which ruled his life. He was extremely intelligent, with an Oxford degree, but totally lacked social skills. He could write letters, pouring out beautiful heartfelt sentiments, and he had sent some to her, but in reality, when this beautiful goddess was standing right in front of him, all he could really do was marvel at her beauty.

He was unaware that she was giving off signals of not wanting to get involved with him. His obsession with her was so powerful it was in total control of him. His lonely flat had pictures of her everywhere, every wall of every room had her beautiful eyes gazing across the room. She was so much a part of his life, and had been for the last twenty years when, as a boy of sixteen, he had fallen under her spell.

"Thank you, I have to get in my taxi now," she said firmly after he had taken several selfies.

He nodded, and reluctantly put his phone back in his pocket. He could have happily stayed next to her for the rest of his life; after all she was his life.

Eleanor was relieved to get away from him. He made her feel stifled. He didn't actually do anything wrong, so she could not report him to the police, but she could sense he was more than just a fan. He never really spoke, but was always taking pictures of her, and those love letters, how on earth had he known where she lived? She had always kept her private life just that, but one or two members of the press also knew it now, and these people were such a nuisance, often camping outside her flat, thrusting cameras into her face, especially if she was all dressed up for an awards ceremony or a gala evening.

Peter was hoping his time with her would never come to an end. He had never had a girlfriend. He was aware he was different from other people, he didn't fit in. His parents had separated when he was very young, and the only person who really accepted him as he was, was his mother. His Oxford Degree had led to a job in a computer company; what he didn't know about computers wasn't worth knowing. He had worked hard because it was something that really interested him, and he now did most of his work from home, occasionally checking into the head office in London when required.

When Peter's mother had died from a terminal brain tumour, inside he felt dead. He couldn't cry, he had never been able to, it was an emotion he didn't understand, but the void she had left in his life was something so deep inside, and he had no one to share it with. His cousin Colin had accused him of being heartless when he found him looking up details about brain tumours. Just because he didn't weep and wail at the funeral like his female cousins, that didn't mean he was uncaring, but he just had to know the details of the vile illness that had robbed him of the one person who had accepted him as he was.

There was something about Eleanor that reminded Peter of his mother; her big eyes and doll-like face resembled a photograph of his mother he kept at home, taken when he was a very small boy.

His mother had been a beauty, but had chosen to spend her life bringing him up, resisting all attempts from her sisters to join a club and find a new partner. They had accused her of spoiling Peter and denying herself a proper life, but Mary Grant had stood firm; her son was her life, he was misunderstood by so many but she accepted him as he was, and chose to have him to live with her after he came home from university. Her ex-husband had not understood his own son, nor bothered to stay in contact with him, so why should she trust another man to enter her life? It was best just to stay as they were.

Eleanor was thankful to get finally into the taxi and be taken home. She kept a smile on her face whilst the driver chatted on merrily. He was her regular driver now. She had given him her autograph for his teenage daughter, who apparently wanted to be an actress and felt it was very cool that her father was now Eleanor Harrison's regular driver.

"There you go, Miss Harrison, I'll walk you to the door."

"No need, I am fine, you can call me Eleanor." She smiled, then opened her purse and enquired how much it was.

"Oh, £10 to you."

"Thanks so much, Max," she said, handing him a twenty pound note, and waving away his efforts to give her change. He watched her climb the steps to the main door of the very exclusive apartments. She was such an independent young woman, but with her baby face and big eyes, as well as not being that tall, it aroused all his protective instincts. It was true she had a secure entry system to her home, but she lived alone, which was surprising for a looker like her. If she had any men friends she kept them quiet, as none of the newspapers had managed to reveal much of her private life.

Eleanor let herself in, walked across the hallway, and then opened the door to her apartment. The smell of furniture polish greeted her, and all the furniture was shining, just as she liked it. Her cleaner had been in earlier and, knowing how fussy Eleanor was, she had made sure that the smell and the look of the place would please Eleanor when she got home. There were extra little touches, such as a vase of daffodils, some After Eight mints beside her dinner plate, and the aroma coming from a slow cooker of a beef dish cooked in red wine. In the fridge was a bottle of Chardonnay, nicely chilled. Eleanor didn't just need a cleaner, she needed a housekeeper, and Faith Brian was just that.

She served Eleanor well, and she was loyal. On the occasions that she did see Eleanor, she had learned, just like a dog does, to accept whatever mood she was in and weather it. She was well paid for what she did. Others had left before her, but Faith had an easy going nature and liked the idea of working for such a well known celebrity.

Faith had gone home about an hour earlier, realising all the fans had made Eleanor later than usual, and right now Eleanor was thankful to slip her shoes off and sit down. With all the money she earned, she could afford to have food sent to the house, but Eleanor didn't want delivery men coming to her door and spoiling her peace. And, anyway, Faith was there to pander to all her whims. She was perfectly happy with that situation.

Eleven o'clock at night was late to eat, but the aroma of the meal attracted her, which is exactly what Faith had intended. Sometimes when she was late she had left a salad untouched, and of course there was always her figure to worry about, but Faith was like an older sister, she might be tiny, and slim, with mousy brown hair and a quiet manner, but she was never backward in coming forward in reminding Eleanor that she needed to eat. And Eleanor didn't mind that she seemed to care, it reminded her of her own mother, before 'he' had come along and wrecked their relationship.

She poured herself a glass of wine, and served out a plateful of the beef and red wine. As well as mixed vegetables, it had mushrooms and diced potato, and as the meal slipped down and warmed her inside, Eleanor felt peaceful and relaxed.

She had by now switched off her mobile. She could see the landline flashing which meant there were messages, but she could always leave them until tomorrow. Curiosity got the better of her, so she refilled her glass, and picked up the handset and switched on the loudspeaker.

First came the voice of Alfie, her ex-husband, reminding her she still owed him half for all the furniture that she had 'stolen' from him when they had parted. His voice had gradually become pleading, as he reminded her that she was comfortably off, whereas he had to start again, and now he had a child to support. She angrily clicked off the message; let him suffer, she didn't care, not after he had walked out on her! The man who had been the love of her life, or so she believed, had been unfaithful, and with plain dumpy Angela, which had somehow made it all seem worse.

The next message was from her sister Isabel. It had been a special day for Isabel's daughter Amy; in the afternoon she had performed a violin recital, and Eleanor suddenly remembered she had promised to go, but then forgotten all about it. But Isabel wasn't mincing her words as she berated her for being selfish and uncaring and, of course, she reminded her, Amy was devastated.

"Emotional blackmail as always!" she said angrily to the silent flat. Could nobody ring up and be nice to her! She finished off the

15

rest of the wine. With a full stomach, she was now feeling sleepy. What did she care about them and their sad telephone messages? Her public loved her, she was a rich woman with a great career, and her miserable and uncaring family could go to hell!

She ignored the little voice inside her, which seemed intent on reminding her that she still loved her errant ex-husband, and she wanted to punish him. As for her sister, Isabel had never forgiven her for having the looks and talent in the family, and Amy wasn't her responsibility, her choice had been not to have children, whereas Isabel had always been mother earth.

She left her glass and plate in the lounge for Faith to deal with the next day. Once in bed, she put everything negative out of her mind; no sleeping pills needed tonight, and she was asleep as soon as her head touched the pillow.

Chapter Two

Alan Clarke had been in the police force ever since he had left school. First as a training cadet, but now, at the age of twenty-seven, he was DCI Clarke, which sounded OK to him. He was ambitious, a man of action, always very athletic at school, and his desire to do a job that stretched him to the limit, coupled with wanting to protect people from unsavoury types and bring them to justice, was his driving force. His promotion to detective chief inspector, although still quite young, came off the back of a drugs ring he had bust. The culprits were now safely locked up, and the girls who had been controlled by them, and forced into prostitution, were now getting help and support. He really hoped they could turn their lives around; some as young as fourteen had been lured into the evil web from which there appeared to be no escape. But Alan and his team had blown the whole operation apart, and that gang would be inside for a very long time. He still felt a little glow of satisfaction when he thought about it.

Alan had a girlfriend called Zoe. They had been dating for about two years, she still lived with her parents, but he was not in a rush to settle down right now anyway. He was a catch for any woman, with his well toned lean body, hazel eyes and brown hair. His eyes could look kind and sympathetic, but equally they could flash with anger and passion when he had a job to do. He knew how to control his temper with the most arrogant and provocative of prisoners, but his eyes and expressions spoke for him. He could also display empathy when dealing with anyone in a distressed state.

He had come into work this Tuesday at midday, thinking that he would be investigating the disappearance of a sixteen-year-old girl who was causing her parents much distress, and today they were going to do a plea on national television for her safe return. But as soon as the call was put through to him from the switchboard, he knew he would have to pass that over to someone else.

"Sorry to spring this on you, Alan, but a woman named Faith Brian has rung us in deep distress. Apparently she is the housekeeper of Eleanor Harrison, the actress, do you know her? She arrived at her apartment, only to find her dead."

"Dead!" echoed Alan disbelievingly. Everyone knew who Eleanor Harrison was. He was thinking that surely death cannot strike a national treasure who is so young. But then his professional side took over.

"How did she die?" He hoped it wasn't drugs or alcohol; his vision of her was as a clean living and very lovely woman. The Holly Willoughby of the acting world.

"Well, she didn't really say, she just found the body on the floor in the lounge."

"We need to get over there, forensics need to go too, and I will need Sarah with me, no matter what she is doing. We have a family to inform, and that is never easy. Please arrange someone else to cover the missing girl case and support her family today."

Isabel Phillips was banging away in her kitchen, still feeling angry and upset about Eleanor's snub the day before. It felt like a snub to her, anyway. She was so proud of Amy, she was such a talented violinist, and Eleanor, selfish as always, couldn't even bother to come to her recital. She had seen Amy's face light up when she told her about Eleanor coming. With an aunt who was so talented herself, Amy's ability to play the violin was further proof of talent within the family.

Why oh why did she still get upset when Eleanor let them down? Surely she should have learned by now just how self absorbed her sister was? She had prided herself on being mature; at eight years older than Eleanor, she had always felt responsible for her. She had felt no jealousy when her mother championed Eleanor's talent. Isabel, although reasonably attractive, did not share her sister's stunning looks. They didn't even look like sisters, as her hair was mid brown and straight, and her blue eyes were not as large and expressive as Eleanor's.

Isabel didn't have a flair for the arts either. She couldn't dance or sing, and lacked imagination, so had never aspired to be an actress. Instead she had graduated with honours from university and followed a career in law, setting up her own practice with Sam, whom she had met and fallen in love with at university. Their marriage had survived for nineteen years. Sam was still the love of her life, and she couldn't imagine her life without him. Together they had made their money in a different way to Eleanor, but they were all very comfortably off in their own right.

Isabel had stepped up when Eleanor had left home at just fourteen years of age; there was no way she could turn her back on her, and Eleanor had shared their home until she was seventeen. It had been a relief then to let her leave and share a flat with a friend. Isabel had weathered her sister's frequently changing moods, but had trusted and believed her when she had learned her secret.

But it had caused a huge rift with their mother that could never be repaired. Their mother Jean had put her husband Dan above them all, and when he left her some years later, it had broken her. She had a nervous breakdown from which she had never properly recovered. To add to her problems, although now only in her mid sixties, she had developed dementia, and was in a care home. Isabel had attempted to visit her, but Jean didn't appear to know her, and she lived in the past, insisting that Dan would be home soon, and Eleanor would one day become a great actress.

Isabel didn't blame her mother for forgetting her own achievements, that would be just too childish, and she frequently berated Eleanor for not visiting her mother, reminding her how hard her mother had pushed to get her drama lessons. Without her strong mother, would she have had the same success, who knows?

Eleanor had said all the right things; she would go soon when she wasn't so busy, but once again, even though she loved her sister, Isabel didn't believe her, but she tried to forgive her. She had forgiven her for so many things all her life.

She sighed to herself, and wondered if her sister's selfishness was in any way her fault, as she had always defended and stood by her. As usual, her anger was gradually subsiding, life was just too short. Eleanor was just Eleanor, and for all her faults, there was a lot of good in her too. Her generous sister supported many charities, and spent time with her fans, saying she would never forget the people who paid good money to come and see her, nor forget it was their support that helped her to be so successful.

Eleanor had also spent money on Amy, paying for and encouraging her violin lessons. She had insisted on, and she was also paying for her driving lessons. When she was in a generous and giving mood, she just wouldn't take no for an answer, but Sam had insisted that they would buy Amy her first car when she passed her test, and not Eleanor.

Isabel had always felt a bit caught up between the two of them, and sometimes felt that Sam was a bit jealous when Eleanor treated Amy to something new. She had worked hard to keep the family peace, as she felt blood ties were so important. Amy had always admired and respected her famous aunt, and like her was interested in the arts, so could relate as to why Eleanor got such a buzz out of performing. She shared her aunt's beauty too, and thick curly hair, although at eighteen had now changed its ordinary brown colour to a reddish auburn, which really suited her. Her build was slim, but she had the long legs of her father, whereas both Eleanor and Isabel were not so tall. Isabel was incredibly proud of Amy. Her only regret was that Amy had no siblings, as she would have loved to have given her a brother or sister. But the years had passed, and so she had just done her best not to spoil Amy because she was an only child.

Sam would have given his daughter the moon if he could, and there was certainly no shortage of money, but he fell in with Isabel's wishes not to allow Amy to have everything she wanted on a plate, and they were both content to see that she was growing up to be a daughter to be proud of, with all the right principles in life. She had so far not been a troublesome teenager, and threw herself into her music, and was never happier than when she was doing a recital.

When she wasn't at work, Isabel was more than content to be an old fashioned housewife, making cakes and pastries which Sam enjoyed eating. He was naturally tall, built like a greyhound, and not prone to putting on weight. At forty-two, he was a very handsome man with dark wavy hair and very expressive grey eyes.

Isabel had never thought of herself as a beauty, and after all these years together, she marvelled that this Adonis was her husband. But maybe the reason they had stayed together was her patient and forgiving nature. Together they shared a very powerful secret, which even Amy had no idea about, it was a secret that could have broken them forever, but Isabel had chosen to accept the inevitable, and it had strengthened, rather than loosened, the bond between them even more.

Cooking felt very therapeutic to Isabel. Never mind all this fast food, she loved to feel she was pleasing Sam, so she put all her energy into mixing up an apple and sultana cake which was a favourite of his. It was maybe for the reason that she always sampled her own cooking, that Isabel, not being very tall, was plump as well as curvy. When she was young she had been as slim as her sister, but her rounded hips, and the thickness around her waist as she had now, was because of her sweet tooth and liking for cakes. Sam seemed to like her that way, he said there was more of her to cuddle, so she saw no reason to change her lifestyle.

She heard the doorbell go as she was lifting the cake out of the oven, and smiled to herself. That would be Eleanor, apologising for messing up yesterday, and wanting to take them out to make it up to Amy. No one knew Eleanor like she did; first she messed up, and then she tried to make up. She knew her sister was not a bad person, just an unreliable one, but then nobody's perfect.

Sam appeared at the door flanked by a policeman and a WPC, his grey eyes were full of concern.

"The police are here to see us Isabel," he said, and she gazed wondering why they were there, and when she saw their serious expressions, she felt the cold hand of fear clutching at her, and instinctively she knew that something was very seriously wrong.

Alfie Mason was fed up, he hadn't meant to sound pleading last night when he had telephoned Eleanor. For five years he had been married to her; five years too long. He had put up with her tears and tantrums, she was so incredibly self centred, until one day he snapped, and walked out. Of course, that was the worst thing he could have done. She had the apartment, and all the furniture, he had nothing except the clothes on his back, but at least he was free of his demanding and unpredictable wife.

At thirty years old he had started a new life with Angela, who was now his wife and the mother of his new son. She might not have the beauty and vivaciousness of Eleanor, but she was supportive and calm to be with, and she had provided him with a son. Eleanor had never wanted children. Children would have cramped her style, he thought viciously. Eleanor might be adored by the public, their golden girl, but he knew the real Eleanor, and she had proved impossible for him to live with.

In the beginning he, too, had fallen under her spell. He was a fervent fan, seeing every one of her films, and then her theatrical productions. The day she came out to greet her fans when she was at The Adelphi Theatre was his first meeting with her. Alfie had been immediately smitten. It probably helped that he looked like a Greek god, with his steely blue eyes and well tanned torso. His blond hair glinted in the sun, and when she smiled at him, he melted inside. But marriage had disillusioned him, it was all an act, and sometimes he wondered if she actually needed some sort of medical treatment, as she was a woman with many faces.

Obviously she was a rich young woman, and no expense had been spared at their wedding. Her wealth had also been an attraction, as Alfie was frequently in and out of jobs, and Eleanor had so much money she didn't much care about it.

He regretted his rash decision in moving out, as he had no claim on anything, but being free of her and having his new life with Angela was worth it. Angela couldn't work at all right now because of junior, and his income only stretched to a very modest flat. Half of the value of the very expensive furniture Eleanor and he had chosen together would have helped tremendously, but it wasn't to be.

Honestly, last night he had felt such hatred towards her, the force of his anger even surprised him, and he felt like he wanted to kill her, to squeeze her neck as hard as he could, silence her forever.

This morning he felt nervous and jumpy, so when his office door opened, to admit a police officer and a young WPC, it was a shock. There could be many reasons why they had come to see him, his conscience kicked in, and he tried to remember all the things he had done wrong. Parking where he shouldn't, speeding, but usually you got a ticket for that, not a personal visit from the police. And judging by their sombre expressions, it wasn't good news.

"Good morning, Mr Mason, I am afraid our visit is not a social one. We have some tragic news."

Chapter Three

Alan was back in his office with the team, outlining his thoughts about the case. It was clear that Eleanor had been hit over the head with a very blunt object. Whether it was planned or done in anger, right now they didn't know. The culprit had removed the offending item. Forensics seemed to think it was a very heavy ornament, possibly a bronze sculpture, but there was no sign of it anywhere.

"We have just informed the immediate family, her sister and her ex-husband, who all appeared to be devastated."

Even as he said the words, Alan himself was finding it hard to comprehend. Eleanor was held in affection by everyone, he had never heard a bad word spoken about her. Who on earth would want to extinguish such a bright light? What a tragedy this was!

He quickly reverted back to his detective mode. They owed it to Eleanor and her family to find the evil brute who had attacked her so savagely and caved her head in. It had been a gruesome sight, her beautiful face covered in blood, and her eyes staring blankly at them. He should be used to all this by now, but it was almost like he felt he knew her, and she was part of his family.

"Everyone is a suspect. Her sister, her ex. We need to get out there and interview anyone connected to her, we also need to find out the state of her mind prior to this."

Sarah nodded her agreement. "Sir, are we going back to look around the flat again? We need to find her mobile, and also check her incoming calls on the landline."

"Good thinking, Sarah. I must admit I thought her sister Isabel

24

was cagey. After she had got over the shock, she seemed to be keeping things to herself, did you notice that?"

"Yes, she was adamant we should never meet their mother, said she was in a care home with dementia, and nothing she said made any sense any more."

"Well, then, we must visit her. Didn't she say she was in Peacehaven? Get someone to find out the details, and we will make an afternoon call on her, and in the meantime, we need to interview the housekeeper, then her ex-husband, we can return to her sister after we have seen Jean Harris."

Sarah smiled at her boss, telling him not to do something was the wrong thing to do, a policeman has to have a suspicious mind. Experience had taught them both that it was often the most unlikeliest of people who committed the crime. At twenty-five years old, Sarah had also been in the police force for a good few years. It was always her driving ambition to have an action packed job, and one that made you think; working out who and why a crime had been committed could sometimes be a brain teaser, but she enjoyed the challenge, and then the satisfaction of bringing the guilty person to justice. To look at her, you would think she was a model, rather than a policewoman, her long black hair, and fascinating green eyes set in a perfectly proportioned face, and then her height, she was almost six feet tall without high heels. Her looks were arresting, and she had been used many times as a decoy in night clubs, when unsuspecting criminal males had been drawn to her, but never guessed she was part of the force.

"I am ready to go whenever you want."

Alan smiled absently at her, his mind still working overtime. He had known Sarah for so long now; with her height and powerful looks, some people found her a bit intimidating, but he was used to her forceful personality, and they shared a great working relationship, although he had never thought of her as anything more than a very competent WPC. He knew Zoe was a tad jealous of her, but she had no need to be. Time spent with Zoe was escapism, as his job was very demanding, especially when he was heading a case like this one.

The door opened, and a uniformed policeman stood there, looking rather agitated.

"The press have got hold of it, sir, apparently they are

b

swarming round the home of the deceased like demented bees, and not only that, the public are in meltdown. You might not be able to get near to the place, there are weeping women all over the show, and a sea of flowers, which stretches way past the entrance to the apartments, causing people to walk in the road, and holding up the traffic. Nothing like that has ever been seen before! The public have gone crazy!"

"My God, it sounds like the nation is out of control. Trust the press to leak it, they just can't help themselves!" Alan said angrily. But when he thought about it, was he really surprised? Many women aspired to be like Eleanor. She was the most well known and photographed woman in the public eye, almost like a member of the royal family. Knowing she was dead, a woman who positively oozed life and vitality, many people would grieve for her, especially when they found out she had been murdered, because there was no way she could have done it herself.

But none of this was going to deter Alan. He thanked the policeman for his information and, with Sarah striding along behind him, they left the headquarters and got into his car. When they got close to the area of Chelsea where the apartment was, the traffic slowed up even more, and was eventually at a standstill. Neither of them were prepared for the amount of flowers, they stretched way past the apartments, covering the steps up to the flats and the pavement beyond. Women had flung themselves prostrate among the flowers, weeping and wailing. Alan had never seen anything like it, and a man was busy videoing it all, no doubt to put on the nationwide news later. It was clear how well loved Eleanor had been, and although he was wondering how they could reach the entrance to the apartments, it didn't stop Alan being moved, and in awe of this overwhelming expression of just how much people cared about Eleanor. She had touched so many hearts.

"Come on, Sarah, we have to get the caretaker to let us in," he said, spotting a gap in the flowers. Alan didn't want to appear disrespectful, but he needed to get away from this mass hysteria.

"Right there boss," she said, gently parting some flowers so she didn't squash them. They stood on the step, and pressed the buzzer several times before the caretaker came shuffling to the door. Alan showed him his identity, and they were taken in the lift up to the top floor. This was no ordinary block of flats, it had an elegant marbled floor, and he had noted earlier the opulence of the apartment. It was spacious, with a very modern kitchen, there were fitted carpets in every room, expensive furniture, and the curtains and furnishings were of the very best quality.

When they reached the door, Faith Brian was standing in the corridor outside, waiting for them, as had been arranged earlier. Her face was pinched and white, and her eyes were red and puffy, it was obvious that she was very distressed. Alan spoke kindly to her.

"I am DCI Alan Clarke, and this is WPC Sarah Stevens. I know you have had a tremendous shock, and we don't want to add to your grief, but we need to ask you some questions."

"I know you do. I am struggling to believe this, who would want to harm Eleanor?"

They had by now moved inside, and could revisit the scene. There was blood on the white carpet, which was the only remaining evidence that an attack had taken place there earlier.

"What time did you arrive and discover her?"

"It was about eleven this morning. I come in to tidy up, and prepare supper for when she comes home."

"Somebody hit her with a very hard object, traces of bronze fibre were discovered, does she have any bronze ornaments?"

"Well, she keeps all the trophies she has in a locked cabinet." Faith pointed towards a wall unit with glass doors, which housed an array of statuettes and cups. But commonsense told Alan that it was unlikely that anyone would unlock a cabinet, even if they had a key, and then return the ornament afterwards. It seemed to him that it had been an act that had been carried out in anger, possibly after an argument.

"Wait a minute, the bronze horse is missing!" exclaimed Faith, crossing to the fireplace mantelshelf. "This is the gap where it was."

Alan noticed the shelf was quite close to the spot where the body of Eleanor had been discovered.

"Do you know where the horse came from?"

"Oh yes, Alfie got it for her when they were married. She has always loved horses, used to ride when she was a child, but had to give it up when acting took over her life. But where is it now?"

Alan was wondering the same thing. The culprit had removed

it and thrown it away somewhere, it obviously had their fingerprints all over it. Sarah voiced his thoughts.

"Even if we find it, it's unlikely to help us much, the DNA will have been removed."

Alan was already thinking it might be significant that her ex-husband had bought it, and it had been used as a weapon. And when they listened to the voice mails, he realised that not only was Alfie Mason upset and angry with Eleanor, but also her sister Isabel. Both of them had a motive to kill her. How had the golden girl managed to upset them so much?

"Was their relationship amicable? Obviously they were divorced; and how did you find Alfie?" He asked Faith.

She looked uncertain, not knowing quite what to say.

"We won't divulge anything you say, or even mention you told us, but we are desperate to find this very dangerous killer, they could strike again at any time."

Faith took a trembling breath, even in death she felt she owed Eleanor a loyalty. Her killer needed to be found. She spoke falteringly.

"Eleanor was a person who liked to keep her private life away from the press. She married a man who was five years younger, and she shut herself away when they split up. He was a fan who followed her around, very persistent, very young and handsome, and she fell for him, and after a very short while they got married."

"You sound as if you don't approve of him."

"My opinion doesn't matter. But I know Eleanor was madly in love with him, and when he left her, she couldn't fool me like she fooled the public, she was heartbroken."

"Did they remain friends?"

"Not really, he married someone else, and was always trying to get hold of some sort of payout, but Eleanor had a flourishing career before he ever came on the scene, and he wasn't always in a steady job. To me it felt like he was taking advantage of her, but, of course, that is only my opinion."

"I see, well thanks for your help, you have given me a much clearer picture. Can we drop you off at home, or anywhere?"

"Thank you, that would be nice," murmured Faith. It was only mid afternoon, but it felt like it had been such a long day. She was still trying to digest the horror of finding Eleanor, with her face covered in blood, and her eyes fixed and lifeless.

After they had dropped Faith at her bungalow, Alan and Sarah voiced their thoughts.

"Well, I don't think she's a suspect, what could be her motive?" stated Sarah, "but the ex-husband sounds like a probability."

"Indeed, now let's put the cat among the pigeons and go to Peacehaven and speak to Jean Harris. Isabel said her mother didn't really take it in when she heard about Eleanor's death, so we might not get anywhere with her."

"True," sighed Sarah, "the staff might not let us, but we have to try because Isabel seemed to be hiding something."

When they arrived at the care home, it looked surprisingly inviting. It was set in very pretty gardens, bursting with colourful shrubs and an abundance of trees. There were wooden benches ranged around the gardens, some were occupied, one lady was sitting with a carer next to her, who was encouraging her to do some knitting. The carer smiled at them, making them feel very welcome. No one likes the thought that one day they might end up in such a place, and for Alan and Sarah, old age seemed an eternity away. But, Sarah thought briefly, if they were all as pretty and welcoming as this one, maybe it wasn't so bad.

The grey-haired lady with her hair in a bun, who opened the door to them, did not seem surprised to see them. Her smile was friendly when she shook hands with them.

"It's such a tragedy about Eleanor, everyone loved her. Because of her dementia, Jean hasn't quite grasped that her daughter has passed away. So, yes, you can interview her, but you may not be able to make much sense out of what she says. Obviously it can't be for too long."

Alan gave her his most ingratiating smile. There was something hidden within this family, and Jean might be the person to let it loose, or she might be still trapped in her confusing world, but it was certainly worth a try.

They were escorted to Jean's room, and introduced by a member of staff, and when she looked at them blankly he couldn't help wondering if this would be a waste of time. He spoke gently.

"Mrs Harris, may we call you Jean? We are so sorry about Eleanor, and we want to find out who killed her."

"Killed her?" echoed Jean. And Alan noticed, although only in her mid sixties she was very thin, and her face was lined, and her eyes showed much confusion. Her next words took him and Sarah completely by surprise.

"She killed her stepfather and me, don't you care about us?"

"How did she do that, Jean?" asked Sarah very gently.

"Of course we care," added Alan gently. Her eyes looked wild with anger, and he wondered what sort of tale they would hear.

"She left home, and then told wicked lies about him. She wanted him in prison, she failed with that, but he left me!"

"So you feel Eleanor was to blame for your husband leaving you?"

Jean carried on angrily, she was now in full flow: "Then she moves in with Isabel, I told her what she was like, but she never listened, and then she went after her husband. That girl had everything, fame, money, but she always wanted more. She killed us, so whoever killed her did us a favour!"

Alan wondered how much of this was true, it was a very far fetched story, but something useful to refer to when they interviewed Isabel. She must have guessed that her mother would go off like this. Maybe there was a grain of truth in what she said, otherwise why would Isabel try to stop them from interviewing her?

But the image of Eleanor that he had, and was presented to the nation, was of a clean living, loving and caring National Treasure. If any of this story was true, then she had fooled everyone, including him, and he felt regret coursing through his insides that she might just be another man-eater, and marriage wrecker, and he really didn't want to think that was true of Eleanor.

Jean's fury passed, and now she grabbed his arm desperately, and Alan felt such pity for her, poor little soul, what a foul condition this was, robbing someone of their mind.

"Please help me, I can't eat anything, they are trying to poison me!"

Sarah moved quickly to comfort the weeping woman, and did her best to reassure her that she was safe. It was uncomfortable to see someone with such a confused mind, so it was not surprising that the grey-haired lady re-appeared, and told them that was enough.

"Jean, my dear, I will take you down to the dining room. How do you fancy a cream tea? The Detective Inspector and Sarah are going now. We are playing bingo too, you like that."

Alan was relieved to see Jean allowing herself to be led away. At least the home understood her needs, and it seemed she still hadn't quite grasped that Eleanor had been murdered.

When they were back in the car, they discussed what Jean had said.

"I think she now lives in a fantasy world, but how sad she has turned against the daughter she loved and supported in the past," commented Sarah.

"Maybe, but it has to be Isabel we interview next; let's see her reaction to her mother's words."

"Yes, I think she will be angry that we went to Peacehaven."

"Tough, we have a murder to solve, and we can't worry about upsetting people, it's our job!" said Alan firmly.

When they arrived at Isabel's home, she greeted them politely, but her face still bore the strain of the news she had been given earlier that day.

"I am sorry to bother you again so soon."

"You have your job to do, and my sister did not deserve to be so brutally murdered."

"We have just come from Peacehaven, it seems your mother has not quite grasped that Eleanor has been murdered."

Alan watched Isabel's face change; firstly a look of panic, which swiftly turned to anger.

"I told you not to bother her. She doesn't even know what day it is!"

"When we are investigating a murder enquiry, we have to leave no stone unturned, and interview anyone and everyone connected to the victim. It's the way to find out what motive the killer had. Perhaps you can now tell me why your mother has turned against the daughter she used to be so proud of. She seems to think Eleanor ruined her marriage."

Isabel took in the steeliness of Alan's gaze and the firmness of his words. There were so many secrets in this family. For years they had stayed within the family, because no one in Peacehaven took any notice of her sick mother's verbal ramblings. But she could not lie to the police, she was far too honest for that. Whether she wanted to or not, she would have to tell this determined man what he wanted to know. She covered her face with her hands and sobbed.

31

"My sister was not a bad person, you know, everyone loved her including me, but she made some bad mistakes during her life, and I have always tried to protect her."

"Would you like me to make some tea," said Sarah, moving to put an arm around her crumpled shoulders. She sensed that important revelations were about to be unleashed.

Isabel nodded assent, and she waited whilst Sarah found her way around the kitchen, busily putting mugs on a tray and making tea. Alan handed her a box of tissues, and watched whilst she made an effort to regain her composure.

She seemed to be calmer when they were all sipping their tea, and in a faltering voice she explained.

"Our father died when Eleanor was ten. I was older, and I left home to go to university. According to my mother, Eleanor became very difficult after she remarried, and didn't like my stepfather. At the age of fourteen she ran away from home. I found her on the streets and brought her home to live with us. Not only was she pregnant, but also she said she had been raped by our stepfather. I believed her. She was traumatised, and said she could never go home. We paid for her to have a private abortion."

"I see, did either of you report the rape?"

"We wanted to, but could you imagine how it would have affected her career, and also tarnish her perfect image? There would always be someone who would suggest that it wasn't true."

Alan and Sarah exchanged glances. This was huge! It certainly wouldn't do for the press to get hold of it.

"So you let him get away with it."

"Not exactly. I told our mother, but she didn't believe Eleanor, she took his side, and that is what caused the family rift. Not long afterwards he left my mother, and she had a massive breakdown, that evil man was her whole life, and without him she just folded right up. She had treatment for her breakdown, but tests revealed she was in the early stages of dementia. The rest you know, we sold her house to fund her care in Peacehaven, and although I have tried to maintain contact by visiting her, she doesn't really know me, and never stops talking about how Eleanor 'ruined her marriage'."

"Did Eleanor visit her and try to explain her side of things?"

"She was always saying she would go, and now it's too late!"

Alan knew his next words would really offend Isabel, but they had to be spoken. He watched her reaction carefully.

32

"Your mother spoke as though Eleanor and your husband had a relationship. Did you know anything about it?"

Isabel drew a trembling breath, forcing her expression to remain as impassive as she could. She didn't have the acting skills that Eleanor had been blessed with, but she was determined that this nosy detective chief inspector and the WPC were not going to know her most closely guarded secret. Her big mistake in the past had been confiding in her mother, she had been desperate to talk to someone, not knowing which way to turn, and she had also thought her mother might rouse herself from her own apathetic state. But it had been the worst thing she had ever done, giving Jean ammunition to blame Eleanor for her own marriage breakdown. But that had been a different situation to this one, she had never forgotten the distress of her fourteen year old sister when she had brought her to live with them.

She hid her anger, and her tone was cold and hard: "My mother imagines all sorts of things, including that the staff at Peacehaven are trying to poison her."

Alan was trying to see any sign of panic in her demeanour, but he just got the impression that Isabel was getting tired of the conversation, and would soon ask them to go. There was still more he wanted to know, and as if sensing he needed some back up, Sarah asked gently.

"Isabel, we realise it has been a very traumatic day for you, and we will leave you in peace soon, but before we go, can you think of anyone who would benefit from your sister's death?"

"Financially yes, Eleanor hasn't altered her will since she split up with Alfie, and he is still trying to get a payment after the split."

"Really, why didn't she alter it, they have been split up a while now?"

Isabel sighed. "It was typical of Eleanor, all the things she meant to do, but never got round to. I also think deep down she hoped he would come back, she still loved him."

"Did you think he might go back?"

"No, he is now married to someone else with a baby son. I don't like to speak badly of anyone, but Alfie fell on his feet when he married Eleanor, he had no money or a job, and he is very handsome. He made it his mission to follow her around until she noticed him, and she fell very heavily for him."

"Did she ever complain about him being violent during their marriage?" persisted Alan.

"Never! I know they argued, and he was being unfaithful to her with Angela, the woman he is now married to. I think he was always with Angela, and he married my sister to get his hands on money. She certainly lavished it on him, and could deny him nothing until they split up. She could never get her head round the fact that he preferred someone plain and dumpy to her; it affected her so badly that she was having counselling for it."

"I see, all this is very staggering, we will certainly need to interview Alfie. Eleanor appeared to be so serene and in control of her life."

"Yes, my sister was a woman with many faces, and acting was her strength, so she was able to maintain an outwardly happy appearance. But she had the kindest heart, she helped many people worse off than herself. Having said that, in all fairness to Alfie, she was not that easy to live with."

Isabel couldn't help the jumbled emotions that raged around inside her. She knew only too well that Eleanor had her faults, but there had also been a lot of good in her heart. She had not had a good start in life, losing her adored Daddy, and then suffering at the hands of her evil stepfather, being raped and abused until she had run away in desperation. That had always haunted Isabel, and was maybe why she had forgiven Eleanor's other faults and made excuses for her behaviour. She felt absolutely desolate now Eleanor had gone; her baby sister had been murdered. It had also affected Amy and Sam as well.

"Isabel, you have been very helpful, we won't prevail on you any longer," said Alan gently. They had a lot of revelations to discuss, Alfie Mason would have to be interviewed tomorrow and then there were her associates at the theatre. They would also take a trip there tomorrow. But one thing seemed certain, Eleanor was not how the public perceived her. Even he felt disappointed to find out that the golden girl wasn't quite how he had expected, but he commiserated with himself, realising that nobody is perfect.

Chapter Four

The hysteria over the death of Eleanor continued. It was the main topic of the news, with re-runs of some of her films dominating the TV channels. And the public were reminded of all her good charity works, and her missions to foreign countries, publicising the need to help and support children who were often orphaned by war and separated from their families. In death, Eleanor the National Treasure had become Eleanor the Saint. The British public were so totally under the spell of the carefully constructed image she had portrayed, that Alan and Sarah both remarked that it was unlikely that any adverse press would affect the legacy she had left behind, because Eleanor was a symbol of how every woman would want to be; beautiful, powerful, kind and dearly loved, and because of all that, they would forgive her anything.

Alan was determined that no one would know about her abuse as a child, although sometimes the press got hold of things they shouldn't. It seemed that Isabel had managed to keep this secret hidden within the family. Alfie was the next person on the list to be interviewed, and having had a picture painted of him by Faith and Isabel which hardly flattered him, Alan and Sarah were both anxious to make up their own minds. When they arrived at the modest flat he shared with Angela, it was clear to see that Alfie was not wealthy.

"He might not know about Eleanor's abuse by her stepfather, so we best not mention it," decided Alan as an afterthought whilst they were waiting to be let in.

"Yes, we mustn't betray Isabel's trust in us," agreed Sarah.

Alan's first impression of Alfie was not a good one. He could see he was a good looking man with his blond hair, and blue eyes set in a very handsome but rather feminine face. He almost looked gay, but as he was with Angela, and they had a child, in this instance looks could be deceiving. His clothes were loud, he wore a red check shirt with very tight jeans, earrings, and his white blond hair was obviously dyed. He wouldn't have looked out of place operating dodgem cars at a fair, his skin had tattoos up his arms, and his complexion was brown and swarthy. It looked like smitten Eleanor had been married to a gypsy. Angela too had tattoos on her arms, she was short and dumpy with lank brown hair, and Alan couldn't help wondering why beautiful Eleanor had been dumped for her. Her expression was one of wariness, she didn't smile, nor did she stay long, as a baby's cry could be heard coming from another room. The flat itself smelt damp and cold, the paintwork was marked, and it clearly had not been decorated for years.

There wasn't much furniture either, a shabby sofa stood on the wooden floor, with a threadbare rug in the middle which had seen better days. It must have been quite a step down for Alfie to leave the beautiful luxurious apartment he had shared with Eleanor and then move into here.

Alfie's expression also looked wary, what did he have to hide? Alan decided to jump straight in, and try to find out.

"Good morning, Mr Mason, it seems your ex-wife was very well loved, judging by the reaction of the public."

Alfie looked a little disconcerted. "Yes the public loved her, she worked hard to achieve that sort of adoration."

"You were married to her for five years. Why did you split up?"

"It's none of your business!" Alfie's manner became guarded, and his eyes flashed with suppressed anger.

"Oh, it is my business, your ex-wife was brutally murdered, hit over the head with what we believe was the bronze horse that you bought her. You left a message on her phone asking for money, and according to your sister-in-law, she hasn't altered her will since you split up. Knowing all this I would say we have a perfect right to ask you any questions that we feel are relevant." said Alan smoothly.

Alfie felt like he was under attack, so he defended himself by explaining his side of things.

"I was married to her for five years, and believe me, she was not an easy woman to live with. She was very different when she was off the stage, and our life was always full of her dramas. She was self-centred, and a little crazy at times. Once she flung herself down the stairs for no apparent reason outside the apartment, and then said that I had pushed her."

"Did you?"

"Of course not. Eleanor had issues, in spite of all her money and fame, she was very insecure. I blame her mother, pushing her onto the stage, and depriving her of her childhood."

"Can you think of any other issues that she had?"

"Not really, I know her father adored her, and it hit her badly when he died, and she didn't get on with her stepdad, but that was all long before I met her. She never spoke much about him, only to say he had got through her mother's money and left her, so when her mother had to go into the care home, Isabel had to sell her house for her. That didn't really bother Eleanor or Isabel, as they had both made their own way in life."

It was clear from what he said, Alfie didn't know about the abuse from her stepfather, and Alan wondered briefly if it was true. Eleanor might well have lived in a fantasy world, but then he remembered Isabel had said she was pregnant, and they had organised a private abortion for her. It had been a very well kept secret in the family if she hadn't even confided in her then husband.

"When we got married, I wanted a family, but Eleanor said she didn't like or want children. That really surprised me, all those orphans she visited in Africa, but of course it's all publicity, it helps to maintain her caring image."

Alan noted the bitterness in Alfie's voice; he really didn't seem to like his ex-wife, and there was no loyalty towards her, so would he be capable of murdering her? He had not reacted to the bronze horse maybe being the weapon.

"Eleanor was killed at approximately 10 o'clock yesterday morning, can you tell me what you were doing then?"

"He was here with me. We had a late breakfast, and Alfie was on the laptop, trying to find a job."

Angela stood there, with a young baby in her arms, and she moved closer to her husband, as if she was trying to protect him. Alan noticed the tightness of her mouth, and hostility in her eyes.

"OK, the bronze horse you gave to Eleanor is missing, have you seen it lately?" he said pointedly to Alfie.

"Not for ages, I have not been in the apartment, but she used to keep it on the mantelshelf above the fireplace. It wasn't worth much money, but it reminded her of the short time she rode horses, before she had to give it up because of her career."

"And presumably you knew that she hadn't altered her will, and that you would inherit if she died before you?"

"I had no idea. When I first married her, she had included in her will some money to her housekeeper of all people, and her niece, which after telling me she didn't like children, was weird! I am sure now we are divorced her sister will contest the will."

Alan studied his face, there was animation in his expression. No doubt the windfall would give them a better life, if he got it. Alfie had a motive, and he bore a grudge towards Eleanor. Of course, it was inevitable that Angela would give him an alibi. This man was definitely a suspect.

They left them then and discussed the situation in the car.

"So Eleanor included her housekeeper in the will, and her niece," commented Sarah. "That gives them all a motive if it's true, but maybe we need to go and see Isabel again. She only mentioned Alfie to inherit, so maybe she doesn't know, but she will do when the will is read."

"Good idea," said Alan. This was all getting quite complicated. "But first I think we should go back to the office and try and check out the background of all these people. Let's not forget, Faith Brian found the body, the ornament is missing, and she probably knows a lot more than she told us, as frequenting the house as she did, not only would she see letters and documents around, but would also hear conversations between Eleanor and Alfie."

"Yes, and we need to check out who was Eleanor's counsellor, although they won't want to tell us much; patient confidentiality will be the reason."

"But they will tell us," said Alan, very firmly. "This is a murder enquiry, and because Eleanor was held in such reverence by the public, there will be a lot of pressure on us to solve this and find someone accountable. The grief of the public is extraordinary, I have never seen anything like it."

Once back in the office, with his team around him, Alan pinned up photos of Faith, Alfie and Isabel. After checking police records, they found Alfie had been convicted for stealing cars when he was 16, and spent time in an approved school, and they failed to find anything about Isabel. Faith, however, had married a man called Joseph Brian fifteen years ago. She had been his housekeeper, but inherited the bungalow where she now lived when he died some three years ago. Joseph's sister Keeley had been convinced that Faith had deceived Joseph to gain control of his money and home, and Keeley filed a complaint to the police. But nothing had ever been proved, so the file just lay in the records, having never been closed. They had decided that Keeley was just another disgruntled sibling, who had been expecting to inherit and become bitter when she didn't, but now Alan wasn't so sure, this put a whole new perspective on things.

Alan addressed his team. "The other beneficiary of the will is Isabel's 18 year old daughter Amy, we have not interviewed her yet. We also want to speak to people she worked with, her make-up artist, and her PA, apparently Eleanor shared a PA with other celebrities, so I don't know how close they were."

"Yes guv, leave it to me," said Ross Green, a very enthusiastic PC. Alan decided that he would. It was physically impossible to be everywhere all the time, and there were quite a few people to interview.

"OK, do that and report back to me, then I will take Sarah with me to interview Amy. I am sure Isabel will be very protective of her daughter."

Alan wasn't sure about Ross Green. As well as enthusiastic, he also had a trace of arrogance about him. He hadn't been in the force long, was only 21, and Alan felt he had a lot to learn. He had the reputation of being quite a ladies' man. His almost latin looks, and lean frame were obviously a hit with women, but Alan felt if he was going to do well in the force, he needed to have a bit less ego and a bit more empathy with people. He still had years to learn all this. Alan had discovered himself that often to get the best out of people you had to gain their trust and show empathy.

When Ross returned later in the day, his words made alarm bells ring in Alan's head.

"I have interviewed Lyn Cartwright, who was Eleanor's make-up artist, and she has told me about a weird stalker who Eleanor found rather intimidating."

"I see, weird in what way?"

"He rarely spoke, but continually took selfies with her, and attended her performances at the Adelphi every night. He also found out where she lived, and plagued her with love letters. He couldn't get into the apartment, but he waited on the doorstep until she arrived in her taxi."

Alan interrupted him: "Get onto the taxi firm, someone, and find out if she had a regular driver."

"No need, I found out, it's Max Taylor. Lyn told me, and he works for SAFECARS."

"Good for you." Alan was pleased to see Ross was showing initiative.

"Shall I go and interview the weirdo, guv? His name is Peter Grant and he lives in Wimbledon."

Alan wasn't sure, but today he had to interview Isabel again, with Amy and Sam too, and they would also have to return to Faith now that they knew about her past. He realised he had no choice really.

"Yes, but weirdo or not, treat him with respect. Just because he's unusual, it doesn't necessarily mean he is a murderer."

"Point taken guv," laughed Ross, as he exited the room.

Sarah went out to get them a sandwich, and Alan organised some coffee for them both. He sat there, biting the end of his pen whilst he pondered, and then Sarah appeared with the food.

"We'll see Faith first, and find out more about her," he said, and Sarah nodded in agreement.

Chapter Five

Ross felt very important being allowed to interview this man without either Sarah or Alan breathing down his neck. He was confident he could get the necessary information from the weirdo, and he took Wendy, a junior WPC, with him. She wouldn't say boo to a goose, unlike Sarah. Wendy was much better for his ego. She agreed with everything he said. He preferred women like that, rather than strident Sarah, who was tall and threatening, even though she was a very good looking woman.

They arrived at the building where Peter Grant lived, left the police car with its driver, and finding the entrance, pressed the buzzer for number four. Ross had not made an appointment, he was just hoping Peter would be at home at lunchtime. He was certain the bastard had done it, and determined to get a confession out of him. That would make Alan Clarke sit up and notice him. Ross intended to make his way up the ladder of success, he didn't think it could be that difficult.

Peter heard the buzzer, but he didn't feel able to answer it. The woman he revered above all others was dead, his life no longer held any meaning, and he was sitting here in the flat with such pain inside him, although no tears would come. The television was on, and the murder of Eleanor dominated every channel. He could feel a huge panic building up inside him. He licked his dry lips, then he peeped out of the grubby net curtains, which had not been washed since his mother had passed away, because Peter didn't notice things like that. When

41

he saw the policeman in uniform, and the WPC, fear took control of him, and his voice shook when he said, "Yes?" He did not dare to ignore the police, they were all powerful.

"Mr Peter Grant, can we come in and ask you a few questions? We are investigating the death of Eleanor Harrison."

Peter's heart lurched, he felt so stressed, he wasn't sure if he would be able to speak to them, but he clicked open the communal street door and then stood at his own front door whilst they climbed the stairs. He was trying to fight panic inside him. She had gone, and now they wanted to talk about her, and he wasn't sure that he could.

Ross noticed how agitated the weirdo was. His body language was evasive, he didn't even speak, but just inclined his head towards the living room, and even though it was afternoon, the curtains remained closed. They were not offered a cup of tea, and there were no pleasantries from this man, which convinced Ross even more of his guilt.

Wendy was quietly thinking that maybe Ross's bold manner was making this man feel very uncomfortable. She could see that he struggled with social skills, this is why Ross called him a weirdo. Peter didn't look after himself properly, his hair needed styling, and he suffered with spots; that obviously wouldn't help his self esteem. His clothes were creased and shabby. That was her opinion, but she didn't voice it, she hadn't been with the force long, and she found Ross's manner a bit intimidating.

"Are we doing this in the hall, or are you going to draw the curtains back, it is afternoon you know."

She winced at the sarcasm in Ross's voice, and spoke gently to the man, who moved like a robot to open the curtains. "This is PC Ross Green, and my name is Wendy, we understand you were a fan of Eleanor Harrison, and we are here to investigate her death."

"A fan, I should say so!" sneered Ross. Once the light was revealed, they could see nothing but pictures of Eleanor. She graced every wall, all along the hall, and then the lounge, her beautiful face, alight with animation and that smile that always reached her eyes, making everyone who came into contact with her feel special.

Ross could see he wasn't just a fan, the man was obsessed with her, and obsessive people were dangerous and unbalanced. It was

42

obvious to him that this bloke must have done it. More than likely hit her because she spurned his advances. She must have let him into the flat because she knew him from his frequent trips to the stage door. Now he was cowering in the dark because he was as guilty as hell!

"What were you doing yesterday morning at about ten o'clock?" he barked fiercely at Peter, his eyes showing his anger.

"I don't know, can't remember." Peter choked out the words. His brain was letting him down, the panic he felt inside had robbed him of his memory. This tall man with the controlling manner was getting right inside his head, and he couldn't think straight.

"A fine excuse, if you can't give me a proper answer, then you will have to come along to the station."

"I. . . I. . . I think I was here, working, I work from home."

"We need to search this flat."

Ross was hoping he could find the bronze horse that Peter might have hidden in the flat after the attack. This bastard was acting as guilty as hell!

Suddenly Peter snapped. He couldn't bear confrontation, or being touched, and he certainly couldn't bear to have anyone violating his space by touching things that were a part of his life. He gave a howl almost like a wild animal, then covered his face with his hands, rocking backwards and forwards.

Ross totally ignored this, and would not be thwarted from his plan. In his opinion this weirdo was oozing guilt. He whipped out some handcuffs, and nodded at Wendy to help him, whilst chanting with great enthusiasm:

"Peter Grant, I am arresting you on suspicion of the murder of Eleanor Harrison. You do not have to say anything, but it may harm your defence if you do not mention when questioned something you later rely on in court. Anything you do say may be given in evidence."

Peter was struck dumb, he didn't really care about what happened to him now. His beloved Eleanor had gone, so what did he have to live for? He allowed himself to be led away into the waiting police car, and Wendy followed afterwards, wondering why on earth Ross had arrested Peter. In her opinion, the poor man was petrified of him, but that didn't mean he was guilty.

She usually went along with what Ross did, but this time it

seemed wrong that he was arresting somebody without any evidence. She could see that Ross was so full of his own importance. It would be wrong to question him in front of Peter, but to her Peter seemed like the victim. So she was going to say something at the station, because in her opinion, Ross was bullying Peter, and that was not right.

Back at the car, Ross sat behind the driver next to Peter, and she sat beside the driver. Peter had his head bowed, not looking at anyone, and because she could sense that he was in deep distress, her heart went out to him. She didn't think he was acting in a guilty way, but Ross had already condemned him. She sat quietly, thinking about what she would say when they got to the station.

Alan and Sarah opened the gate leading to Faith's bungalow, and he noticed what an attractive garden she had; mature trees, with colourful shrubs in abundance, and the lawn looked like green velvet. It was very well looked after, so either Faith was a keen gardener, or she employed someone. It wasn't just an ordinary bungalow either, it was long and spacious, and he could see into the back garden, which was also well kept, and there was a swimming pool and a patio area, and it all looked very well looked after.

"Wow, this is nice!" remarked Sarah, looking around her. "How does Faith get the time to be a housekeeper? This all takes some maintenance."

"I was thinking the same," remarked Alan.

Most of the properties around the outskirts of London were Victorian terraced houses, but this bungalow was set at the end of an unmade road, which was more like a lane, and it was set on its own. Alan was guessing that maybe Faith's husband Joseph had bought the land and had the bungalow built for him. Of course, living alone she must rattle around in it, but it was certainly a very nice home to inherit.

Faith opened the door to them, her face was pale and wan. It appeared that the death of Eleanor had hit her badly, but was this an act, and did she go around marrying men and inheriting through their demise? The police records didn't mention if she had been married before, only that she had been married to Joseph for fifteen years.

44

"Good afternoon, please come in."

They both greeted her, and Alan glanced around, taking in the spacious hall with its polished wooden floor and various paintings of country scenes adorning the walls. The door was open, leading into a large lounge which housed elegant furniture and curtains. Straight ahead was a kitchen with shiny worktops, a centre unit with bar stools, and the polished floor continued on right through the bungalow.

"Please come into the lounge and sit down. Would you like tea or coffee?"

Because she was a housekeeper, it was an automatic thing for Faith to say no matter how she was feeling. She had a duty to take care of her guests.

"Yes please. Tea with milk for both of us, and I need some sugar in mine," said Alan.

Faith went into the kitchen, and soon re-appeared with a tray of tea and biscuits. She sat opposite them, twisting her hands together, clearly feeling uncomfortable.

"Aren't you having any?" enquired Alan, munching on a custard cream.

"No, I had some tea earlier. Please tell me you have found out who did this terrible thing."

"Not as yet, although we have our suspicions." Alan met her gaze when he said this, was it guilt making her so uneasy? He just couldn't be sure.

"They are playing her films all day on TV, she is really missed."

"Yes, the reaction has been extraordinary, but Eleanor seemed to appeal to so many people. Many watched her grow up from a talented little girl to a very accomplished actress."

"I can't believe she upset anyone enough to want to kill her."

"Her husband claims she was very difficult to get on with."

"Well he would, he left her. In all honesty, like any actress, Eleanor was temperamental, she got tired and snappy sometimes, but all these things are part of normal life."

"Did you find her difficult?"

"I didn't see her much. I came in to do my work whilst she was out. She never complained about anything I did, but when Alfie was here, sometimes I heard them arguing, and she could give as much abuse back as he gave to her."

"Was he ever violent towards her?"

"I never heard any violence, only shouting and swearing. Eleanor did tell me once that Alfie had pushed her down the stairs outside their apartment because she tried to stop him from going out, but I never saw it. He was going to Angela you see."

"How long have you worked for Eleanor?"

"Three years. I took the job a few months after my husband died."

Alan noticed that she was now a little flushed, probably realising that they might have found out about the complaint from Joseph's sister. So he didn't mention it yet.

"It appears that Eleanor had made a will leaving her flat and assets to three people; yourself, her ex-husband, and her niece Amy. Did you know you were included?"

Faith now looked even more uncomfortable. When he met her eyes, she glanced away.

"Eleanor did tell me she had made provision for me in her will. She had a succession of housekeepers, but I stayed, so last year she included me. I felt uncomfortable about it because when I was married to Joseph, he also left me his house and money, and his sister Keeley took it badly and reported me to the police. I felt like a gold-digger, but we were married for fifteen years. In the end I sent Keeley five thousand pounds, but it wasn't enough, she said it was 'guilt money' and reported me to the law. But I was never charged with anything."

"Yes, we know about the inheritance from your husband. Thank you for explaining it all so well. Do you know why Eleanor would have included Amy?"

"She has always been close to Isabel, so maybe it's to please her sister."

Alan put down his cup, and Sarah drained hers too, remarking, "Thanks so much for the tea, it was very nice. We won't take up any more of your time."

When they were in the car, travelling towards the house where Isabel lived, they compared notes. "She did look relieved when we left," observed Alan.

"Yes, but I think that is because we knew about her past," commented Sarah. "I don't see her as a suspect. She has a beautiful home already, and she seems to live alone, I can't see why she would work on Eleanor to be included in her will."

46

"I'm not sure. She started working for Eleanor just after her husband died. That is quite a co-incidence."

"Well she must have felt lonely when her husband died. Maybe going back to work was her salvation, rather than a need for more money."

"I am still keeping her on the suspect list," said Alan,

"Of course," said Sarah. "And now to meet Amy, and speak more to Sam. He kept his distance last time and let Isabel do all the talking."

When they arrived at Isabel's home, which was a detached Georgian style house although built within recent years, she was out in the garden instructing her gardener just where she wanted some new shrubs planted. Sarah thought longingly how nice it must be to have the sort of money that meant you just gave out the orders and someone else did the work. It certainly wasn't going to happen to her whilst she was a lowly WPC, but maybe her Mr Right would be a rich man, she could but hope!

Sam opened the door to them, and then called his wife inside. He seemed a quiet sort of man, although Sarah did notice he was easy on the eye. His dark wavy hair and expressive grey eyes were arresting, but he didn't have much in the way of banter, he just smiled politely and showed them through into the spacious lounge overlooking the big garden.

"We need to speak to your daughter Amy, too," said Alan when Isabel appeared.

"She's not here, she's out shopping with her friend," volunteered Isabel. "Why did you want to speak to her anyway?"

Alan decided to jump in with both feet. "You told me that Eleanor had still included her ex-husband in her will, but according to him, more recently Eleanor also included her housekeeper and Amy. Were you aware of that?"

Isabel became visibly agitated, and Sam looked equally uncomfortable. Isabel had never been able to tell lies, she always felt her face would betray her, because she was unable to hide her expression. She loved Sam with all her heart, but experience had shown him to be a weak man. She knew exactly the reason why Amy had been included in Eleanor's will as did Sam, and she now felt caught like a rat in a trap.

Sam could see how distressed his wife was. He knew he was a lucky man, she had loved him, and stood by him when he didn't deserve it, and now she was suffering for it. He would never forget what he had done. The guilt still haunted him, and he never wanted Amy to know. How she would despise him. But maybe if he owned up now to what he had done, the police would be obliged to keep it a secret, and it would be a relief to him, and also the pressure would be off Isabel. He looked Alan straight in the face, and spoke softly, but with determination.

"Amy is Eleanor's daughter, but she doesn't know, and we don't want her to know."

"I see, so you both adopted her?"

"She is my daughter too. I had a one night stand with Eleanor and I have always been deeply ashamed of it. Not only did my wife forgive me, but she also became a mother to the child that Eleanor didn't want. I didn't deserve her love and forgiveness, but she gave it to me; she is a remarkable woman. Eleanor always felt money solved everything, so this is why Amy has been left money."

Isabel felt such fear flood through her that their secret was now out. She had not been expecting Sam to confess, but no matter what, he was her husband, the love of her life, and she would always forgive him anything. He had made her sound like some sort of martyr, but her reason had been a selfish one. She hadn't wanted Eleanor to have an abortion.

Isabel hadn't been able have children of her own, and she desperately wanted to have a child by the man she loved so much, and Eleanor's pregnancy had been her only chance. She had taken care of Eleanor during the pregnancy. It was the only stretch of time that Eleanor hadn't worked, so they went away and rented a cottage in Cornwall until the baby arrived. Isabel had been with Eleanor when she gave birth to Amy, and actually seen Amy being born, so in her mind the bond had been instant, and Sam had to wait until afterwards to see his daughter. When they returned from Cornwall, Eleanor had returned to work, and Isabel had contacted everyone they knew to announce the birth of her baby daughter Amy. Because it was such a huge burden carrying this secret, she had confided in her mother, and always lived to regret it.

"Amy is our daughter now, we have been bringing her up together for eighteen years. Eleanor didn't want children, she didn't have that maternal streak," she said firmly, meeting Alan's gaze head on.

Alan looked at her with new eyes. What strength of character this woman had. She had forgiven her sister and her husband, and even made a success of her marriage. How many women would be able to do that? But already his mind was working overtime. Had her love for her sister turned to hate, especially when she neglected her own daughter by forgetting her special event. Love and hate were so closely linked. Regrettably, because he actually did admire her, Isabel was also a suspect. But not so Sam, that man didn't have the balls, handsome is as handsome does, and the man.

Amy Phillips had felt like she had the world at her feet. She had the best parents in the world, she knew she was pretty, and her ability to play the violin left others in awe of her. She was never more happy than doing a recital. It was cool to know she had inherited her aunt Eleanor's talent for entertaining.

Then everything had changed. Her beloved aunt had been murdered, and nobody knew who had done it. Her poor mother had a funeral to arrange, and still Amy felt like it was a dream, it rocked their own little world, dad was sad too. Mum had suggested she went out with Chloe. She didn't really want to, but both herself and her mum had sobbed so much, and it wasn't going to bring Aunt Eleanor back, so she had gone out. But then her mum had texted to say the police were here, and they wanted to speak to her, so she had come home.

She came in the side gate and made her way towards the kitchen door. Because it was a hot day, the patio doors were open and she could hear the conversation. When she heard her father's confession she felt like her world was tumbling down. She felt dirty, she was the result of his grubby little affair with someone she had believed was beyond reproach; her beautiful perfect aunt, whom everybody loved. In her anger, she didn't pity her mother either, she had been two-faced and not told her who her true mother was, and now she felt like she didn't know herself any more. She was a person without an identity, and everything about her family was a lie. She rushed out into the garden and vomited over a flower bed, this was too much to take in.

Isabel heard the sounds of distress and ran into the garden, only to be confronted by a very angry Amy. Guessing Amy had overheard the conversation, she tried to put her arms around her, but Amy pushed her away furiously, and ran inside. She met her father's guilty eyes, and he could see the pain in hers.

"How could you Daddy, you adulterer, didn't either of you think I had a right to know?"

"We tried to protect you," Isabel said anxiously, but Amy pushed her away, she was not going to be calmed down by anyone.

Alan could see she was her mother's daughter. Her anguish had become a huge drama, but none of them had known she would hear what they said. Maybe when she calmed down she would realise that it wasn't her aunt that was the saint, it was her mother.

"I don't need protection, I needed the truth!"

"I am sorry you have had such a shock, but I am duty bound to ask you if you knew that Eleanor had left you an inheritance?"

"Of course she didn't!" Isabel said quickly.

"Amy?" asked Alan.

"My parents don't tell me anything, as you can see, they treat me like a child. Of course I didn't know, and now I know about her and my dad, I don't want her filthy money, I want out!" At that moment she flounced from the room and ran up the stairs, watched with open mouths by Sam and Isabel. The normally meek and mild, and very compliant, Amy had changed into a very unforgiving and irate person.

"Give her time to get used to it, she'll come round," said Isabel. But her heart was heavy with worry. She had hoped to keep this a secret forever, it was causing so much pain.

"Not much more we can do here boss," said Sarah. All those years of hiding the truth, and it would have probably stayed hidden if Eleanor hadn't died. She felt as if they had caused havoc by coming here but, she reasoned with herself, it wasn't their fault that this family had so many guilty secrets.

Alan agreed with her. You could cut this atmosphere with a knife. But judging by her reaction, he didn't think Amy had killed her aunt, so she was off the list.

"So Jean was right, she knows more than they give her credit for," he remarked to Sarah on the way back to the office.

"Yes, this is why Isabel didn't want us to meet her."

"Well we are not going to share it. They are happy with the situation, so it's not really our business. It's a shame that Amy came in when she did."

"Yes, the truth usually does come out," said Sarah musingly.

Chapter Six

Ross was impatient for Alan and Sarah to return to the office, he felt he should be commended for bringing in the weirdo. People like him were just a blot on society. Right now Peter was cowering in the interview room, being watched over by a duty PC.

"Well Wendy, what a good day's work!" he said smugly. "There's no flies on me!"

"I don't agree, Ross. I think you were too overbearing with him. You have no evidence to prove he did it, just a very confused and intimidated man who clearly cannot handle this sort of situation."

Ross couldn't believe it, it looked like the worm had turned. His reason for taking Wendy, the mouse-like WPC, with very ordinary looks and absolutely no personality, was because he needed a yes man or woman to boost his ego, and now she had dared to disagree with him. But what did she know?

"Since when did you become the fount of all knowledge?"

"I have a brother who has Asperger's syndrome. He is very clever, but he cannot speak up much for himself, and he would have found it so hard, just as Peter did, in that situation. There are obvious traits that show themselves too, lack of eye contact, and his obsession with Eleanor, hence the photos everywhere."

"Excuses, and more excuses, it's the obsession that has driven him to kill her. After all, she did know him, and she let him in. Whether he has Asperger's or not, he is a killer. All we need to do is find that ornament and then the evidence will be complete."

Wendy could see it was useless speaking to this very biased

51

man. She disliked Ross strongly. Having seen her own brother being bullied at school for being different, she had immediately picked up on the signs with Peter, and felt she owed it to him, and others like him, who found it hard to have a voice to defend themselves. But her words had fallen on stony ground. She had always found Alan Clarke had empathy, and no arrogance, so she intended to put her side of things when she saw him. She got herself a coffee from the vending machine and sat there drinking it. She was ready for further instructions when the boss returned, and from where she was sitting, she would see him the moment he entered the building. She knew Ross had returned to the office they shared and she could imagine him on the telephone, legs stretched out, telling everyone what a catch he had made; and the thought of it made her feel sick inside, so she was going to stay where she was.

When Alan and Sarah entered the police station, Alan was surprised to see Wendy, the young WPC, come up to him, her manner was very determined, so he could see she had something on her mind. Normally she was quite a shy and retiring girl, so it must be very important.

"Can I speak with you sir, in private."

"Sure, come into my office," said Alan, and Sarah left him to go and get herself a coffee, but not without wondering what was wrong with Wendy.

Wendy followed Alan, his office was at the other end of the building to the one she shared with Ross, and she heaved a sigh of relief when she saw it was empty. She had been wondering if Ross would be waiting for him, all full of himself, but now she had the opportunity to explain the situation from her own perspective. He sat at his desk, which was covered in papers, and she perched herself on a chair the other side. He looked enquiringly at her. She took a deep breath.

"Sir, I went with Ross to interview Peter Grant, and I didn't like the way Ross treated him. The man clearly has difficulties, I suspect he is autistic, and instead of being tactful and polite, Ross bullied him and reduced him to a shivering wreck. Then he arrested him and read him his rights."

Alan was surprised to hear this, and immediately wished he

hadn't let Green interview Peter, he was just too full of himself that one.

"Why did he arrest him? Was his place searched?"

"No, he went into meltdown when Ross suggested it, but that doesn't mean he is guilty. I know a lot about it sir, because my brother also has Asperger's, and would have reacted in the same way."

Alan remembered that Wendy had an autistic brother. It wasn't something that had touched his life, but he knew enough about it to realise that anyone suffering would have been very hard to interview, and there would have needed to be a lot of patience involved. He wished now he hadn't given it to Green, it sounded like it was a right mess.

"So where is Peter Grant now, and more importantly, where is Green?"

"Peter Grant is in the interview room waiting for you, but he has been in a cell, and last time I saw Ross, he was in his own office. I know he will be angry with me, but I don't care, I hate injustice!"

Alan looked admiringly at her, she had guts to come to him like this. He certainly wouldn't condone any suspect being bullied, especially one with special needs.

"You have done well Wendy. Don't worry, I will sort it out."

Alan's first thought was to find Green, so he went along to his office, where Ross was busy regaling anyone who would listen to him about his arrest of Peter Grant. Alan could feel a distinct dislike of him and his methods, so he wasted no time on preliminaries when he entered the room.

"What's this I heard about an arrest you made today?"

"Oh yes, you have me to thank. The weirdo is nicely locked up. He was as guilty as hell, so I arrested him."

"So you found some evidence then?" said Alan through clenched teeth. This upstart was leering at him, and his tone was incredibly arrogant for a lowly PC. Alan held on to his temper, but only just.

"I didn't have to. It was so obvious, he couldn't hide it. When I suggested searching his flat, he went into meltdown."

"So you haven't even searched his flat yet?"

Alan was incredulous. Ross had just arrested Peter on a whim, this was ludicrous. His tone was icy. "I suggest you come up to

53

the interview room with me, and when Peter Grant comes in you apologise. Don't you realise he can sue us for arresting him for no good reason."

For the first time Ross looked a little crestfallen. He had been expecting a pat on the back, and now he was being told to apologise.

"He was acting suspicious, boss," he repeated, but he could see it was falling on deaf ears, so he made his way towards the interview room.

Alan would have liked to take Wendy as well, because she seemed to know about autism, but he didn't want PC Green to take out his frustration on her, so he quickly filled Sarah in on the situation, and made his way to the interview room where the PC was waiting for them.

It wasn't long before Peter was brought in by a duty officer, he was shaking with fear, his head bent, clearly out of his depth, and Alan immediately felt an empathy for him, and cursed himself for allowing Green to have anything to do with him. He could just imagine the press headlines if this got out: VULNERABLE MAN BULLIED BY POLICE IN MURDER INVESTIGATION.

Sarah was the first to speak, as Alan had thought maybe he would be less scared of her.

"Hello Peter, my name is Sarah. We are sorry you have been put in a cell, all we wanted to do was ask you a few questions about Eleanor, as we know you were a fan, and we are trying to find the person who killed her."

Considering she was such a tall and positive person, Alan thought it was nice to see that Sarah had a soft side, and shared his empathy. This man had to feel comfortable with them, otherwise he would tell them nothing, and for his own sake, Alan really wanted to rule him out of their investigations.

Sarah's soft voice was comforting, and to Peter it could almost be his mother again, so he reluctantly raised his bowed head and met her gaze. But then he saw that PC, and he became scared again, he found him so intimidating.

Alan had watched all this carefully. He could see they wouldn't get much out of him all the while Ross Green was in the room. Ross had to apologise to him and then get out.

"PC Green has something to say to you before he resumes his duties," he said, very pointedly.

Ross was furious, were they blind? He had done them a favour, rounded up the weirdo, and now they were going to release him, and expected him to apologise. But as arrogant as he was, looking at Clarke's face, he could see his job might be on the line here. He swallowed uncomfortably, this apology was going to hurt him, but he didn't mind playing the long game. When they discovered he had been right all along, then they would be apologising to him, and he would get his deserved promotion. He spoke quietly, in contrast to how he was feeling inside.

"Mr Grant, I apologise for arresting you without sufficient evidence, and for causing you distress."

"Thank you, now report to the desk for your further duties for today," said Alan, whilst Sarah held open the door for Ross to leave the room.

After he went, Peter looked up, and Sarah resumed her conversation with him.

"I know you got very upset when PC Green suggested searching your flat, and we fully understand that it isn't nice to have strangers going through your personal things. But if you do give your permission, unless we find anything incriminating, then you will be free to go."

"I didn't kill her, I couldn't!" Peter's trembling hands covered his face, and somehow Alan didn't believe he was acting. If they could just carry out a search, then rule him out, he could go home. But although they could get a warrant, it would be much better if he would comply with their wishes.

"OK, but don't touch any of the pictures, they are very special to me."

Alan heaved a sigh or relief, and assured him that nothing would be interfered with.

"You don't have to be locked in a cell, I can't apologise enough about that. We will send someone to do the search now, and I expect you will be going home later," he said encouragingly.

"Now, how about some tea, we all need that!"

Wendy heard later that Peter had been brought back from the cell, and Ross had apologised to him. Someone had gone to search his flat for evidence, and she was sure they wouldn't find anything, and then the poor man could go home. She didn't care if Ross had a go at her, this man needed some support, she was doing it for him and her brother, and all people like them who were very often misunderstood.

She was sent out during the afternoon to accompany another PC. Some children had been caught shoplifting in town, and her job was to be there whilst the children were cautioned in front of their parents. After that it was time for her to go home, and although it had been a long day, she was confident in her mind that by now Peter Grant was probably back in his flat. She sat down taking off her lace-up shoes, and searching for her slippers, and whilst she was putting them on, her mobile rang. It was Ross, now whatever could he want now?

"It was him, and no one would listen to me Wendy, the buggers even made me apologise to him. But they did a search, and guess what, the bronze horse was found in his kitchen. He had wiped his own DNA off, but it still bore traces of Eleanor's blood."

Wendy was stunned, she had been so convinced of Peter's innocence, and she hated the way Ross had been towards him. It was so hard to believe. Peter had struck her as a man who absolutely adored Eleanor and certainly wouldn't want to harm her. But if they had found the bronze horse, it must be true.

"I suppose that is why he didn't want us to search," she sighed, trying to remember. They had been in the hall, and then the lounge, they hadn't gone in the kitchen.

"Course he's denying it, says it was planted. But he is being held for further questioning. Not quite arrested yet, but only a matter of time."

"Maybe it was." Wendy's mind was working overtime. The killer might have planted it, but how had they got in? Unless it was someone Peter already knew. She really wanted to believe he was innocent, and as she had Alan's mobile number, once she got rid of Ross, she would ring him.

"Thanks for letting me know, Ross," she said, and cut him off. The sneer and jubilation in his voice had really got to her.

When Alan answered his phone, she rushed in quickly, before he could say anything.

"Ross has told me that the bronze horse was found in Peter's kitchen, and yet Peter is saying he was framed."

"Yes, that is true Wendy. Like you I really wanted to believe he

56

was innocent, but unfortunately the evidence is there, traces of Eleanor's blood are on it."

"I understand what you are saying, but autistic people don't lie, and I believe him. Do you know if he has a solicitor? Because he needs someone who has experience of people with autism."

"I am not sure Wendy, but when I go in tomorrow, come and see me, and together we will make sure he has the help he needs."

"Thanks so much, boss."

Wendy felt she could do no more right now, but her DCI was a good man, thank goodness.

There were quite a few things that Alan didn't understand in this case; that didn't add up. Forensic had discovered that Eleanor had sex shortly before she died. It didn't appear to be forced, she had no marks or bruises on her, and the DNA didn't match with Peter's DNA. Maybe the person she had sex with hadn't murdered her, but as she died at about 10 o'clock in the morning, and not at night when most murders took place, it certainly seemed like she had had a busy morning.

Isabel had no knowledge of her having a boyfriend, so maybe it had just been a one-off act. Alan's rosy ideal of Eleanor was fast disappearing, she had been put on a pedestal by her fans, but was no different to anyone else. He didn't look down on her, who was he to judge? He just admired the way she had built herself an image that in death made her untouchable, as he certainly wasn't going to leak it to the press. He had ordered DNA tests for every man that had any contact with her that he knew of, Sam, Peter and Alfie, but they were all in the clear. None of the neighbours had seen anyone visiting her that morning, but most of them were professional people and not in. The porter had confirmed that Peter Grant hung around there sometimes, but he had not seen him that morning.

Peter Grant remained with them for further enquiries, and because Alan couldn't be sure that this man wasn't being taken advantage of, with Wendy's help, he had found a solicitor who specialised in representing people with special needs. Charles Lambert would know how to get the best out of Peter, and also how to stop him from having a meltdown. He had even suggested that his client should be released, but because of the seriousness of the crime, that wasn't possible. Peter was going to be interviewed by a psychiatrist to ascertain whether he would be fit to stand trial if he was charged.

Then there was the text on Eleanor's phone, it simply said: 'I am outside now.' Was this sent by the killer, and where was the mobile it came from? It didn't appear to belong to any of the suspects.

Alan and Sarah went back to see Isabel again, to ask her if she could think of any other man who was connected to Eleanor in any way.

Isabel wasn't feeling very helpful, as since Amy had found out about her father and Eleanor being her parents, she had taken off to go and stay with a friend, saying she needed to sort her head out. Isabel knew it wasn't really both their faults, it was hers, for concealing the secret, but Amy had never been a difficult teenager until now, and she didn't know how to deal with it.

"I don't know what else I can tell you," she said. "Amy has gone walkabout. I know she is safe, but she has turned against both of us."

"I am sure she will come home once she can digest what has happened. You have both been her parents together, not Eleanor, and she knows how much you love her," said Sarah soothingly.

"Did you say she was staying with her friend Chloe at the moment?" Asked Alan.

"Yes, Chloe's father, Max Taylor, was Eleanor's taxi driver, he was enlisted on a regular basis after Peter Grant kept stalking her."

Alan and Sarah exchanged glances, they both had the same thought.

"Can you give me the address?" asked Alan.

"Oh, you mustn't go round there and say anything to Amy, we want her to come home of her own accord!"

"We wouldn't dream of it, don't worry," said Alan. "We just need to have a few words with Max Taylor."

Chapter Seven

Max Taylor opened the door to them with quite a startled look on his face. Alan guessed his age to be about forty-five. He was tall with dark hair that had tinges of grey and his face had a ruddy complexion. Alan could imagine him as a hail-fellow-well-met type of bloke in the pub. He lived in a Victorian terraced house at Tooting, and his cab was parked outside. This was one road that didn't have yellow lines or parking permits, which was unusual in the area.

"I hope this isn't about Amy. She's just spending a bit of time with Chloe; they have been friends for years."

Alan assured him it wasn't. "I am DCI Alan Clarke, and this is WPC Sarah Stevens, we have come about a very serious matter, the death of Eleanor Harrison."

Max's face showed concern. Alan was trying to decide if it was genuine.

"Oh yes, terrible, Amy's aunt. We were all very upset to hear about it."

He had by then shown them into the lounge, which looked spacious and comfortable with sofas and a rug covering the polished wooden floor. He offered them a hot drink.

"No thank you, time is getting on, so we won't take up too much of your time," said Alan. "How long have you known Eleanor?" he continued, watching Max's face very carefully.

"Um, must be a couple of years, it was because the girls are friends. I heard that Peter Grant was bothering her from Chloe, so I took the liberty of offering my services on a regular basis.

Eleanor never acted like the big star she was, and she used the underground. I suggested she would be safer if I took her home, even though it wasn't that far."

"So you know Peter Grant?"

"Well, I knew of him. His mother was known to everyone. She was a seamstress, she made dresses and also did alterations. She shortened some trousers for me, and made my wife some summer dresses. I believe she made wedding dresses too. Unfortunately she died, and I think Peter has been very lonely since she passed away, and then he started stalking Eleanor."

"How well did you know Miss Harrison?" said Alan rather pointedly, which was not lost on Max.

"Not that well, although she did insist I call her Eleanor. She was such a smiley and nice lady, but somehow I felt she wanted me to think that she was happy."

"So, on the morning that she died, can you explain your whereabouts?"

"Yes I can. I had arranged the previous evening to come and pick her up about ten, as she had some sort of fashion shoot for a magazine. I arrived just before ten and sent her a text to let her know I was waiting, but she never came down. I guessed she had changed her mind. I was a little miffed that there was no answer, so I waited for a few minutes, and then went on to do another job."

Alan was startled. Max had been there virtually at the time she was murdered, they should have interviewed this man earlier.

"Show me your mobile please."

Max complied, although he still looked very nervous, Alan wondered what else he was hiding. This was the number they hadn't been able to trace, right under their noses.

"Did you see anyone else near to the flat? You do realise you were there almost at the time she was murdered?"

"Yes, I saw it on the news, but those apartments have very high security, lots of wealthy people live there. I didn't spot anyone outside except one man, who I knew lived there. He exited the building at about ten-twenty, and so I then decided to go."

"What did he look like?"

"I know who it was: Matthew Roberts. He is a psychiatrist, and he has a practice in Harley street. I have often taken him home at night, and picked him up. But not that day. I wound down the window and offered, but he barely acknowledged me, and scuttled away like a frightened rabbit."

"I see, that is very interesting. Why didn't you tell us that you were near to the crime scene before Eleanor died?"

Max looked very awkward. "I have been very busy, and as I know I didn't kill her, I didn't think it was relevant."

Alan used his severe tone. For all he knew Max Taylor might have been let in by Eleanor and done the deed, and be trying to push the blame onto Matthew Roberts, who would clearly be the next person to be interviewed, although it would have to be tomorrow.

"It's up to us to decide what is relevant, not you! That was very important information, and you should not have suppressed it. Somebody had sex with Eleanor at about that time. You need to come to the station to have your DNA checked, so we can rule you out."

Max didn't look particularly worried by that, and he replied immediately.

"Of course, whenever you want. I have nothing to hide."

"One more question. Did you ever take Peter Grant in your cab?"

"Once or twice, and he was a bit of a nightmare. He was always losing his key, and didn't always have any money on him. He's a very clever man, but doesn't cope with everyday life. His mother knew that, this is why she worked from home."

"And you are sure you didn't see him that morning."

"Definitely not!"

"Well, thanks for your time. Come to the station at nine tomorrow morning and see the police doctor."

Amy was upstairs in the bedroom she had shared with Chloe for the past few days when they saw the police car arrive. They had been experimenting with eye make-up; anything to try and keep her mind off that revelation about her father and Eleanor. She had found it almost as devastating as the death of Eleanor, and it felt so private. As close as she was to Chloe, she couldn't bear to share it.

Chloe and her parents both believed that it was her grief that had caused Amy to come to them, and they had welcomed her

61

with open arms. She had kept busy with Chloe, but at night, when Chloe was asleep in the bed beside her, Amy had tried to make sense of the situation.

Her darling daddy had always felt strong and brave to her, and she wouldn't have imagined him capable of sleeping with his wife's younger sister. It seemed sordid, he was like some dirty old man, and she felt heartbroken. He had made a mistake, a very bad one, and she had been the result. But now she started to see her mother in a different light. She had forgiven him, and also Eleanor, and been willing to bring up Amy as her own daughter. What a deep love her mother must have had, not only for her sister, but also for her husband.

Amy had no doubt that her parents loved each other deeply. She had always felt safe and loved by them, and in her mind Isabel was her mother, not Eleanor, who hadn't wanted her apparently. That did hurt, she had always looked up to Eleanor, and thought she was perfect, but realisation had now hit her.

Amy didn't want anything to change at home, so if her mother could forgive daddy, maybe she should do, because nobody's perfect.

"The police are here," stated Chloe.

"To take me home, no doubt," said Amy.

"You don't have to go, you are eighteen," Chloe reminded her.

Amy didn't reply to this, but she was now missing all the familiarity of her own home. When she didn't get called downstairs, she was surprised, and then they heard the door close and watched the police car drive away. Inside she almost felt disappointed, was there no pleasing her?

She had always looked up to her dad, but she realised now he had shattered all her ideals about him. Being away from home didn't help either. She needed to talk to her mother and try to understand why he had betrayed her, and why she had been able to forgive him, and then maybe Amy could forgive him too.

Life had felt normal before Eleanor had died, but now it felt like it had all disintegrated into a thousand pieces. It was making her feel very insecure, and she now needed to be back home with her parents. She was very grateful for the way Chloe's family had supported her when she felt at her lowest, and even though she wanted to return home, she would not forget their kindness.

She brought the subject up at dinner, and they totally understood that she needed to go home.

It seemed like a good idea to go in the morning of the next day, so during the evening she picked up her mobile phone to contact her mother.

When they were travelling back to the police station, Alan and Sarah discussed the case.

"You know, boss, I was wondering how anyone could have planted that bronze on Peter, but now we know that he's always losing his key, that means anyone could have come in and done it whilst he was at the station with us."

"Yes," mused Alan. "And of course that makes our job a whole lot harder. There are several of them that could have done it, each with their own reason, so tomorrow we must go and interview Matthew Roberts, the man who was trying to sort out Eleanor's emotional problems."

"We also need to interview Dawn Fraser, Eleanor's PR lady," Sarah reminded him.

"Yes, but as they didn't really meet face to face, it all seemed to be done by email, I am not sure how much help she can be. Apparently she manages several celebrities, that is how it's all done nowadays."

"So what is going to happen to Peter? We can't hold him indefinitely, boss. His solicitor is right, he should go home. I know he could have done it, but then so could any of the others," remarked Sarah.

"I agree, I think we will let him go home, providing he returns tomorrow, and then we will question him about this key business with Lambert in the room with him."

"Yes, it's late in the day now. We need to go home and then regroup with the team in the morning. Sometimes after a good night's sleep, things make sense."

"I hope so Sarah. Right now I feel we are groping in the dark."

Alan sighed, they just seemed to be going round in circles, and there were so many suspects. It was amazing that so many people would have a reason to extinguish Eleanor from this life. Like everyone else, she was not perfect, but she wasn't a bad person either. She didn't take drugs, or drink heavily, there was no evidence of that, but it seemed her life's path had been a rocky one, and she had borne the scars.

When they pulled into the station car park, Alan told Sarah she could go home, and he watched her with amusement as she fitted her long legs into the racy little sports car of PC Bright, who was giving her a lift, and they roared off with her hair blowing in the wind.

He guessed that Wendy would still be there, as she would be concerned that Peter had been kept in for further questioning all day. She jumped into his path when he entered the door, and went to pass the desk of the duty officer.

"Sir, what is happening with Peter? Charles Lambert has said either charge him or send him home."

"I know Wendy, and we have decided to send him home. Apparently he can't hang onto his front door key, so if he didn't kill Eleanor, then someone else might have had access to his flat to plant the bronze horse. It's all supposition at the moment, because like you, I don't believe that he's capable of murder. If you like, tomorrow when I interview him, you can sit in on it. With your knowledge of Asperger's, and Charles Lambert's experience, we can find out from Peter whether he has mislaid his key."

"Thank you so much sir. I will see you in the morning."

Alan opened the door to the interview room. Charles Lambert was seated in a chair next to Peter. He was a tall thin man, with iron grey hair, probably in his fifties. His navy blue suit was well cut, and his blue shirt and navy tie looked immaculate. Alan shook hands with him.

"You must be Mr Lambert, I am DCI Clarke. I apologise for keeping you here all day Peter, as I'm sure you'd rather be at home. You can go home as long as you come back here tomorrow morning for an interview."

"My client has found it hard to cope today," said Lambert. "Peter, how would you like to come back tomorrow?"

"No, I wouldn't, but I will come back. I didn't do it!"

Alan studied him. This man had problems functioning in everyday life, so being locked up here wouldn't have helped. He looked too tired to be interviewed tonight, and Alan himself had had enough too. Tomorrow was another day.

"Let's all start again in the morning after a good night's sleep."

He smiled at Peter, hoping it would give him confidence. Everything seemed to centre around this man, and whether he was guilty or not.

Isabel and Sam had been in bits ever since Amy had taken off. Sam was heartbroken because he had lost his daughter's respect, and Isabel felt desolate because first her sister had died, and then her daughter had left home.

Every time the telephone rang, they had both rushed to answer it, and the last few days had felt like years to them. Isabel knew Amy would be struggling to reconcile what her father had done, and she so wished she could make it better for her. She felt her daughter's pain as much as she had felt it when she realised what Sam and Eleanor had done.

But the landline remained persistently silent. Amy was taking things cautiously. Then the text came through on Isabel's mobile:

> MUM, CAN I COME HOME? I NEED TO TALK
> WITH YOU, BUT NOT DAD YET.

Well what else could she expect in the circumstances? It was a start, and she would tread very carefully because her heart ached at the loss of Amy:

> DAD WILL BE AT WORK TOMORROW. I AM HOME,
> SHALL I COME AND PICK YOU UP?

Amy then replied:

> NO, MAX IS GOING TO DROP ME, I WILL BE HOME
> ABOUT TEN.

Relief flooded through Isabel. Amy really was coming home, and they would sit down and talk together. She would do everything she could to lessen Amy's pain. For the first time since Amy had gone, Isabel managed to sleep for a few hours. She was pinning all her hopes on tomorrow.

Alan was looking forward to going out for a nice quiet meal with Zoe tonight. Zoe was twenty-four, she had short curly blonde hair, and a very happy and friendly way about her. Zoe was not unlike Eleanor, who had been his pin-up since he was about seventeen, so maybe that is why he had been attracted to her.

She had found her vocation when she trained to be a nurse. Her natural empathy and caring attitude made her very popular with the patients, and it was rare to see her without a smile on her face. The first time Alan set eyes on her was when he had come to interview a man in the hospital who had been wounded in a fight. He could see she was so much more than just a pretty face. With his job he was often called away, so there wasn't much time for a social life, but Zoe had always understood. Sometimes she also worked long shifts, so the time they did spend together was very precious, but rare. Because of that, they had an unwritten rule not to talk about work, but just to enjoy their time together.

They both had a rare night off this evening, and no matter how tired he felt, he was determined to go. All he hoped was that nothing urgent would come up. Sometimes he really cursed his mobile phone, but he couldn't turn it off, he had to be ready for any eventuality.

They were celebrating their two years together, so he decided not to go out in jeans or shorts, even though the weather was hot. It was good to get out of his working suit, and to jump in the shower. Maybe one day Zoe would move in with him. His flat was certainly large enough, although he wasn't really home long enough to feel lonely. But it would be nice to wake up next to her every morning, even though they had to spend the day apart. Her dad often joked about her still being at home, but nurses' wages didn't really stretch that far, so they preferred she stayed with them and saved a bit for her future.

He dressed in some light trousers, and opted for a blue patterned short sleeved shirt. He had chosen quite an expensive restaurant, so his trainers might not go down that well. He had some light beige shoes, which would look OK, so he slipped them on, and left the top button of his shirt undone, as the emphasis was on casual during this really hot summer.

When he arrived at Zoe's house, she must have been looking out for him, as he didn't even get out of the car before the door opened, and out she came. She was wearing a blue dress that really suited her; it accentuated her eyes, and the fitted waist and straight skirt really suited her slim figure and tiny waist. She wasn't wearing tights, her legs were tanned, and the white sandals with the silver straps really complemented the dress. Her blonde hair shone in the sunlight, with the curls springing out at the side. He felt so proud to be with her, and her ready smile helped him to temporarily forget all about the puzzling unsolved murder.

"You look gorgeous baby," he said, as she leaned over to give him a welcome kiss.

"My new dress," she said proudly. "It's nice to give it an airing."

"I hope you are hungry, it's a great restaurant," he said enthusiastically, realising it was some hours since he had eaten.

Zoe gently touched his arm. "I know we don't usually talk shop, but as I haven't seen you, I just wanted to say how sad I am about Eleanor, I know you always admired her."

"Yes, Eleanor our National Treasure," he said sadly. "But tonight is for us. And right now it's a cow of an investigation."

Chapter Eight

Alan's evening out with Zoe had been such a tonic after the last few very intensive days. When they were sitting outside her parents' house in the car, he took the plunge.

"Zoe, it's been two years together, lots of time our jobs take us separate ways, but how do you feel about moving in with me? Since I met you, I haven't wanted to be with anyone else."

Zoe could scarcely believe her ears. To her Alan wore many hats. He was a very professional police officer, meticulous in his job, strong and unyielding when he had to be, but he also had a gentle side, and showed empathy and respect towards others.

She had fallen in love with him when she first saw him interviewing someone at the hospital. It hadn't take him long to bag her phone number. And two years later, she loved him even more, and the prospect of moving in with her Prince Charming was overwhelming. The only problem was, she earned much less money than he did.

"You must let me share the rent," she said quickly.

Alan looked at her reproachfully. "Zoe, my love, I didn't invite you to share my home because I want your money. That is not important, it's your company I crave."

Zoe was touched by his words, and she was determined she would pull her weight. She could look after him, wash his clothes, clean the flat, and cook him nice meals, just like a wife would. She shivered with excitement at the thought of that word. Maybe one day, but living together would be the testing time, seeing just how well they would get on.

"I will tell Mum and Dad, and then I can get all my stuff together sometime next week. Does that sound OK?"

"Perfect, as long as they approve," said Alan, kissing her gently.

"They will," said Zoe confidently. She refrained from telling him how her dad had teased her about hooking up with Alan. Nothing must spoil this or make him feel pressured. She didn't believe in playing hard to get, or keeping him guessing, she felt they knew each other inside out, and had trust and honesty.

Isabel waved Sam off to work the next morning. She hadn't told him anything. It had been very hard, but she had to make sure he wasn't around when Amy arrived, because then they couldn't talk, and it was so important. She was hoping that they could rebuild their relationship, which had taken such a battering. Amy had to know how loved she was, she was their world.

When Max dropped her off, Amy thanked him again for the kindness the whole family had shown her. She turned from the taxi and spotted Max waving. He was waving at her mother, who waved back, as she was standing at the front door.

Isabel stood at the door with her arms open wide, and, with a sob, Amy ran into them.

"I love you Mum. I have missed you."

"We both love you so much Amy. It's so good to have you back."

They linked arms and went inside, and Amy left her holdall in the hall. Right now the only thing on her mind was talking to her mother. Isabel put the kettle on, and made them both a cup of tea.

"Have you had breakfast?" she enquired.

"Not really, I couldn't eat," admitted Amy. Isabel could see how pale her face was, and her eyes looked tired. A wave of pain stabbed at her heart, what had they done to Amy? All she had ever tried to do was keep her safe, and to avoid all this.

"How about some toast then?"

Amy was already at the fridge door. "A yoghurt will be fine Mum. I am not that hungry."

Isabel didn't argue. Maybe after they had spoken, Amy might feel different. She nervously launched into conversation.

"I am truly sorry that Dad and I kept that secret from you. Dad felt ashamed when Eleanor became pregnant with you. She would have had an abortion because she was also ashamed at what had happened."

"I never thought that my dad would sleep with your little sister," said Amy, wrinkling her face with distaste.

"But it was my fault," said Isabel quickly. "We had an argument. I was hell to live with at that time. I could not conceive, we had all sorts of tests, and then we tried IVF. Our love life didn't really exist, it was more like a training programme to get me pregnant. Your dad must have felt a bit like a robot, and he did something which is not how he is normally, he went out and got drunk. When he arrived home, I had gone to bed. Eleanor was still up, she had been out with a friend, and also had a few drinks. She shouldn't have because she was only sixteen, but looked older. It happened, but neither of them really remembered much about it afterwards."

"And when did she confess to you? When she was pregnant?"

"No, your dad told me the next day. He expected me to leave him, he was distraught at what he had done, and it was a few weeks before Eleanor knew she was pregnant."

"She didn't want me, she couldn't wait to hand me over to you," said Amy bitterly.

"No, it wasn't like that. Your dad suggested an abortion to save me any hurt. And maybe I was selfish, but I had always wanted to have a child by him, and it hadn't happened, so here was my chance. Eleanor and I went to Cornwall for a few months, and I was with her when you were born. It always felt like you were mine right from the beginning."

"She didn't want me anyway."

"You have to try and understand Amy, and not judge. Some women don't have a natural instinct to be a mother, but I can assure you that after Eleanor had given birth to you, she did bond with you, and she shed many tears when she gave you to me. But it was the right thing to do. She was always a doting aunt to you, and I am so grateful that she gave me the opportunity to be your mother."

"Mum, I am grateful too, you are the best mother in the world. I need time to forgive Dad, but if you did, then I must, because we have always been a close family, and I think that is because you are such a caring and forgiving person."

70

Isabel blushed slightly. "Well, it was of benefit to me too, and I believe that Eleanor tried to show her love for you by leaving you a part of her estate, and you must take it and use it, she would have been so proud of you."

"Yes Mum, I will," said Amy, now she had come to terms with it, and her family was still intact.

After their talk Isabel felt like she was making headway with Amy, but she was still nervous about how she would react when Sam came home. She sent him a text explaining that Amy had come home and they had talked, but she was still fragile, so when he came home, he needed to be prepared to tread on eggshells, because that is what it might take to reconcile with Amy.

Sam was so relieved. He had worried incessantly since Amy had gone to Chloe's house, and he had fought against going round there and asking her to come home. He had always carried such guilt about his one-night stand with Eleanor, but if he hadn't done it, they wouldn't have had Amy, and she and her mother were his whole world. Isabel's loyalty had been truly amazing, and he didn't deserve her. My God, he was such a lucky man!

He entered the house with great trepidation, not knowing what to expect, and made his way towards the lounge where he could hear the sounds of the TV. He saw Isabel sitting on the sofa, her face etched with worry, and next to her was Amy, her face pale and her eyes cloudy, and he hated himself once again for what he had put them through.

Amy rose from the sofa, and he held his breath as her eyes met his. He didn't want to see reproach in them; his heart ached. There was a pregnant pause, then suddenly Amy sobbed and ran towards him.

"Oh, Daddy, I missed you!" and Sam could feel the tears unashamedly pouring down his face. Was she giving him a second chance?

"I missed you too Amy, thank god you are home!" he said, wrapping his arms tightly around her. Then Isabel was there too, and they all silently hugged, grateful to be back together again.

Back at the station, Sarah volunteered to go and interview Dawn Fraser. It was just a formality because Dawn hadn't actually known Eleanor that well. Their business relationship had been conducted mainly via the internet. She knew that Alan was going to interview Peter again about his door key, and that Wendy was going to sit in and take notes, because she had the experience of having a brother with Asperger's syndrome. Sarah didn't know anyone with the condition herself, so she felt it made sense for her to be doing something else.

When she arrived at Dawn's apartment, she pressed the entry bell and was admitted. Dawn lived on the ground floor, and she stood with the door open waiting for Sarah to come across the hall. She smiled politely, and Sarah introduced herself.

As they entered the flat, Sarah noticed it was in general disarray, and she was shown into a lounge with a desk at one end that was stacked high with computer printouts, and there were open files also on the desk. She guessed Dawn's age to be about forty, she was of heavy build, not very tall, and she wore a long floral skirt, with a loose silky pink blouse. Her dark hair was long and straight, and her brown eyes were her best feature.

"I have the kettle on, would you like some tea or coffee?"

Sarah politely declined. Dawn had not apologised for the mess, so obviously she lived like this, and didn't notice that there seemed no sense or orderliness. Judging by the pile of files, she had a lot of clients.

"It's very sad news about Eleanor. A beautiful and talented woman, such a loss for the acting world."

"Indeed, did you know her well?"

"Not at all, I met her once when she took me on as a PA. My job was media advertising, and booking events for her. Also, if there was any adverse publicity, it was up to me to dilute it, if you know what I mean. But with Eleanor there was no need, everyone loved her."

"Yes, all except the person who murdered her."

"This is why I found it so hard to believe. How could she have upset someone that much? She had a kind word and a smile for everyone. She was the easiest of all my clients, and I do manage a few."

"Where were you on the morning of her death?"

"I was out of the country; holidaying in Spain, actually."

"Can anyone corroborate that?"

"Yes, my friend Lucy who came with me, and here are our printout documents for the flights and hotel," she said triumphantly pulling out a sheaf of papers from the desk.

Sarah glanced through them all to make sure all was in order, marvelling that Dawn had managed to find them amongst all the mess.

"Thank you for your time," she said. There was no point wasting any more time here. Dawn was not a suspect, and there didn't seem to be a motive. She decided to head back to the station and see what was going on there, and find out what her next instructions were.

Alan sat opposite Peter and his solicitor in the interview room. Wendy sat next to him, recording the conversation. Peter had made some sort of effort by putting on a suit, but it was ill fitting, with the trousers not reaching his black shoes and the tie wasn't tied properly. Alan guessed it had been hanging in the wardrobe for years.

Wendy felt a wave of empathy for him. Her own brother had no idea of dress sense either. She knew that some people with Asperger's were unable to comprehend how important it was to be smart; clothes were just a body covering to them. It was the same with his hair; it had no style, it was just combed to the side and flattened. She had to resist the urge to offer to straighten his tie and sort out his hair, he was here to be interviewed, and her job was to record it.

"Good morning, Peter Grant, we are here to interview you in the presence of your solicitor, Charles Lambert. For the sake of the tape, can you just confirm that you are Peter Grant?"

"Yes."

"You are?"

Charles Lambert cut in quickly: "Peter tends to answer questions with just 'Yes', 'No', or 'OK'." Then, turning to Peter, he said slowly and clearly, "Look at me Peter, and tell me you understand."

"Yes," said Peter, reluctantly meeting his eyes.

"Because this is a very serious case. As you know, the police need as much information as we can give them, so when you are asked a question, instead of just using one word, you have to reply with much more of an explanation. Obviously you know what you mean, but they don't, so when they ask you to confirm you are Peter Grant, instead of just saying yes, you have to say, I

73

am Peter Grant. And also when DCI Clarke asks you a question, you must look at him just as you are now looking at me."

"I am Peter Grant."

Alan looked sympathetically at him. Thank goodness the solicitor had explained to him, and understood his needs. He was even more convinced that this man had been framed by the murderer. The bronze horse must had been planted; he just didn't look capable of murdering anyone.

"Thank you. I remember that you told us that you were working at home on the morning that Eleanor died. You also said you had seen her the previous evening when you went to the stage door after you had watched her in the period production."

"Yes, that is all correct," said Peter very firmly.

Alan remembered that Wendy had said that people with Asperger's tell the truth, so he continued. "One of my PCs came round to interview you. If you remember Wendy was with him."

"I do remember."

Wendy smiled encouragingly at him. "Can you remember locking your front door when you came to the station with us Peter? I seem to remember you pulling it to behind you."

Alan allowed her to continue, as she had been there at the time, and not himself. He was glad Ross wasn't there right now, they could do without his attitude.

Peter still found it hard to talk about Eleanor being dead. It had only been a few days, but he realised that finding the bronze horse looked bad for him. That bullying PC had arrested him, then they had told him he was only being held for questioning, but he could be arrested again, and he was really scared. He had never been a great conversationalist, always preferring to read books or use the internet, but his solicitor had said he must give as much information as he could, and not just say yes and no, which was usual for him, so he turned towards Wendy, whom he noticed had a kind face, she was smiling at him, so he did his best to explain.

"My mother always said I was very absentminded, in a world of my own often, and I always seemed to lose my key. In the end, she used to leave a spare under the plant pot outside our front door. You can always get in the communal door, the security isn't great, and people frequently don't pull it properly shut. The council are supposed to be doing something about it, but it has never happened."

"So is that where you put your key now?"

"No, I don't have a key any more. I just pull the door to, but you can lift the handle up and open it."

Alan looked at him in amazement. This man left his flat open at all times, how on earth hadn't he been burgled?

Wendy said very gently, "So you never lock up. Does anyone else know this? It doesn't sound as if your flat is very safe, Peter."

"I know, my mother used to take care of all that. Yes, people know. Sometimes when I am out, I get deliveries, but nobody has stolen anything."

"You are very lucky. Could you not ask a neighbour to look after a key for you?"

"Maybe, I will try."

Alan was astounded that he didn't have any sort of security to his flat, and clearly didn't realise what sort of danger he might have been in. Locking the door at night when alone was a way of protecting yourself from unwelcome intruders. As for the bronze horse, anyone who knew how careless Peter was could have done it. It was a minefield. It would be so easy to push the blame onto this man, who clearly, as clever as he apparently was, had trouble functioning in his everyday life.

Charles Lambert had been carefully following the conversation, and he calmly addressed Peter.

"Peter, this young lady is right, leaving your key with a neighbour is a good idea. It's much safer, because living alone as you do, you would be an easy target for a burglar."

Peter nodded his head. Right now he didn't even have a key, he had no idea where he had lost it, and he knew that meant he would have to pay for a new lock, which involved somebody strange coming to his flat and fitting it. But what they were telling him was true, he knew he was at risk, his mother had been so careful about security. For the sake of her memory, he must try to put things right. As always, he spoke with complete honesty.

"I need a new lock, I will get it sorted."

Alan was hoping they had got through to him. There didn't really seem to be much more to question him about, so they could wind down this interview. His gut instinct told him that Peter was being honest with them, and he felt Peter had been framed, but now they had to find out who had done that. He nodded at Wendy, who was making notes.

75

"Interview terminated at 11.30am. Mr Peter Grant, you are free to go home."

As they were leaving the room, Charles thanked them both for their patience, and assured them he would make sure that Mr Grant had security at his home in the future.

"Thank you," said Alan. "We may need to call back Peter Grant at any time, so please make sure he stays in the United Kingdom."

"I certainly will," said Charles, shaking Alan's hand. They had managed to get through the interview without Peter having a meltdown, and got information freely from him, so Charles felt a sense of satisfaction. And now he hoped they could find the culprit, as just because Peter had Asperger's, it didn't mean he was a murderer.

Chapter Nine

After a quick lunch break, Alan, accompanied by Sarah, went to interview Eleanor's psychiatrist Matthew Roberts. They were visiting him at his practice in Harley Street, as his secretary had insisted he only had a few minutes spare between clients. Alan had sensed a reluctance to be interviewed, which had been filtered through to his secretary, and he wondered just what this man had to hide.

They were shown into a waiting room, which was empty, it had a fitted carpet, a coffee machine, and a jug with cold water, but the glasses were not plastic, they were crystal. Their surroundings had an air of opulence about them, comfortable sofas and armchairs were ranged around them.

"This is posh," whispered Sarah, sitting on a sofa, and Alan perched himself on the edge of a chair, as he too felt a bit out of his depth. The door opened, and the woman who stood there was almost like a school mistress, and she gave them a disapproving look. She was tall, with her grey hair caught into a bun, her suit was also grey, with a pale blue blouse, and she wore silver earrings which added slight relief. She wore high heels, and Alan guessed her age to be about fifty. There was definitely an attitude about her. She sniffed and then spoke.

"Mr Roberts is very busy, but he can see you for just a few minutes, now!"

Alan bridled, he didn't like her attitude, but he kept anger out of his voice as he smoothly replied to her, "We appreciate him making time, but with a matter as urgent as this, who knows how long it will take."

She glared back at him as she ushered them through to the consulting room. She shut the door and went, and Matthew Roberts rose from his chair to greet them. Alan was privately thinking that maybe she should go back to charm school, as she had a lot to learn.

His first impression of Matthew Roberts was that he was nervous, his body language was cagey and not forthcoming, and his eyes looked troubled. He was a tall slim man, smartly dressed in a blue suit, with a paler blue shirt and a tasteful silky tie. Alan guessed his age at about forty-five. His hair was mid brown, very sleekly styled. A good looking man, with brown eyes, but he seemed jumpy.

"Good morning Detective Chief Inspector. I have a full diary today, but I can spare you five minutes."

"This is a murder enquiry, so it will take as long as it takes, or else we will do it down at the station."

Alan failed to keep the sharpness out of his voice. It felt like this man was trying to obstruct him from doing his job. Just because he was a Harley Street Psychiatrist, it didn't mean that he didn't have to answer questions like anyone else.

"I am as sorry as anyone that Eleanor Harrison was murdered, but I don't know why you should think that I could help you."

"Just answer the questions and, if you give us the right answers, we can leave you in peace."

Matthew looked at Alan's stern and set face. He had tried so hard to keep a low profile since the murder, but he could see this officer was determined to get everything out of him. Oh, how he wished he had never set eyes on Eleanor, let alone been her psychiatrist!

"Where were you at ten o'clock on Tuesday of last week, the day Eleanor was killed."

"Well, every day I arrive here at work at nine o'clock, so I guess I must have been here, as I can't remember one day from another, they all blend in together."

"How do you travel to work?"

"Usually by tube, but if I'm late I get a taxi."

"Well, you were late last Tuesday. You were seen leaving your apartment about nine-thirty, and there was a taxi there, but you hurried away. Why was that?"

Matthew's heart sank. Of course, Max Taylor had seen him, and the reason why he hadn't wanted to get in his cab was because he was upset. He didn't want to listen to that cockney sparrow chirping away about nothing. He was hoping that by the time he got to his practice, he would have collected himself, and nobody would realise anything was wrong. His mind whirled, whilst he quickly tried to think of something convincing to say.

"That must have been the day I got a telephone call at home, which held me up. So, yes, I was late that day."

"We will check your phone to see if that is accurate you know," said Alan, not convinced by the flimsy excuse and the worried look in Matthew's eyes. This man was definitely hiding something.

Matthew did his best to change the subject. "You probably know that Eleanor was my patient, but I can't share anything with you, it's patient confidentiality."

"Not when it's a murder inquiry," said Alan grimly.

Matthew's heart sank when he saw the determined look on Alan's face. Perhaps if he confirmed that Eleanor's state of mind had not been good, it would detract the inquiry away from himself. He had to do something, and she was no longer here to be accountable for her actions.

He sighed. "OK Eleanor came to me because she had many issues, and she needed someone to listen to her. Outwardly she was a talented and beautiful actress, with a ready smile, and a charisma that seemed to envelop everyone. But inside she was trying to cope with issues that had affected her all through her life. Losing her father at ten affected her greatly, then being raped by her stepfather, and not being able to bring him to justice for fear of how it would affect her own future."

Matthew was disappointed to see that his words didn't get much of a reaction. It looked like the police knew about Eleanor's past, well some of it anyway. My god, he had loved her so much, he didn't want to share anything else she had told him. Sadly she hadn't loved him back, she still held a torch for her feckless ex, and Matthew had no idea why.

"When did she last visit you?"

"I can't remember, I would have to check my work diary, but not for about a month."

"So you haven't seen her for about a month?"

Matthew still felt incredibly nervous. It was almost as if this police inspector could see right into his head, and read his thoughts. He knew lying to the police was very unwise, and of course there were always CCTV cameras everywhere. He didn't think there was one inside the apartment corridor though, only outside the main door, so he took a chance.

"I am pretty sure it's that long, but my secretary can check out her last visit in the diary."

"What about at the apartment? You live in the same block, with the same entry system."

"I am not in the habit of visiting my patients at home, detective inspector."

Alan met his eyes, they mirrored uncertainty, and he knew something wasn't right, so he went straight to the point, and watched Matthew's reaction.

"I am glad to hear it, because just before her death, Eleanor had sexual relations with someone, and so far we can't match the DNA to anyone. You will need to go to the station and see the doctor there. If your test is clear, then we can cross you off the list too."

Matthew's face was white now, he was unable to hide his distress, and he felt like a rat caught in a trap. Now his lie was going to be found out, and his reputation would be on the line. If any newspapers got hold of this, his practice would be finished. He had always known that being involved with Eleanor was like playing with fire. Part of the fun of their relationship was the secrecy to begin with, but as he was single, he had wanted a future with her; he wanted to marry her. That morning still haunted him. She had taken him into the lounge and it had happened on the sofa, it was all over so quickly. But when he told her how much he loved her, she had laughed, and told him that was the last time and to treasure it. Why had she been so cruel to him?

"OK, we did have a relationship. It will be my DNA, but I had plans to marry her, I am a free man."

"Did you kill her because she turned down your proposal?"

"No, it wasn't like that. Eleanor liked to keep her private life away from the press."

"How long had you been in a relationship with her?"

"About a year, I think. Since her marriage collapsed."

80

"You do realise you had no right to conduct a sexual relationship with a patient, you could be struck off."

"I know, and I wanted to refer her on to someone else, but she said she could only discuss all her issues with me. I thought once we got married, it would be OK."

Alan looked at him very severely. No wonder he had looked so guilty. Alan's only concern was to find Eleanor's killer, was it this man? Had he lost his temper with her because she didn't want to marry him? He only had Matthew's word for it that Eleanor was going to marry him. Yet another person to add to his list of suspects.

"Get yourself down to see the police doctor today, and don't leave the country, we may want to question you further."

Alan left the room rather abruptly, so Sarah turned as they went through the door, and said politely, "Thank you for your time."

Matthew nodded in response, but all sorts of thoughts were whirling through his head. He could be facing ruin if this got out, and all for the love of Eleanor, who was now not even here. He would never understand why she had been so cruel, but it didn't diminish his love for her in any way. The flame still burnt brightly inside him. He sank down onto his desk with his head in his hands, right now he wished he had died with her.

Zoe had such a spring in her step, every time she thought back to last night and what Alan had said to her. When they first met he had been honest; he said he liked her very much, but had no plans to settle down. She had agreed, as they both had very demanding jobs. Zoe worked in various different wards. Lately it had been the geriatric ward, which in itself was quite a challenge, trying to encourage elderly people not to give up on life when it became hard for them. The idea was to build up their self confidence, which may have been shattered by illness or bereavement. She had seen her own granddad fade away with dementia last year, so she knew her support mattered.

Sometimes patients could be very grumpy and withdrawn, and it took every bit of self control to smile at them, and ignore any rebuffs. But Zoe was always up for a challenge, and it was so rewarding when she saw them smile and respond to all the love and care she tried so hard to give them.

She tried not to take her job home with her, but her nature was caring and full of empathy. That was something she shared with Alan; they both had stressful jobs, but they truly cared about the people they came into contact with. She knew that bringing a criminal to justice was very fulfilling for Alan; it was the relatives of the murdered victim he cared about, and they deserved closure. They didn't talk about work much to each other because their times together were precious. Alan was frequently called away, but she understood. If they were living together that would still happen. But she couldn't think of anything nicer than him coming home late and cuddling up to her in bed, and waking up next to him in the morning.

He had always liked Eleanor, and Zoe could see why. She was a brilliant actress and singer, in fact multi talented, and because she had been a child star, it felt like she had been around for ever, yet still seemed incredibly young. He hadn't said much, but Eleanor's death must have shocked him. It had certainly shocked Zoe, and the reaction of the British public said it all. Eleanor had been greatly loved and respected. It was amazing that during such a stressful case, he should ask her to move in, but when she thought about it, being together when life was so stressful would only make them stronger.

She had mentioned briefly to her mother this morning that Alan had asked her to move in with him, and her mum's response had been happy, as Zoe had expected. Her dad had already left for work, but she knew how much they liked and admired Alan and, after two years together, it was no great surprise. She couldn't wait to start their new life together and see what the future might hold.

They were not seeing each other until Friday of this week, as she was working late, but she had the complete day off. So, as far as she was concerned, that was her moving in day. Alan was finishing early, so he would bring the car round, and everything she had packed would be loaded on board. This was the beginning of a new chapter in her life, and no matter how hard the next three days were at work, she knew she would cope, as she had so much to look forward to.

Alan arrived back at the station after interviewing Matthew Roberts, scratching his head even more. Here was yet another possible suspect. By his own admission he had been in the apartment very close to the time Eleanor had been murdered. He was also having a secret relationship with her, although he claimed they were going to get married. Yet her sister had insisted that Eleanor was still in love with her ex-husband Alfie. Amongst Eleanor's papers, a copy of her will was found, and it was now confirmed that she had left everything to be split between Alfie, Faith and Amy. Was it a question of Eleanor never having found the time to alter her will? Or had she truly hoped that Alfie would return to her? Alan suspected that Matthew had been lying. Maybe he had wanted to marry Eleanor, but were his feelings reciprocated?

He noticed Ross hanging about. Oh, how that bloke got on his nerves; so arrogant, and thought he knew everything. No doubt he would be airing his views. Sure enough, there was a tap on his door, not long after he had gone into his office.

"Can I speak to you guv?"

"Of course." Alan's voice was gruff, and Sarah stiffened, hoping they would play nicely. She wanted to go home soon.

"It's about Grant. I know I shouldn't have arrested him, but as you have the evidence, the bronze horse, surely it's time to charge him now?"

Alan was privately wishing that he would do one, but he had to squash him with dignity. This bloke Ross brought out the worst in him.

"Tomorrow morning come into the main office. I am getting the whole team together to discuss the case. It's not clear cut at all. There are several suspects, including Grant. What we have to be careful about now, seeing as it is 2021, is that we don't pin a crime on a person whose only fault is that he is different. I believe he has been framed, Sarah does too, and because he is vulnerable, the real culprit would be more likely to choose him to frame rather than anyone else."

Ross bit back his annoyance, he could feel that Clarke disapproved of him. His one aim was to make that weirdo suffer for being different. Guilty or not, he would like to see Grant go down for this murder. But it seemed that Clarke and Sarah Stevens were going to do everything they could to prevent it. He would love to vent his frustration, but he was aware of their different rank, and knew he would come off worse. He wasn't used to curtailing to others. And he had pesky Wendy sniffing round him too, and fussing about the weirdo. However, he would say something at the meeting tomorrow. There could well be others who agreed with him, and it would be great if he could ruffle Clarke's feathers.

"OK guv, tomorrow it is then. Goodnight."

"Goodnight," said Alan, relief coursing through him. Maybe there was hope for this bloke yet.

"He's getting very subservient," laughed Sarah, "but somehow I don't believe him. He'll be on your case tomorrow. How he would love to be you!"

"Yes, and thank God he's not," said Alan with feeling. He wished Zoe was at home tonight. He could do with seeing her smile, and putting all this out of his head for just one evening. At least Friday was not that far away.

Chapter Ten

Alan came into work on Wednesday morning after a troubled night. The case was weighing heavily on his mind, and he felt a duty to wrap it up and find the killer. Isabel was anxious to lay her sister to rest, but as yet forensics had not released the body. The public also wanted their beautiful icon to rest in peace, and because of her high profile, it was expected that between them, Isabel and Dawn would organise an event that allowed many celebrities to say their goodbyes to her.

When he headed to the main office, his team were waiting for him, and the buzz of conversation stopped when he entered the room. Sarah appeared with coffee for them both before he addressed them all. Out of the corner of his eye he could see Ross Green, lounging casually against a desk. Wendy was not standing with Ross, as she had in the past, but she was at the front of the group that had gathered round the board, on which photos of all the suspects were pinned. Alan faced his team, and spoke to them.

"Good morning, everyone. Up on the board we have pictures of all our suspects. I am going to go through each one with you, and if anyone has anything to add, put your hand up. We need to get this case wrapped up, and so far it is looking very hard to crack it."

"The press are giving us a hard time!" remarked Ross, very pointedly.

"Well they should try doing our job!"

Alan said this with feeling. He could see Ross was trying to create dissension, but was relieved when no one else added any comment, so he continued.

"It has been eight days since Eleanor was murdered, and it seems like the British public continue to be in shock, and the newspapers are making a fortune out of their distress. She was probably the best known actress in Britain; in fact, well known globally, and also our National Treasure. The girl next door, and greatly loved. So the public are angry, and they expect us to bring the killer to justice." He paused to check all eyes were on him, and his team were listening, and then continued:

"What we do know about her is she liked to keep her private life away from the press, and until her untimely demise, she succeeded. In questioning her family we have discovered this. Firstly, she was very close to her sister Isabel, their relationship survived quite a few family dramas. Secondly, she was still in love with her ex-husband, even though he had married again, as she had left a third of her assets to him. Thirdly, behind the happy exterior that she presented to the world was a woman who, because of past experiences, had issues, and regularly attended psychiatric counselling."

Still nobody spoke, and all eyes were on him. Even in death, fascination surrounded Eleanor.

"She was hit over the head with her own ornament, a bronze horse," looking warningly at Ross, he continued. "We will go into that later, but it would appear that she was hit in temper. The killer picked up the nearest object, so something she said, or did, made that person very angry."

"I can't imagine her making anyone angry. She was lovely," said Wendy, who had often wished she had the looks and beauty of Eleanor, her icon.

"How do you know she was lovely? She was an actress, so she could make people believe anything. Maybe she wasn't," said Ross darkly, and there was a murmur of dismay amongst the team.

Wendy bit her lips together. Why was Ross being so negative? He was hindering rather than helping. First he had bullied Peter, and now he was trying to discredit Eleanor. This man seemed to have such a chip on his shoulder.

Alan looked at him with distaste. They had kept this investigation very discreet and not tarnished Eleanor's name. The team didn't need to know everything, so why on earth was this motor mouth coming out with such negativity. Of course, he was trying to derail him, and get some backing from the others, but so far it hadn't worked.

"Now I am going to tell you about the suspects. You can make notes, and if you have any questions, or observations, then I will welcome your input."

He pointed at the picture of Faith on the board. "Faith Brian, housekeeper to Eleanor, worked for her for three years, has been left a third share in Eleanor's estate. She has always spoken highly of Eleanor, and she found the body. During recent checks through our files, we discovered that Faith's sister-in-law lodged a complaint against her when her brother Joseph died, leaving his bungalow and estate to his wife Faith. She felt Faith had coerced money from Joseph, but after 15 years of marriage, why should he not leave everything to his wife? It seems that Eleanor valued her because she stayed, whereas a lot of other housekeepers had left because of irregular hours. So Eleanor chose to show her appreciation."

A hand went up. Another PC about the same age as Ross, but with a much better attitude.

"Sounds like the sister-in-law was jealous guv, but, as you say, she did have a motive to get even richer quicker."

"She did." Alan used his pen to point out the next picture of Isabel.

"Eleanor's elder sister Isabel. Her motive could be anger, as Eleanor failed to attend a violin recital that Isabel's daughter Amy was giving. She left an angry message on the phone the night before. Her daughter Amy benefits with a third share of Eleanor's estate, and Isabel and her husband Sam both say they were together that morning, a day at home, and Amy was at college."

Another hand went up, a WPC this time. "Was Isabel jealous of her sister's success?"

Alan responded, "I don't think she was. In fact, she played a supporting role to her sister when she left home. I think she has always loved her deeply, and cared about her. However, there is such a thin line between love and hate, so we can't rule her out, as I believe this crime was committed in the heat of the moment."

His pen rested on the picture of Alfie. He noted his face was handsome, but he seemed to lack character. Would he have had it in him to commit murder?

"This is Alfie Mason, started off as a fan, then wooed and

87

married Eleanor, but then left her for another woman. They are now married, but very poor. Alfie also left a message asking for money. Eleanor never altered her will because the family believe she hoped he would come back to her. Alfie has a third share coming to him."

Sarah put her hand up. "It's incredible, guv, that a woman like Eleanor, who could have had anyone, would forgive him for leaving her for another woman, and then wait for him to come back. I would never let a man treat me that way!"

Looking at her, Alan didn't doubt it. Sarah would be a match for any man, and he realised Eleanor had obviously had issues of insecurity. Once Alfie had left her, he had missed all the privileges that he had enjoyed whilst being married to a rich woman. That gave him a definite motive.

"Naturally, Alfie's wife Angela has given him an alibi; said he was at home surfing the net looking for jobs."

Sarah intervened politely: "And we checked it, guv. Somebody was using his computer at that time, but it could have been her, and Alfie might have been out."

"Exactly!" said Alan, "so another suspect."

His pen moved over the board, to rest on the picture of Peter Grant. He was expecting Ross Green to give him grief over this.

"Peter Grant. A very intelligent man, but suffers from Asperger's, which affects his behaviour. He is obsessive, and has in fact stalked Eleanor for a long time. He is besotted by her, and appeared to be devastated by her death. He has trouble functioning in everyday life. His council flat is open house to anyone, as he can't cope with hanging onto his front door key. When he was brought in for questioning, we searched his flat and found the bronze horse, which was the murder weapon, in his kitchen. He denied all knowledge of having it, and actually I believe him. With his lack of security, anyone could have planted it, knowing he would be blamed and would also find it hard to defend himself."

"Guv, it must be him. We could wrap this up today!" said Ross.

Before Alan could say anything, to his complete surprise, the usually quiet Wendy leapt out of her chair, her cheeks were flushed, and her eyes flashed with anger. Her voice was shaking with emotion:

"You are so biased Ross, and it's not right. Peter is vulnerable, and he doesn't need people like you bullying and victimising him!"

"Not bias, just common sense," sneered Ross. But the support he had been expecting didn't come, and there was an embarrassed pause until Alan delivered his blow.

"There's one problem with your theory Green. Whoever framed Peter Grant wasn't very clever. None of his DNA was found at Eleanor's apartment, so he was never there, and could not have killed her."

He had the satisfaction of watching the biased PC's face crumble. He might have thought he could swing the opinion his way, but he had failed. And Wendy looked so relieved, she obviously felt very strongly about it.

"Max Taylor is a taxi driver; we have no motive that we are aware of for him to be the killer. He was Eleanor's regular cab driver, and he came to pick her up that morning, although she never appeared, he said. We found traces of his DNA in the flat, but he has picked her up before."

Alan poised his finger next over Matthew's picture. "And finally, this man is Matthew Roberts, Eleanor's psychiatrist, and probably knows more about her than anyone. He lives in the same block of apartments and we have CCTV footage of him outside her flat that morning. By his own admission, he was having an affair with her, and they had sex that morning. He came voluntarily to the station and was tested, and it was positive. He maintains they were going to get married, but we only have his word for it. Isabel insists that her sister was still in love with Alfie."

"So this could have been a crime of passion, sir. He asked her to marry him, and she turned him down?" remarked Sarah, thoughtfully.

"Maybe. And if you remember when we left this man yesterday he was absolutely in bits."

"Yes sir, but more because his career was threatened due to his affair with a patient."

"I agree, Sarah. In my opinion, this man is the most likely to have done it. But, folks, what are your thoughts? I would love some input."

This announcement prompted everyone to start talking at once, and the babble of conversation grew, as everyone expressed their opinion. Alan let them have their head for about five minutes, and then he rapped on his desk for their attention, and suddenly it all died down.

"Right, let's put this to the vote. Each time I mention a name, if you think it's them, put your hand up. You can only vote for one person, by the way."

After the showing of hands, it was clear to see how divided it was. Alfie was a strong contender, as was Matthew Roberts. Not many people thought it was Isabel or Faith, and because he had stated there was no DNA of his at the flat, only one person thought it was Peter. That was, of course, Ross Green, stubbornly refusing to accept that it didn't seem possible. Alan couldn't help smiling to himself. PC Green was something else.

Sarah and Wendy both thought it was Alfie, and Alan himself had veered towards Matthew, who had actually been around at the time. Although Max had been there too, he couldn't find a motive for him. A thought sprang into his mind: could Max also have been having an affair with her? But then he dismissed it, feeling rather guilty. Eleanor may not have been perfect, but sleeping with two men at once? Max had been perfectly willing to do the test, and it was negative, whereas Matthew's had been positive.

"Well, thanks everyone for your input. If any of you think of anything else, please let me know."

It was whilst he sat drinking another coffee with Sarah, that Alan saw Ross coming back into the room. He had an excited look on his face, and Alan wondered what else he was going to come up with.

"Guv, I just checked up on Matthew Roberts, he has a criminal record."

"Go on then," said Alan patiently. At least he had abandoned the vendetta against Peter Grant.

"Ten years ago, a patient brought a complaint against him for attempted rape. It was never proved, and soon after she committed suicide. It was thought she was severely depressed because of the case not being proved. This was in Birmingham, so Roberts moved here and bought this practice.

"Good work, Green," said Alan. Credit where it was due, he had come up with something interesting. "Sarah, I think we should visit him again. Something here doesn't seem quite right, although forensics did say there was no sign of a struggle."

"Well, if she liked him, there would not have been a struggle," pointed out Sarah.

"Yes, liked him, but didn't want to marry him," said Alan. Whatever the truth was, only Matthew knew now. He seemed to be the main suspect, so another visit to his Harley Street practice was imperative. Were they finally getting there?

Matthew had spent a sleepless night since the visit from the police. To lose everything because of his relationship with Eleanor would cut him deeply. He had built up a good base of clients, and enjoyed a great lifestyle with all the luxuries that this afforded him. He had naively imagined that, if they got married, then the relationship would not affect his working life. But it had all changed when Eleanor died. He could still remember that bitter sweet morning when he had gone to see her, and they had made love. But when he asked her to marry him, she had laughed, and said she didn't think of him in that way, and that had hurt him deeply. Surely he had been a much better proposition than her leech of a husband, who was the main reason for her insecurities?

Matthew was aware of his own failings. Ten years ago he had fallen in love before with a patient. Melissa, in his eyes, had been a beautiful goddess. But in fact she had turned out to be a call girl with one intent; to make as much money as she could out of him. He had been swayed by her beauty, and her apparent vulnerability, and he felt he wanted to love and protect her forever. They had enjoyed a brief sexual relationship, and then she had stopped being his patient, and dumped him. Whilst his heart was healing, he was amazed to then find out she had accused him of attempted rape. He had been taken to court, but apparently Melissa had done it before. Her past had not exactly been without incident. The case was thrown out, but he knew he was still on police records. So he had left Birmingham, and come to London to set up again. Shortly after he started his new life he had heard that Melissa had committed suicide. He certainly knew it wasn't because of him, it was more likely that she was heavily in debt and couldn't see a way out of it. But he also knew that it would look as if it was because of him. It seemed, even in death, Melissa had done all she could to ruin his good name.

As the years passed, and his clientele grew, he started to relax, and put the past behind him. Then one day Eleanor's PR lady had phoned him, and asked if he could take on Eleanor as a client. He already knew her from her TV and film appearances, it was impossible not to, and like everyone else, he was captured by her beauty and charisma. Eleanor poured her heart out to him; the effect the loss of her dad had on her, and her evil stepfather, who had raped and made her pregnant at such a young age. How Isabel had helped her, and her shame that she had then had a daughter by Isabel's husband. Her candid honesty completely won him over, and he saw her as a damaged person, rather than a bad person,

Sharing a closeness like that, he felt that it was inevitable they would fall in love, and he had truly believed that Eleanor had loved him too. He had even moved to the same block of apartments, so he could be close to her. He knew for sure that, this time, Eleanor would not be using him for money. She was richer than he was and, for a time, being so near allowed their relationship to flourish. He was confident that all the pain and rejection she had felt from Alfie leaving her was diminishing, and she could now see Alfie for what he was, a man who had used her to get his hands on her money.

He felt he knew Eleanor inside out. His job as a psychiatrist was to give people peace of mind, and he believed she had been coming to terms with everything that life had thrown at her. But he realised he hadn't really known her, when she laughed at his marriage proposal; that had hurt so much. Now he was in a situation where he had allowed two women to ruin his life and his reputation, and he wasn't sure he could come out unscathed this time.

When he finally dozed off out of sheer exhaustion, he awoke with a start at the sound of his intercom buzzing. He answered it with a feeling of fear deep inside. He just knew the police were not going to leave him alone. He was like a rat caught in a trap, and there was nothing he could do, and nowhere to run and hide any more.

"Yes, who is it?"

"Good morning, Mr Roberts, we would like you to accompany us to the station to help us further with our enquiries."

"I have told you all I know."

Alan grimaced to himself. They had hardly got started yet.

This man had a past, an unsavoury one, and Alan was convinced he had been lying about marrying Eleanor. He was acting in such a guilty way; so a spell at the station being interrogated was necessary.

"We'll be the judge of that."

"Do I need to have a solicitor present?"

"You well might."

Matthew conceded defeat. There was no other choice, so he let them in. Although polite, there was a steely edge to Alan Clarke's voice, and Sarah, the WPC who accompanied him looked very serious. Whilst they were waiting he made a call to his solicitor, who arranged to meet him at the station in about half an hour. They accompanied him out to the police car, and he got in, praying that none of his neighbours were watching, but maybe it was too late anyway. The cold hand of fear was clutching at him. He felt sure he was going to be charged with Eleanor's murder, and he had absolutely no idea how he could escape punishment.

Chapter Eleven

"Have you got a key to Eleanor's apartment?"

Matthew was so glad they couldn't see how hard his heart was hammering. There was no point lying to them, they would find out, and it would only be worse for him. He sat in the bare and forbidding interview room, his solicitor sat next to him, and opposite was Alan Clarke, and his WPC Sarah.

"Yes. Sometimes I finished before she did, and she didn't like coming home to an empty house," he said miserably.

"Did you ever see her housekeeper?"

"No. She came much earlier, Eleanor didn't want anyone to know about me."

"Do you know Peter Grant?"

Matthew licked his dry lips, and tried to swallow before speaking. There was something about Alan Clarke that reduced him to a blubbering wreck. He knew more than anyone, that keeping himself calm and just answering the questions was what he needed to do, but he carried so much guilt inside him. This was the second time he had been brought down by a woman.

"I have not met him, but I know of him. Eleanor was being stalked by him, and she spoke about how tiresome it was."

Alan was trying to decide whether he was telling the truth or not. Here was a man who had managed to be involved with two women in the past ten years. He had abused his position, so he could well be capable of murder.

"We know that ten years ago Melissa Simpson accused you of

attempted rape. The case was never proved, but shortly afterwards she committed suicide."

"I didn't try to rape her. We were lovers. At least I thought we were, but I later found out she was a call girl, and she tried to get money out of me by bringing the charges. Luckily my innocence was proved."

"And very shortly after that she took an overdose, and the subsequent inquest verdict was that she committed suicide," Alan reminded him.

In spite of all his fears, Matthew felt angry. He was getting the blame for everything, but Melissa had been the author of her own misfortune. Her drug taking had been nothing to do with him, he hadn't even realised she was sniffing cocaine. But she had tried to use him to fund her disgusting habit, and when that hadn't worked, and she found herself so heavily in debt, she had ended it all, knowing that he would be blamed for it.

"She didn't do it because of me, it was because she had so many debts!" he shouted desperately. "I know it looks bad, but I am innocent!" he said, turning to his solicitor in desperation.

The solicitor was a stocky insignificant man in a dark suit, but he interjected.

"That is all supposition. My client was found innocent of the attempted rape, and he is not responsible for what happened afterwards."

But Alan continued with his theories. "I suggest to you that you did know Peter Grant. He was well known because his mother was a local seamstress. You knew where he lived, you panicked when you hit Eleanor over the head with the horse, and took the murder weapon home with you. Later you went round to Grant's flat. It was common knowledge that the flat was left open most of the time, and you then planted the bronze horse there."

Matthew was pale with fear now. He could not prove otherwise, so now he would be charged. He felt he had nothing left to fight with. But his solicitor was still trying.

"If you have any evidence to back this up, then arrest my client, if not then you must let him go home. It seems to me that all you have are theories, not facts!" he finished triumphantly.

Alan knew he was right. Just because he felt in his bones that Matthew Roberts had killed Eleanor in a flash of anger after being rejected, it wasn't enough. They had no hard evidence, and couldn't prove it. The bronze horse had been carefully wiped of any fingerprints. He had no choice but to let him go home, and all he could hope for was that they would eventually find out something incriminating about him.

"OK, Mr Roberts, you can return home, but we may need to interview you again, so please don't leave the country," he said, rising from his chair. He felt Roberts had guilt written all over his face, but proving it was hard.

He watched them leave the room, turning towards Sarah for her opinion.

"Well Sarah, everything about him, his body language and the fear in his eyes, makes me convinced he is the killer. Your thoughts?"

"Mmm, he could be, but he doesn't seem to have a very strong character. I would think that Alfie would be more capable of doing it. He was ruthless enough to leave her, and she was his money tree. Now he's broke, and he needs his inheritance."

"You have a point," mused Alan. "Honestly, we just keep going round in circles here. Let's see what happens tomorrow."

Although Isabel had got over the immediate shock of losing Eleanor so suddenly, she was finding not having her sister around was devastating. She had loved her ever since she was born, and always tried to protect her. Having Amy back home again was such a relief; she hated herself for putting her through such turmoil. Sam, too, had suffered a terrible attack of conscience, but life was beginning to settle down now. Amy had realised that both her parents were less than perfect, but had understood that everything they had done had been meant for her own good. Sam had shown his weakness of character to her now, but she had forgiven him, he was still her dad, and she still loved him. If he had not made Eleanor pregnant, she would not even exist. Isabel was the only mother she had ever known, and she had always been close to her. Now that it was all out in the open, it somehow strengthened the bond.

To Isabel, not being able to arrange her sister's funeral made her feel she would never have closure. Without the culprit being brought to justice there was no chance of moving on. It felt to her that the police were being very slow. Nothing could bring her beloved Eleanor back and she would always miss her. She had been a complex character, inspiring love wherever she went, but always having her issues to contend with. Eleanor's judgement of men was hopeless. Alfie had been no more than a freeloader, and if Isabel were trying to solve this case, he would be the main suspect. She had always felt that Eleanor had thrown herself away on this man, and he hadn't been worthy of her. She had been careful not to malign him too much to the police, feeling that in circumstances like this it was better not to sound too bitter.

She had wished so many times that they would make an arrest; maybe then Eleanor's body could be released, and she could start to organise the funeral. She didn't care who they arrested. Just to have someone accountable for the crime would help, then the public might also calm down. There was huge pressure on the police, she knew, but they had to solve this murder.

It wasn't a great surprise when Alan Clarke and Sarah paid her another visit. She opened the door to them and immediately enquired, "Have you found the killer yet?"

"We are not sure," said Alan. "But did you know Eleanor was having an affair with her psychiatrist, Matthew Roberts?"

Isabel stared at him, trying to digest this new revelation. "Are you sure? Surely it would have been unethical for him to have an affair with her."

"It was, and right now Mr Roberts is acting in a very guilty way. He insists they were going to get married."

"He took advantage of my sister. He was there to help her with her issues, not to take advantage of her. She was very vulnerable you know!"

"Did she not confide in you about their relationship?"

Isabel became angry now. If truth was known, she felt that, as they were so close, if Eleanor was having an affair with Matthew Roberts, she should have been told.

"What relationship?" she scoffed. "My sister would not have been planning marriage without telling me. She was still licking her wounds after Alfie's betrayal. I don't believe it."

"We do have evidence that your sister had sex with him that day, and he also admitted it. There were no signs to indicate it was forced upon her."

Isabel's mind was whirling now, and she felt hurt that Eleanor had kept such an important fact from her. However, she didn't

97

want to let her guard down to this nosy chief inspector, who seemed to be dissecting everything.

"The reason why she didn't tell me was because it was unethical, and she knew I would have put a stop to it."

"How?"

"By going to see him, and threatening to report him if it didn't stop."

"It would have ruined his career and his reputation."

"I don't care. He took advantage of Eleanor. Why are we even discussing this anyway now?"

Alan studied her; she seemed very angry. He tried to read Isabel's mind. She appeared to dote on her sister, even to the point of trying to over protect her, and always blaming the other person when something happened to her. But was this just an act? Had she been consumed with jealousy that Eleanor had it all, and angry because she had missed her own daughter's violin recital? Had she gone round there just after Roberts had left, maybe even seen him leave, and had she just snapped? There was such a fine line between love and hate. Had the worm finally turned?

"We are discussing it because we want to solve the case," remarked Sarah, also noticing Isabel's agitation, and wondering what she was so sensitive about.

"Well, if he was having an affair with her, and was at the apartment, then he probably killed her. She wouldn't have married him, so maybe he was cross about that," retorted Isabel.

Alan was interested to see how she was trying to distract the conversation away from herself and blame Roberts. But he wasn't about to discuss the case with her. It was time to go.

"Well, Isabel, you have been very helpful as always. We will be in touch again soon."

"All I want to do is lay my sister to rest. It's distressing for the whole family."

She didn't add 'except my mother', but she was thinking it. Jean was getting worse by the day, now, convinced that Eleanor was causing harm to herself and Dan. She thought he was about to leave her, and Isabel found it distressing to realise just how much harm that man had done to her mother and her sister. And to think he was still out there somewhere, lording it up with her mother's money. Thank goodness he hadn't managed to get his hands on the house, otherwise it would have been much harder to get her into Peacehaven.

"We want to wrap up the case as much as you, but several people had a motive," said Sarah.

"I hope you are not including me or Sam when you say that," said Isabel indignantly.

"We have to include everyone, and it's often the most unlikely person, so we can't rule anyone out," Alan said firmly. Isabel certainly seemed jumpy, and Amy would soon inherit her third share. What was she hiding?

In the car, whilst travelling back to the station, Sarah studied all the notes she had made.

"You know sir, this case is doing my head in. First I thought it was Alfie, her feckless ex. Peter Grant was a possibility, and then I decided it must be Roberts, because not only did he live in the same block of apartments, he also had a key, and was there at about the time she was murdered. He could have put the bronze horse in his briefcase, and planted it at Peter's council flat, knowing that Peter could probably be talked into confessing. . . "

"Yes, I go along with that. I am actually thinking about bringing him in for further questioning. . . But I am not sure now. Isabel definitely was acting strangely today, and somehow she seems too good to be true as a sister. How many sisters would accept an affair between their husband and their younger sister without falling out with them?"

"I have wondered that myself, but she has an alibi; she was at home with Sam."

"That means nothing!" pointed out Alan. "He would give her an alibi anyway. He may have been the unfaithful one, but Isabel wears the trousers in that household. He is too weak to do it himself, and if she did it, he would protect her. After all, he will always have a lot to make up to her."

"Yes, but they still strike me as a very happy and in love couple. She clearly adores him, you can see it in her eyes," remarked Sarah.

"Don't expect a mere bloke like me to notice those sort of things, and don't go all Mills and Boone on me," laughed Alan.

"Just giving you a woman's opinion," said Sarah lightly.

*   *   *   *

99

Isabel heaved a sigh of relief after they had departed. She had never been able to tell lies. Her character was straight and honest, but, over the years, there was so much she had had to conceal.

On the day of the murder, she had been at home and, for some of the time, so had Sam. He had popped out about nine o'clock to fill the car up with petrol, as they were going to Bath the next day for a lawyers' convention. But they had never gone, because after she had the news about Eleanor, she hadn't been able to focus on anything else. Her mind had been so full of her sister, she hadn't even considered going, so Sam had rung up and made their apologies.

And when Sam came back that day, Isabel had nipped down to the shop in her little runabout to pick up some dry cleaning, as she needed the dress for the convention. The shop was very close to Eleanor's flat, and when she left it, she remembered it had been nine-forty, because she had glanced at the clock on the wall as she walked out.

Knowing how suspicious the police were, she realised that it would look bad for both of them if they had admitted to being out at that time, and they would be hauled in for questioning again. When Sam had gone on his own, she had to trust him, and she did trust him, their marriage would never have survived this long if she hadn't. She truly believed that he had never been on his own with Eleanor, or even given himself an opportunity to make that same mistake again, so he wouldn't have visited Eleanor that morning. The fact that Eleanor's apartment had both Sam's and her DNA meant nothing, as they were frequently visiting her. But every time the police came round, she was nervous. Apparently the CCTV had failed that day, it was an old system that needed to be updated, so the police had to rely on those who had been around at the time to inform them.

But the knowledge that they had both left the house in that time frame made her feel so guilty. Hiding anything from the police was never a good idea, and it only needed someone from the dry cleaners to remember she was there, or from the garage to remember that Sam had been buying petrol. She just wished someone would be charged. And in her eyes, Matthew Roberts deserved to be, after taking advantage of Eleanor. She felt that her family had been through enough. How on earth would Amy cope with her parents being taken to the station to be questioned about

100

Eleanor's murder? Isabel wasn't going to let that happen. They had to stand united, because surely soon the police would find someone accountable. Their lives had been totally shattered with the death of Eleanor, and now they had started the process of rebuilding the bonds between them, with still a long way to go, she couldn't let the police shatter their family again.

Chapter Twelve

After being questioned by the police, Matthew had gone home and, with shaky hands, opened a bottle of whisky. By the time he had downed the third glass he felt better. His life was in ruins now. He was convinced at the very least he would be struck off, and maybe even charged with Eleanor's murder. How he wished he had not gone to see her that morning; that bitter sweet morning when they had made love, and it had meant so much to him that he had asked her to marry him.

It hurt when she said she didn't think of him that way. It made him feel so rejected. He had fallen deeply in love with her, and knew all about her insecurities, and all he wanted to do was to love and protect her for the rest of his life.

Try as he might, he could not remember what happened after that. He didn't recall leaving the apartment, but he had noticed Max Taylor in his taxi. And all he had inside him was this huge pain of rejection. The woman who meant everything to him had turned him down, and he knew his life could never be complete without her.

His relationship with Eleanor had started off as a professional one, and then it progressed to a trusting relationship, and one day they had become lovers. She had said he was the balm she needed after Alfie's betrayal, and he hadn't minded that, as he wanted her to feel safe with him. His love for her became an obsession to him. He could not eat or sleep properly, or even stop thinking about her. She seemed so happy in his company, and he had convinced himself that she was over Alfie. She barely mentioned him.

Eventually his hand flopped down. The unfinished whisky trickled slowly onto the cream carpet, but Matthew had by then fallen asleep.

He woke up the next morning stiff and uncomfortable, and still fully dressed. He couldn't face going in to work. He imagined the look on his secretary's face when they arrested him, then walking past any waiting clients, and finally being torn to pieces by the newspapers with all his previous past gleefully exposed. He knew they would love to reveal any scandal.

After telephoning his secretary to cancel all clients for that day, he opened yet another bottle, then he steadily drank himself into oblivion. Matthew was a broken man. He had neither the strength nor the courage to fight back. Just to make sure, he downed a bottle of pills as well, and then he lay down on the floor, and welcomed death. Soon nobody could touch him any more.

Alfie was hoping that the police would have arrested someone for the murder of Eleanor by now. Every day that passed made him more nervous because he hadn't been completely honest with his alibi. Luckily Angela would stick by him, and insist they had been together that morning, and they had been for some of the time.

But the morning after his phone call, when there had been absolutely no response from Eleanor, he had told Angela that he would have to go and see her. They were desperate for money, he couldn't find work, and they had a young baby. Angela agreed he had no other choice but to see Eleanor face to face. He still had a key to the front door, she had never asked for it back, and so he planned to get there before she left to go to the theatre. He knew she usually left late in the morning, so around ten o'clock she would be there, up and eating breakfast. It was before her housekeeper came in too.

So he had gone to try and remonstrate with her, maybe even to appeal to her better nature. His biggest fear was whether he had been caught on the CCTV camera, and if so, when would the police come back knocking on his door?

Angela hadn't really liked the idea of Alfie visiting Eleanor. It wasn't that she didn't trust him, she knew that he was done with

Eleanor, he couldn't cope with what he referred to as her 'Diva' behaviour. He said she brought out the worst in him, and although Angela had never experienced Alfie's temper, he had admitted to her that once, in a fit of anger, he had pushed Eleanor. He felt ashamed, as he didn't condone violent behaviour towards women, but he said she really knew how to get under his skin, and it was shortly after that incident that he had left her.

When he returned home, he had said Eleanor had refused to discuss money with him, and that was it. He didn't mention it any more. And then within a couple of hours, the police had come to give them the news. Alfie had looked very shocked and upset, and the police had gone away, but returned later to check their alibi. She stood doggedly by her husband, and she hoped and prayed that no one had seen him that morning. They had carried on with life as normal since then, and Alfie had said he was hopeful that once all the estate was settled, he would be getting some money. But Angela couldn't feel happy about that. There was an unspoken question that hung between them. It was threatening their happiness and their future, and she didn't have the courage to ask it. Had Alfie killed Eleanor?

Ross was pleased that it looked like Matthew Roberts was now in the frame. Naturally he would have preferred it to have been the weirdo, but he had been made to look a bit foolish by Clarke, and he hadn't liked the fact that no one had supported him. But then he had been the one to think of checking Robert's past, and he had come up with that gem of information that he had been charged with attempted rape. The fact that he had got away with it meant nothing, he had a police record.

The more he thought about it, the more it all seemed to fit like a jigsaw. Roberts lived in the same block of apartments, he was having an affair with Eleanor and probably had access to her flat. She would have confided in him, during the psychiatric counselling, about Peter Grant stalking her, so it would seem that Roberts came up with the plan to plant the offending bronze horse in Grant's kitchen. It had nearly worked too, except that he hadn't thought about it properly. Peter Grant had never been allowed access to her flat. He only ever hung about outside, as stalkers do. She would never have let him in. He was a nuisance, and she was constantly trying to get away from him. So as his DNA was not in the flat, it could not have been him. Roberts had admitted having sex with Eleanor that morning, and his DNA results proved he had been there, so without a shadow of a doubt, he was the killer. Ross was going to make sure they all remembered that he was the one who checked out Robert's past. He was taking credit for this one. Clarke might sit up and notice him after this. Arresting Roberts would make everyone happy, especially the public.

Personally, Ross didn't think Eleanor deserved all the accolades. After all, she had used men for her own pleasure and then dropped them. He didn't think of her as a National Treasure, more of a slag, but it was more than his job and reputation were worth to voice these thoughts. He had been a fan of hers at one time, but during this investigation, when facts started coming out, he had changed his opinion. He slowly took out the photo of her that he had always carried in his wallet, and ripped it in half, dropping it into the office bin. Now Eleanor Harrison was well and truly out of his life.

Faith was hoping the police would have arrested someone by now. The sooner that Eleanor was laid to rest the better. Her face still dominated the TV and newspapers, and the mass hysteria demonstrated by the public had now subsided into a sullen silence, everyone wanted to know who was culpable, and to see them brought to justice.

Every day that passed without the police returning to question her, she felt was a bonus. She had never wanted to be deceitful, but it just seemed easier to say she came to work and found Eleanor on the floor. They didn't need to know that she had let herself in when Matthew was there, and made good her escape before they heard her. She had seen the taxi driver outside, but Eleanor was too busy with Matthew to heed him. She had also seen the other visitor, and she didn't know whether they actually got in to see Eleanor because she went for a coffee. When she returned, they had all gone, and she had let herself in, fully expecting Eleanor to have left for work.

With her previous involvement with Joseph, and her inheritance, she really couldn't afford to have the police probing into her past. It was all done and dusted now, and all she wanted to do was move on, and get on with her life.

Chapter Thirteen

Alan's mobile rang out impatiently that morning, and he grimaced. Today was his day off. Zoe was moving in, and he had taken the day off to help her. He felt with all the crime and violence that he came into contact with, Zoe felt like the one good thing in his life. She was used to trauma in her own working life, but like him, she didn't allow it to drag her down. They both had the same desire to help people who needed it, and he felt the thought of coming home to her after a stressful day would be both soothing and calming. To wake up to that smile in the morning would put him on the right foot for the day ahead.

They both worked irregular hours, but it was not something he thought would come between them. They respected each other's ability to do their job properly, and accepted there would be times when one or other of them would have to stay later, or be called back to work for an emergency. As Alan picked up his mobile to answer it, he had a feeling that this might be one of those times.

"Good morning, sir. I am afraid we have a new development today. The body of Matthew Roberts was found in his apartment this morning. He appears to have taken an overdose of pills."

"Oh, no. Who found him?"

"His cleaning lady. She arrived at nine o'clock. Usually he would have gone to work, and she found him fully dressed on the floor of his lounge with two empty whisky bottles beside him, and an empty bottle of pills."

Alan knew what this meant. It was a huge shock; but was it really? Roberts had appeared to be very nervous when

106

interviewed. Had he taken his own life to avoid being brought to justice? Had this last act of desperation cemented his belief that Roberts had killed Eleanor? He couldn't be sure, and he needed to go into work, and get up to speed with the investigation yet again.

"OK, I will be in the office shortly. Get the team together, we need to review the case again."

He looked at the clock beside his bed. It was nine-thirty, he had arranged to take his car to Zoe's about eleven o'clock. Here he was letting her down again, but duty had called. He picked up his mobile and called her. Her excited voice came over the line.

"Hi Alan, I am nearly packed."

"I am so sorry, Zoe. We have had a new development in the case, and I have to go in, I can't avoid it."

Zoe gave a nervous giggle. It was no great surprise to her, and she wouldn't have cared so much about Alan if he had delegated his job to someone else. He wanted to wrap this case up for the sake of the grieving family, and the uneasy public. No one could rest easy until the culprit had been exposed. She knew he was doing the right thing.

"Don't worry. Daddy has offered to help me. I am afraid I have a lot of clothes. Do you want me to bring an extra wardrobe?"

Alan thought briefly about his flat, which right now was typically a bachelor's haven. Sometimes his clothes didn't even make it into the wardrobe, but instead they were lined up on the chair beside the bed. Would there be room for another wardrobe in the bedroom? There had to be, as Zoe would need her own because, knowing how orderly she was, her clothes would be hung up and treasured. He made an unconscious promise to himself that he would try harder to be tidier. His greatest problem seemed to be never having enough time. He always meant to tidy up, but then his mobile rang, and he found himself off again, trying to solve a case.

"Now what a good idea that is. My wardrobe needs to be sorted, much better for your clothes to be in their own space."

Zoe smiled to herself at the other end of the phone. During visits to Alan's flat, she had realised that he didn't have much sense of order, and he resisted all attempts by her to have a cleaning lady. He said he didn't want anyone poking into his private things, which was fair enough. But she felt certain that,

107

with her help, he could get his clothes into some sort of order. He always asked her advice when buying something new. He told her she had very good taste, which pleased her. In her eyes Alan always looked smart. His suits were of good quality, and his casual clothes, when he wore them, were well co-ordinated. But even if he hadn't dressed so smartly, his handsome looks alone, and expressive eyes, would have captured her interest. She felt she had definitely met Mr Right, even if he didn't know it yet. She had no intention of telling him this, because moving in together would be the true test to see whether they were compatible and if their love could last, but her womanly intuition felt that it would.

Zoe had already planned the evening meal, as, until now, she knew that Alan lived on takeaways and ready meals. She had cooked a chicken in readiness. They could have it hot or cold at whatever time he got home. She could now make sure he ate properly, and she couldn't wait to take care of him. She had seen her mother do the same for her dad for all of her life, and no matter how old fashioned it might be, she wanted to emulate them. And, who knows, during the times when she was later home, Alan might even take the reins and prepare dinner for her.

Alan felt so grateful that Zoe understood. He did feel guilty, because although he had often been called into work before, today had been a special one, with Zoe moving in, and he had really wanted to be a part of it. The thought of going home to her later was a comforting one, though, as this case was getting more complicated by the day.

He said goodbye to her, just in time for his mobile to ring again. This time it was Sarah ringing from work.

"Sir, I expect you heard about Matthew Roberts. I have been asked to visit the apartment whilst forensics are there."

"Yes, I am going to meet you there!"

"Are you sure, sir. I thought it was moving day for Zoe?"

"It is, but this case has to be sorted. I have to know whether he did commit suicide, and was it through guilt?"

Another stab of guilt went through him. Was he putting his fascination for Eleanor, and the desire to know who killed her, before his feelings for Zoe? But his head argued back with his heart.

He had earned his position as DCI, but he couldn't rest on his laurels; this case had affected the whole nation, and it was his duty to solve it as soon as he could. The reason why he cared so much about Zoe, even though his intention had not been to settle down so quickly, was because she was special. She understood the importance of his job, and she was not a demanding person who expected to be put first. In fact, it was because she was so special to him that he had asked her to move in. Zoe didn't know it yet, but he intended to marry her, he wasn't about to lose the love of his life to someone else. Knowing this gave him a glow inside, and made it easier to get on with the job in hand.

"Zoe is one in a million, and she understands. I will meet you outside the apartments in half an hour."

"OK boss. I am leaving now."

As Sarah left the building, and got in the car, she thought how lucky Alan was to have that sort of support. She had lost boyfriends in the past because of her job, and was currently single. It seemed her model figure and startling looks were not enough to keep a man when she wasn't always available to go out on a date. She sighed to herself, maybe she just hadn't met the right person yet, but then she was already devoted to one man.

When she arrived, she saw Alan standing outside the entrance to the apartments, and she fiercely squashed down her feelings of wanting to stroke his forehead, and ease the lines of worry from his face. She had been in love with Alan ever since she had been consigned to accompany him on investigations. But his body language had always stopped her from declaring it. Alan was firmly in love with Zoe, and she knew it, so it was a hopeless situation. The only time he was hers, was at work, and so she lived for her work, and the chance to be his working partner.

Her feelings about him refused to go away. And she hadn't shed any tears about the death of Eleanor. Eleanor had been Alan's pin up for years, and now she had gone. But there was still Zoe, and Sarah realised that no matter how striking her looks were, it was petite blonde curly haired women that Alan was attracted to, which was the complete opposite of herself. In her wilder moments she had even wondered how she could find a way to discredit Zoe in Alan's eyes, but that was difficult. She barely knew Zoe, only having met her once, and she seemed too damn perfect, and never put a foot wrong. With her passion for Alan getting stronger every day, all Sarah could hope for right now, was that some way of discrediting Zoe would present itself, and if it did, she would grasp it with both hands.

Alan pressed the buzzer to alert the caretaker, and he arrived very promptly. To Alan it was like history repeating itself when they went in, but this time the apartment was only one floor up. He nodded his thanks, and they entered the apartment, which had been cordoned off. Men in white coats were there, and Alan greeted them, looking past them to the body on the ground, fully dressed.

"It looks like an overdose, empty bottle of pills on the floor, and two empty whisky bottles beside him," said the white coated figure.

"Deliberate or accidental?" enquired Alan,

"Can't tell yet, and we may never know. It depends what state of mind he was in."

Alan had a mental picture of Matthew's face when they had questioned him. He would have described him as desperate, but was it because his career was over, or because he had killed Eleanor? Had he been a violent man? Matthew's job was to support people with mental problems, so he must have been compassionate. Had his passion for Eleanor been his downfall?

The white coated man removed the sheet which covered the face, and Alan looked at the eyes staring glassily at him. Apart from that, his face looked peaceful, and the worry lines on his forehead were relaxed. So maybe he was finally at peace. After all, no one could ever get at him again.

"He is out of it all now, but we have to inform his family," Sarah reminded Alan.

"Yes, if we go and see that frosty secretary she will probably have contact details," said Alan gloomily. He had broken bad news to so many families during his career, and it never got any easier.

They left the apartment, and it wasn't long before they arrived at Harley Street. When they entered reception, the grey haired secretary was sitting at her computer, and judging by her worried face, she knew something was wrong. Alan noticed she was wearing a badge with her name on, 'Hilda Webb', so he didn't need to ask. He glanced at Sarah, and she nodded, knowing what was expected of her.

110

"Good morning, detective inspector, I am afraid Mr Roberts has not come in today, or yesterday. It is quite unlike him."

Gone was her cold and unfriendly manner. She had genuine concern written all over her face.

"I am afraid we have some bad news for you. The body of Mr Roberts was found in his apartment earlier this morning by his cleaner," said Sarah gently

Hilda Webb's face took on a greyish hue, and the shocked look in her eyes was soon replaced by tears rolling down her face. This was not what Alan had been expecting, loyalty was one thing, but this woman seemed to genuinely care about Roberts. Surely she hadn't been in love with him?

"Why didn't his cleaner contact me? How cruel of her not to let me know!" she sobbed out.

"Well, she rang us first. She probably didn't want to give you such upsetting news," suggested Sarah. Hilda Webb certainly seemed to care deeply for her boss.

"I am his only next of kin. I should have known first," she insisted.

Alan was surprised to hear this. They had no idea she was a relative.

"Matthew was my young brother. I looked after him when my parents died, and we have always been close. Until she came along, and then he moved out, and bought an apartment close to her. But I knew she wouldn't make him happy."

"She?" enquired Alan, knowing full well who Hilda meant, but wanting to hear her admit it.

"Eleanor, of course. She was so crafty. First his patient and then his lover, but she used him."

"He told you they were lovers?"

"Of course, we didn't have secrets from each other. We were very close."

"Did he tell you he had asked her to marry him?"

"He did, but she said not right now."

"Do you think he was upset by this?"

"A bit maybe, but I knew he would ask her again, although I didn't trust her to say yes."

"Do you think your brother was upset enough to end his own life?"

"Certainly not!"

111

Alan was finding this interesting. So Roberts had lied to him about Eleanor agreeing to marry him, but told his sister the truth. Now why had he lied?

He decided to see if Hilda knew about her brother's past.

"When your brother was working in Birmingham he became involved with a patient called Melissa, who later accused him of rape. . ."

". . .That call girl, you mean, who tried to bring charges of attempted rape just so she could get a nice little payout from him! Well it didn't work. He was proved innocent, and then to add to his troubles, she took a drug overdose. She did that to spite him, but it went wrong, and she died."

"So you think she didn't mean to kill herself."

"I don't care whether she did or not. She was heavily in debt, and she tried to ruin Matthew's life. He had to come to London and start all over again."

Hilda's loyalty to her brother was apparent. She didn't think her brother had committed suicide, so maybe it had been an accidental drug overdose.

"Was your brother on medication?"

"He was, ever since our parents were killed in a plane crash. He was only nine years old, and I was seventeen. They wanted to put him with foster parents, but I was working, and I fought to keep him with me, and I brought him up. He suffered bouts of depression, and I think the reason he became a psychiatrist was because he wanted to help others like himself, because he knew what it was like to struggle in life."

Her eyes filled with tears again. "I was always telling him not to mix his pills with whisky. He was partial to a glass of whisky after a difficult day. I believe he accidentally overdosed."

Sarah was wondering whether he had taken a lot of pills, as, so far, no one knew how many pills he had in the bottle. If he had taken a lot, what would they actually achieve by upsetting his sister even more, so she made no comment about that. As if reading Sarah's thoughts, Hilda said, "My brother was the kindest man ever, with a big heart. He may have made unwise choices for girlfriends, but he didn't have a mean bone in his body. I don't know how I will cope without him."

She buried her head in her hands, sobbing loudly, and Sarah attempted to console her by putting her arms around her. Alan stood looking on, wondering if their questioning of Roberts had been too harsh. He didn't always get it right, and sometimes he felt the job was too much. Occasionally trying to get to the truth destroyed people's lives.

After the police had gone, Hilda tried to compose herself a little. She was devastated by the loss of her 'young brother'. She had always thought of him that way, being eight years younger than her, and because of trying to be mother, father and sister to him for so many years. She had kept boyfriends at bay, always putting Matthew first, but when Matthew went to Birmingham to set up his practice there, although she had toyed with the idea of going with him, Hugh had been around, and it seemed she would have a chance of happiness, and her job for Matthew was done. She was at that time a school headmistress, and Hugh was deputy. She had known Hugh for years as a friend, and then he had left for a while to take care of his wife who had cancer.

When Hugh had returned to school after the loss of his wife, he really needed a friend, and she became that and more. They had always worked harmoniously together, and with Matthew's blessing, they got married. She had been very happy for a couple of years, but one day Hugh collapsed at school with a blood clot and died instantly. It was a huge shock to her. He had not been ill, and was only fifty-two, and it made her feel really cheated that cruel fate had taken away the man she loved so much.

She had left her job, not being able to face going into school any more, and had for a while been totally wrapped up in her own grief. It was during that time that Matthew had become involved with Melissa. She totally blamed herself for not being in contact with him. It had been a huge relief when his innocence was proved, but it still meant that Matthew could no longer work in Birmingham.

She had persuaded him to return to London, and it had all worked out well until now. He had a clientele of the rich and famous, but he also dealt with the local community, because Matthew had a good heart, and genuinely wanted to help people who had troubled lives. She remembered how he had tried to help Peter Grant after his mother had died. Getting through to him had been a challenge, the young man suffered from Asperger's syndrome, and it must have

113

taken all his courage to even book an appointment. Matthew hadn't charged him much, he said he couldn't, Peter lived in a council flat and probably didn't have much money.

The only time she had ever seen Matthew angry was when he was about fourteen. A girl he liked had laughed when he told her so. They were standing outside the house they lived in at the time. She went skipping off, and he was so angry he almost kicked the front door in. She had been shocked to see him behave like this. It was quite out of character, and she had told him so angrily. It had never happened again. In recent years her brother had seemed calm and in control of his life, so that incident had been pushed to the back of her mind, where it belonged. She knew if she mentioned it to the police, they would assume Matthew was a violent man.

He had become more emotional since becoming involved with Eleanor, so in one way her death had been a relief to Hilda. But she had soon realised that Matthew had not only been around at the time she was killed, but also had been hurt by her rejection. He told her Eleanor had turned him down. His behaviour at work had been jumpy and nervous, so she had tried to protect him from the police, but she hadn't done enough. She couldn't bear to think that he was so desperate that he had committed suicide. She would never know for sure if he had killed Eleanor because she rejected him, but her own love for him would go on, and she would always miss him. Her job now was to protect his memory and let him rest in peace.

"Did you believe her?" asked Alan, on their way back to the station.

"I am not sure really," mused Sarah. "He was her kid brother, so she would protect him with her life."

"That is what I thought. But you know, if he did kill Eleanor, he has paid the price with his own life. It's a very distressing set of circumstances. Do you think I went too heavily on him when I questioned him?"

"No I don't guv. You don't shout and bully, not like Green. He got himself into a corner because of his past, I reckon, and that wasn't your fault."

"Thanks, Sarah. You've made me feel better now."

They got out of the car. Alan thought briefly about Zoe and her dad, probably busy unpacking at his flat now. He couldn't go back yet. He needed to call a team meeting, but hopefully some time this afternoon he could get back.

"It's lunchtime now, guv. Shall I go and get coffee and sandwiches?" suggested Sarah, and Alan realised how hungry he was.

"Yes please, whilst I arrange a team meeting. One o'clock should do it," he said, glancing at his watch. It was now almost twelve-thirty.

Sarah sped off, hoping there wasn't a queue. As usual, he wasn't giving himself much time to eat his lunch before he had to address his team. She had known him, at times, actually to address them and eat his lunch at the same time, and then his coffee was cold when he eventually drank it. Working alongside Alan, she had to be as energetic as he was, and she liked to feel she was taking care of him, and making sure that he did eat and drink during the day, even if his breaks were not very long. Their working relationship meant everything to her. She knew what his favourite sandwiches were, and how he liked his coffee strong and sweet. Whilst at work, she could dream that he belonged to her, but when the day ended, he would be going home to Zoe, and not her, and she could feel jealousy ripping through her insides because of her unrequited love.

When she returned with the refreshments, he was already in the room where the meeting would take place. He was studying the board where all the photos of the suspects were pinned up.

"Roberts said he only knew of Peter Grant, but had never met him, when we interviewed him. I just listened to the tape."

"OK," said Sarah, handing him his coffee. "Here you are, cheese and pickle." They had done many interviews, and thank goodness they were recorded, it would be easy to forget what people said.

"Hilda just rang, and told me that Peter Grant was a patient, and how kind Matthew had been to him. She is still defending his honour, but unwittingly has exposed him to me as a liar."

"Did you tell her?"

"No, what's the point? He has gone now, so why upset her further. Although I will mention it at the meeting."

"Of course, guv, they need all the facts," agreed Sarah. She was impressed by his compassion. Surely Alan must be the kindest boss in the world.

115

Chapter Fourteen

Alan faced his team. Once again he had to go through it all, and hope their input would help.

"Good afternoon, everyone. We have had a new development in the Eleanor Harrison case. Matthew Roberts, one of the suspects, has died of an overdose. Whether he committed suicide, or it was accidental, we really don't know. He was a troubled man and, when questioned by us recently, seemed very nervous."

"So you think he did it, guv?" interjected Ross Green.

"I am not saying that. Like several of the others, he might have done it. There were several people with a motive. I will refresh your minds with what we have discovered."

He pointed to the picture of Faith Brian. "Eleanor's housekeeper, who previously married a man and inherited a property and a lot of money. We only know about this because, after his death, his sister complained to the police that she felt Faith had extorted money from Joseph. She was not convicted; it just seemed like sour grapes from a sibling who felt she had missed out."

His finger rested on the picture of Isabel. "Eleanor's elder sister Isabel, who appeared to love Eleanor deeply, but was angry because she missed a violin recital performed by Amy, Isabel's daughter. Amy will inherit one third of the estate when it's settled."

"She seemed a bit too perfect to me," said Sarah.

"OK, anyone else agree?" asked Alan. Two hands were raised in response.

116

"Next there is ex-husband Alfie. He was desperate for money, and left a pleading phone call the night before her death. He will also get a third share, as she never changed her will after they parted.

That is just a brief summary of the main suspects. We ruled out Peter Grant because he had never been in Eleanor's flat. We also ruled out Max Taylor, the taxi driver; he had no motive. Taylor saw Matthew Roberts leaving the apartments about the time Eleanor was killed. He didn't hail a taxi, but hurried towards the tube station. He kept his face hidden, and was acting very suspiciously. He admitted having an affair with Eleanor, said they were getting married, although his sister said Eleanor turned him down. He lied about that, and also he lied about knowing Peter Grant, who was apparently his patient."

"Have you been told this by Grant?" asked Ross, his eyes glittering. Alan wondered what mischief he was about to cause.

"No, but we have Hilda's word about it. We will confirm it with Grant, of course, all in good time."

"So you think Roberts planted the bronze horse at Grant's house, hoping he would be blamed. If that is so, what an awful man he was!" cried Wendy passionately. "That man came to Roberts for emotional help, and he knew he was vulnerable, so he used this knowledge to protect his own cowardly skin!"

Alan held his hand up until she had finished, and made a soothing motion with it.

"No Wendy, I honestly don't know if that did happen. Matthew Roberts was a vulnerable man himself. In spite of the position he held, he had his own issues during his life, so I don't think we can judge. Any one of those four people could have done it, and Roberts is no longer around to defend himself. So I have decided to keep the case open. If it seems more likely that Roberts did it, then he has paid the ultimate price by losing his own life. If any of the other three did it, we can only hope that one day they will do something to give themselves away."

He paused to take a gulp of his now very tepid coffee.

"I am going to recommend that the body now be released so that Eleanor's family can arrange a funeral, and get some closure. Eleanor was murdered by person or persons unknown, and the public will have to accept that and move on. As lovely as she was, and we know she was adored by many, the time has come to lay her to rest and move on."

"Amen," said Green, reminding Alan just how irritating this man was. "But you still think it was Roberts, we all do."

"Who agrees we should move on?" asked Alan, and there was a big show of hands. So that was it then. It was more than likely Roberts had done it, but they couldn't charge a dead man who couldn't defend himself, and there was no way he would steer this investigation into that scenario. As he had stated, the case would remain open, and maybe one day the truth would come out.

Alan was satisfied that he had a majority support. The next thing he wanted to do was to visit Peter Grant again, and find out how well he had known Roberts, and then try and figure out why Roberts had lied about it. As the team filed out, he drank his last bit of coffee with a grimace, it was now cold.

"Sarah, can you arrange for us to call round and see Grant. We best not go on the off-chance. I think he would want to know first."

"Yes, sir. Are you intrigued to know why Roberts said he only knew of him?"

"I am, but he won't need his solicitor this time. We only want to know about Roberts."

"We know how to tread carefully," commented Sarah.

Peter Grant was eating his lunch whilst watching the lunchtime news when he learned about the death of Matthew Roberts. The summary was brief, it stated that Matthew Roberts, prominent Harley Street psychiatrist, who was having a relationship with Eleanor Harrison at the time of her death, had been found in his flat, after what appeared to be an alcohol and medication drugs overdose. This news affected Peter. Although it was hard for him to show his feelings, inwardly he felt it, the pain racked at him, and he felt so sad. Matthew and Peter had history, and he would never forget him. His mother had said what a good man Matthew was, and she had been proved right. Peter sometimes found the strange world of everyday life hard to deal with, and it was comforting to retreat into his own safe personal life at times.

But he knew Matthew couldn't do that. They were not made the same, and it must have been something absolutely devastating to make him overdose, if indeed he had done it deliberately. Peter felt an uncomfortable sense of loss, just like he had when his mother died. But this time the man who had understood was not around to help him cope with it.

He heard his landline ringing. He didn't really feel like talking to anyone whilst he was getting over the shock of Matthew's death. But if he didn't answer, maybe the person might come round to see him, and he didn't want that either, it would be an invasion of his space.

The voice came over the line, soft and soothing, just like his mother's used to be.

"Good afternoon, Peter, it's Sarah here. Have you heard about the sad death of Matthew Roberts?"

Peter gulped, his throat was dry, and his voice was low.

"It's been on the news."

That was as much as he could say. His emotions were hidden as always, but inside he was hurting, and trying to understand.

Sarah had been expecting a short answer, and she used every bit of tact she possessed to carry on the conversation.

"I don't know how well you knew him, but DCI Alan Clarke and I were wondering if we could pop round and talk to you about him."

"If you have to. I don't feel like visitors, but I knew Matthew very well, and Hilda too, so I will speak to you."

"Thanks so much Peter, we really appreciate it. We'll be round within the next half hour."

Peter put the phone down. It was at times like this his own world felt safe. It was so easy to retreat there, but he would never forget Matthew's kindness to him. He was probably the nearest person to a friend that he had had in his life. Matthew had never judged him, unlike some of the boys at his school, so he needed the police to know what a good man Matthew had been.

When the buzzer sounded, he opened the door to let them in. He noted they both had very grave faces, Alan spoke kindly to him.

"Thank you for seeing us again Peter, it's nothing to worry about."

"I heard about Matthew. He was my friend, you know. He was a good man."

Sarah chose her words carefully. "That is a nice thing to say about him Peter. In what way was he a good man? Had you known him for a long time?"

119

"A very long time, before he went to Birmingham. I was glad when he came back. When I went to secondary school I didn't much like it there, I was picked on, but Matthew defended me. He was a prefect in the sixth form. He reported the boy who was bullying me, and he got expelled, not just for me, but others he had bullied. After that Matthew always kept an eye on me, and made me feel safe. His sister and my mother were friends. My mother had made some dresses for her. She was nice too. When Matthew went to live in Birmingham, Hilda was lonely, so mother struck up a friendship with her. Then one day Matthew came back."

Alan had no doubt that all that Peter was saying was true. Matthew had championed him, so this made Alan think that he would not have planted the bronze horse in Peter's flat, which also now led him to believe that Matthew had not murdered Eleanor. It just didn't fit together like it should have, so he would have to go back to his original idea of letting Eleanor's family move on without knowing who had killed her. He glanced at Sarah for back up. Surely they were done here now?

"Peter, you have been very helpful, we will go now and leave you in peace," said Sarah. She marvelled at how well she could read Alan's mind at times. She wondered if Zoe could.

They took their leave of him, and shared their thoughts whilst travelling back to the station.

"No way would Matthew set up Peter!" declared Sarah, and Alan agreed with her.

"So if he wasn't the murderer, then who was?" asked Alan. It could be any one of the others, they all had nice neat alibis, so they had to go back to the board yet again. He looked at his watch, it was now four o'clock. Zoe and her dad had probably unpacked almost everything by now, and he felt that pang of guilt go through him once more.

"Sarah, I will drop you off and head home. I need to think it all through again."

"I think you should put it out of your head for tonight; it's moving day!" said Sarah, secretly exulting that he was so late. Surely Zoe would be feeling fed up by now. Her precious Prince Charming had let her down.

Alan grimaced, not saying much, then drew up outside the station to let her out. He felt like this case had taken over his life lately. But Zoe was important to him too, and he didn't want her to feel left out.

"Are you sure you don't want to come in and see if there are any new developments?" she asked, feeling wicked. Alan was looking very despondent.

"No, you're all right, see you tomorrow."

He made a supreme effort, whilst driving home, to put the case to the back of his mind. Many officers of higher ranks than himself had found their marriages suffer because of this job. Some of them were divorced and alone because most women wouldn't put up with the crazy hours, cancelled evenings out, and everything that the job entailed. Living together with Zoe, and still having to go into work at a moment's notice would decide if they had a future. Alan knew for sure that he wanted to marry her, but would she accept his heavy commitment to the job?

When he saw Zoe's little Fiesta parked in the allotted area, he started to relax a little. A nice meal together, and a glass of the Prosecco he had just bought to celebrate her moving in, would be lovely. He used his key to let himself in, his face alight with a smile, knowing it wouldn't be a takeaway or microwave meal tonight. Zoe was standing in the hall with her nursing uniform on. Her face lit up when she saw him.

"Welcome home, Alan darling. I am afraid I have to go back in. They are very short staffed, and one of my patients, Henry Miller, is not expected to last the night. His poor wife has taken it badly, she needs my support."

Alan's words died on his lips, and huge disappointment flooded through him. His first night with Zoe, and she had to go out. It was ironic; he was arriving home, and she was going to work, just like ships that pass in the night. But however disappointed he was, he knew he had to curb it. He mustn't be selfish. It wasn't all about him, and Zoe cared a lot about her elderly patients. It was the right thing for her to do.

He hugged her warmly. Soothing himself with the thought that this was just the beginning of their life together, and there was always tomorrow night.

"There is a chicken leg in the oven, and a jacket potato cooking, and in the fridge I have done a salad to go with it, and I put a couple of beers in the fridge," said Zoe, as she opened the front door.

f

"That sounds nice," said Alan. He didn't usually bother with salad, but with Zoe around, she would encourage him to eat more healthily. He would now relax with his beer and eat his dinner, and try to figure out if he could ever solve this case.

Zoe knew she was in for a stressful evening. But it was worse for Henry Miller's wife, she was about to lose her husband, so if Zoe could give her some support, maybe it might help her a little. Zoe had been looking forward to waking up next to Alan tomorrow morning, but knew she probably would be coming in as he went off to work. Well, that was their crazy lifestyle. They had both chosen it to be like that, but they were young, with their future stretching out before them, they had time on their side.

Chapter Fifteen

It was three months since the death of Eleanor. The newspapers no longer ran stories about her, and her face was not dominating everybody's TV screen. It wasn't because nobody cared, an icon like Eleanor would live in the hearts of her fans forever. But time marches on, and right now the press were following the rocky progress of the Brexit negotiations, the country appeared to be in turmoil, and there were daily arguments amongst MPs in the House of Commons.

After a recommendation from the police, namely Alan Clarke, who was leading the case, Eleanor's body had now been released so she could be laid to rest. Her will had been read, and Faith, Amy and Alfie had all been awarded their third share. Isabel had been tempted to appeal against Alfie's share, as they had been divorced, and not only that, she had seen how heartbroken Eleanor had been when he left her.

But when she had gone round to speak to him about it, she had been shocked at how poor they were, and how shabby the flat was, and she could see what a difference the money would make to them. It wasn't in Isabel's nature to be spiteful or vengeful. At that moment she forgave Alfie, just as years earlier she had forgiven Eleanor and Sam, and made no move to stand in his way.

She had known that Faith had served her sister well, and stayed, unlike some housekeepers before her. Eleanor had been grateful for her loyalty, and that was her reward. Amy was keeping her share in an investment trust for now. She was still at college, and didn't need it yet. Money was no object in this family, but this little windfall was a token of Eleanor's love for the daughter she had chosen not to acknowledge, and made Amy realise she had loved her, and tried to do the right thing.

It was a relief to know her estate was now settled, and Isabel felt ready to lay her to rest with dignity. There was a big gulf in her heart that could never be bridged, but Alan had explained that Eleanor had been murdered by a person or persons unknown, so now was the time to finally say goodbye to her.

Any ideas that Isabel had about a quiet family funeral were soon dispelled when Dawn Fraser had asked to be involved. Eleanor's celebrity status meant that anyone and everyone connected with her in show business would want to attend. Some would want to make speeches about her, and as for the public, even if they tried to keep it out of the press, it would be leaked, and the streets between her home and the church would be lined with adoring fans, all wanting to say goodbye to her. She would be treated with the same reverence as Royalty, because to her public she was Royalty.

Isabel did understand that, and a part of her felt so proud of what Eleanor had achieved during her life. She had courted and captured the public, and although they had put her high on a pedestal, which was partly fantasy, that didn't matter. An icon is never thought of as a normal human being with good and bad in their character, they are elevated to dizzy heights that are impossible for anyone to live up to, because nobody is perfect. But if the public wanted to think of Eleanor in that way because of the illusion she had created, and if it inspired other young women to be like her, then as far as Isabel was concerned, Eleanor had done good.

Amy had come to terms with the fact that Eleanor was her biological mother, but Isabel had brought her up, and been her true mother, and loved her, even to the point of forgiving Sam for his lapse with her sister. Amy had forgiven Sam too now, and she marvelled at not only how forgiving her mother had been to Sam, but how strong their marriage had been to survive such a betrayal.

One of Eleanor's favourite colours had been red, and she wore it a lot. She would be remembered for her vivacious nature and ready smile. She rarely wore black or dark colours, always preferring pink, emerald green, and deep blue, which matched her personality. So because it wasn't just a funeral service, but a celebration of a bright and lively woman, whose life had been extinguished so tragically and abruptly, Dawn suggested that the guests should be informed they didn't have to wear black or be miserable, because Eleanor's life was going to be celebrated.

At first Isabel was horrified, and thought that maybe seeing everyone arrive in brightly coloured clothes would be a lack of respect. But Amy assured her that it was like that now at funerals. She had recently been to a funeral, when the mother of one of her friends had been tragically killed in a car crash. Everyone there had been brightly dressed because Tara had requested it. Her mother had been very into fashion, and abhorred black and dark coloured clothes.

Dawn was excited that so many celebrities wanted to attend. The list was huge, and three prominent ones had asked if they could say a few words about Eleanor, and how proud they had been to be associated with her. Isabel and Sam both thought that a good idea. It was better that people who worked alongside her spoke about Eleanor, because anything they had to say was private, with memories that would stay within the family circle.

Isabel and Amy went shopping together to choose outfits. They had become closer than ever since Eleanor's death, and Isabel was glad to get her teenage daughter's approval of the cornflower blue outfit she chose with the pencil skirt and matching jacket, set off with a cream hat and cream shoes. She felt she looked more like she was going to a wedding, but Amy assured her it was very suitable. Amy chose a full length red dress, which had tiny cream flowers on it, and a tie belt, which accentuated her slender waist. She wore red sandals with cuban heels, they had cream straps which looked good with her dress. She also had gypsy type earrings and a gold chain round her neck given to her last Christmas by Eleanor, and she lovingly referred to her jewellery as her 'Bit of bling'.

The night before the funeral, Isabel found it very hard to sleep. It was very important to her that it all went off well. It was taking place at eleven o'clock the next day, and the weather forecast was set to be fine. The funeral cars had been arranged, the flowers had been chosen, but only from the family. Anyone else wanting to contribute was encouraged to donate to The British Heart Foundation. This was in memory of their father, who had died from a stroke, and she was sure that was what Eleanor would have wanted.

Isabel's difficulty in sleeping was partly guilt, because after a lot of soul searching, she had decided that her mother Jean could not attend the funeral. It was possible that anything Jean did say would be excused as confusion because of her dementia, but the press would be there, trying to pick up any spicy gossip they could print, and there were certain true things that Jean could remember. She had finally grasped that Eleanor was dead, but now tended to drift back to when she was a little girl, and had first become an actress. Her recriminations that Eleanor had ruined her marriage had been forgotten right now, but Isabel was only too aware that something could set them off again. Jean was just too unpredictable, and they could not risk her putting any sort of slur on this very poignant and special day. She had explained to her mother's carers at Peacehaven that she felt it would be too distressing for her mother, with the illness that she had, and they had politely agreed. But it didn't stop Isabel from feeling guilty that she had stopped the one person who had helped to make Eleanor the celebrity that she was, from paying her last respects to her.

Faith had wanted to come. She was grateful for being included in Eleanor's will, and knowing how highly Eleanor had regarded her, had made Isabel decide to invite her. But Faith was aware she was a servant, and not family, so she planned to come to the service, and not join them at the meal afterwards. She knew her place, although Isabel had never made her feel uncomfortable.

Alan and Sarah were also attending, but keeping a discreet distance. For all they knew, the killer might well be at the funeral, but because of the high profile celebrity that Eleanor had been, it was a mark of respect from the police force that they were there to make sure that everything went off as it should. As Alan put on his pale blue suit and silky tie, he was hoping it would all go off smoothly. It was a sobering thought that the killer might be in the congregation, pretending to pay their respects to Eleanor.

Zoe wished she could be standing next to Alan at the funeral instead of Sarah. She had known for a long time that Sarah carried a torch for Alan, even though she had only met her once. It was in her eyes when she looked at him, and her body language was possessive too. Just because she worked with him, it didn't mean she owned him. It wasn't that she didn't trust Alan. He had laughed when she commented about Sarah, and assured her he didn't think of Sarah in that way, she was just a very efficient WPC. And her commonsense told her this was true. But seeing him looking so smart, and knowing that Sarah would not be in uniform, but done up like a dog's dinner, and walking as close to Alan as she could, didn't help. After three months of living together, she was more in love with him than ever. His only fault was his untidiness. He was gentle, kind and considerate, and they were just the qualities she wanted in a husband. She loved cooking for him. She had changed his diet, and he liked it. Takeaways were very rare now, and because their shifts didn't always coincide, they shared the housework. He wasn't great at making the bed, but he happily ran the hoover over when necessary, and if he was home before her, he peeled the vegetables for dinner.

She never mentioned the subject of marriage, although Alan had once or twice, saying how she had changed his life for the better, and how lovely it was to come home to her at the end of a stressful day, then grinning and adding, "Let's make it permanent one day."

Zoe had smiled back enigmatically, unsure as to whether he might be joking. Even though it was 2021, she didn't want to appear desperate to have a ring on her finger, although she knew deep in her heart that Alan was the love of her life.

She put on her nursing uniform, commented how smart he was, and then watched wistfully as he got in the car on his way to pick Sarah up from the station to go to the funeral. He only had to drive a short distance, which was just as well, as she guessed the public would be out in force saying their goodbyes to Eleanor.

Zoe had known that, like many other men and women, Alan had been a fan of Eleanor since he was a teenager, and she understood why. She had admired Eleanor herself, not only was she an amazing actress and singer, but there was a special quality she had when on camera, which made one feel that she was talking right to you and she cared, there was a certain magic about her that had captured the hearts of the nation, and this was why she would be sorely missed.

With the case left open as it had been, she couldn't help wondering if the killer would ever be found, but in the meantime, it would be a relief to know poor Eleanor would finally be laid to rest.

Apart from lining the route to pay their respects, many of the public would be outside the church, and also near to the graveyard where Eleanor was to be buried. Police would be around to keep order, and nobody other than family and the invited celebrities would be allowed in the church. Alan and Sarah were the only exceptions.

Zoe had thought about going to the graveyard to pay her respects. Alan had agreed it was a good idea, although he wanted her to go when the burial ceremony took place. But Zoe felt she might look like a spare part, whilst Sarah would be standing with Alan gloating, not that he noticed that. So she had decided to work, and then go later in the evening to quietly pay her respects after everyone had gone. Having made that decision, she went off to work. She was ashamed of herself for feeling jealous, but it wasn't Alan she mistrusted, it was Sarah. However, there was no way Sarah would have him, she could dream on about that!

Faith was sitting quietly at the back. That was where she wanted to be, as insignificant as possible. The front part of the big church was filled with celebrities. Many of them had worked alongside Eleanor, and the speeches made about her were glowing and sentimental. Having seen her at home off stage, Faith knew that Eleanor was just a normal woman, sometimes bright and happy, and sometimes stressed, and at those times, difficult. But she had understood that, because the world of show business held many uncertainties. An actress could never rest on her laurels, and she had to make enough money to survive when the work was not coming in. Eleanor was luckier than most. She had always been in high demand, but sometimes she had come home after working with a difficult co-star feeling jaded and irritable. Faith wasn't always there to see her, as Eleanor's hours were erratic, but her patience had paid off. She had never even thought about being remembered in Eleanor's will. With her being a mere housekeeper, the windfall had been a huge surprise, and she had fully expected Isabel to contest it, just like Keeley had done when Joseph died.

If anyone had seen her sumptuous bungalow, with its vast grounds and swimming pool, they would have wondered if she actually needed money, and even queried why she had gone back to work as a housekeeper for Eleanor after Joseph died. She hadn't needed to work, but with no children of her own, and being the right side of sixty, Faith knew she would be very bored if she didn't work. Working for a celebrity like Eleanor had felt like a privilege. She had gone through a rigorous process of being vetted and been successful in getting the job, and there had been a lot of other disappointed women. Now that Eleanor was gone, she wasn't sure what to do. With even more money, working seemed futile, but maybe she should take more holidays. Being on her own hadn't suited Faith, maybe she might meet someone on a cruise or some sort of holiday.

The sound of 'The Lord is my Shepherd' filled the church, and she stood with her head bent like the others, remembering Eleanor, the woman whom so many had loved. And yet someone had hated her enough to snuff her life out without a second thought. She prayed that Eleanor's soul would rest in peace.

Alfie had not been invited to Eleanor's funeral, and he had not intended to go. He felt that her family would not want him there. He was the errant ex-husband who had left her. But after he received his inheritance he was troubled by his conscience. He had loved her once, but he had found her very temperamental to live with. Any feelings of animosity that he had harboured had died with her. He now remembered her with affection, because the windfall he had inherited had allowed himself and Angela to move into a flat that wasn't damp and unhealthy. They had money left over for furniture, carpets and furnishings. All he could feel now was gratitude, and although he had no plans to go to the church, he was going to the graveyard to pay his respects to her.

He had explained all this to Angela, and she had agreed it was only right. She had looked at him a little strangely, maybe wondering why he had a change of heart towards Eleanor. In previous fits of anger he had called her many names, but then Alfie was a hot-headed man, who acted on impulse and then regretted it after. If going to say goodbye to Eleanor by paying his respects made him feel better, then Angela was all for it. But she still felt anxious deep inside. There was still a niggling feeling that she didn't know her husband as well as she thought she did. Had Eleanor pushed him too far that fateful morning when she died, and was this his way of trying to ease his conscience?

She wasn't sure she wanted to know. She wanted to bury her head in the sand and forget it all. Maybe it was a coward's way out, but ever since she had known Alfie, her life had been full of drama, and all she wanted now was to get on with her life. They had a lovely new home, and some spare money, courtesy of Eleanor, so all she hoped was they could continue to enjoy it.

Isabel was sitting between Amy and Sam, at the very front, whilst the funeral service took place. The amount of celebrities who had come to pay their respects to Eleanor had been far more than she could have possibly imagined. Famous stars had jetted over from places such as America and Australia to be there. Her popularity was mind-blowing.

Isabel and Dawn had got together to arrange it all, and the news about it had spread very quickly. They had been besieged by celebrities' agents, saying how honoured they would be to be invited. So the invites went out, and everyone had accepted.

Three separate celebrities had spoken about Eleanor, her beauty and grace, her infectious smile, and her talent. Greg Wise had spoken about how she had been a joy to work with, and her ability to stay grounded and interact with her fans, always willing to give them her time after shows.

These were the things that Isabel wanted to remember about her sister, and their glowing speeches brought tears to her eyes. She found the whole service very emotional, and the sight of her sister's coffin, adorned with the flowers marked 'SIS' she found heart-rending. She could feel anger that someone still in the prime of her life could have been taken like this, and guilt that her last words to her beloved sister had been said in a very angry telephone call. She wished she could rewind to the evening before, and not react the way she did, but it was too late now, and she had to bear her guilt for the rest of her life.

Sam stood silently at her side, touching her hand gently when he saw her tears. His empathy was comforting to her, so she gently wiped her eyes with a tissue. Sam had always allowed her to be the driving force in their marriage, but he had consistently stood by her, and right now, more than ever, the touch of his hand was as comforting as any words he could have said.

Several rows behind them sat Hilda. Isabel had invited her. Knowing she had recently lost the man who Eleanor had cared about, it seemed the right thing to do. In the beginning, Hilda was not inclined to go. Just a couple of months previously, she had arranged a very quiet send-off for Matthew after it was confirmed he had taken an overdose of prescription drugs; accidentally or not, wasn't clear. She had invited Isabel and Sam, not expecting them to come. But they had come, and expressed their sadness at her loss of Matthew.

Peter had also come to Matthew's funeral, but could not be persuaded to come back to the house for refreshments. Hilda understood that. She was well aware of his awkwardness in social situations, and she appreciated his loyalty to Matthew, knowing it had probably been quite a difficult thing for him to do.

As the strains of 'The Lord is my Shepherd' again filled the church, the family party was invited to stand and file out, followed by the rest of the congregation. Isabel composed herself, knowing that there were many people to meet and speak to outside before they headed to the hotel where refreshments would be served. Sam gripped her hand, and Amy put a comforting arm around her mother's shoulders. It was this display of unity that gave Isabel the courage to hold her head up high, and smile at everyone, even though her heart felt like it was broken and beyond repair.

"Let's go then," she said determinedly.

Chapter Sixteen

Eleanor's burial place was as special as she had been. After a lot of discussion, it had been decided that as a mark of respect, she should have her own private area. There was always the fear that if the grave was accessible to anyone, it might get damaged or desecrated, especially as her killer was still somewhere out there.

So, at the back of the churchyard there was a wooded area, with a winding stream passing through it, which had been fenced off. A very high fence and a sturdy gate with a padlock were erected, but it was agreed that, on the first evening, the gate would be left open and, with police present, the public could file past her grave area to pay their respects.

Isabel had mixed feelings about it. She didn't like the idea of Eleanor being locked away, but at the same time she could see she needed protecting. On the anniversary of her death every year, the gate would be open for that day, although family would have a special pass to go at any time.

On the day of the funeral, as was to be expected, the public filed solemnly past her resting place, some taking photographs, until late in the evening. The police were present, but apart from some women being emotional, it was relatively calm, with no troublemakers appearing.

Isabel and the family had long gone by then, so had Sarah, but Alan was still around, as he knew that Zoe would come after she finished her shift at six. When she arrived, he greeted her warmly, noting how tired she looked.

"Hi babe, have you had a busy day?"

Zoe smiled. "No busier than yours, I hope it all went off OK."

"Yes, very sad of course, but a lovely ceremony, and many beautiful speeches about her."

"Well she was probably the best British actress we ever had, as well as her other talents. We will all miss her!"

This was spoken with absolute sincerity. Zoe had looked up to and admired Eleanor ever since she had been a young girl, and had always been delighted that she shared a slight resemblance to her with her blonde bubbly curls and doll-like face. She had been with Alan to see some of her films and stage performances, and had wished she could meet her, but it was too late now. She had fully understood why Alan had admired her so much, and felt no jealousy about it. Everyone was entitled to have someone to look up to. She herself admired Greg Wise, Eleanor's leading man, and had enjoyed watching the chemistry when they performed together.

Alan linked his arm through hers, and they made their way towards the group slowly filing past the grave. There was a respectful silence, with just a faint sound of a young girl sobbing in the queue. Alan glanced towards her. She was only about sixteen, she made an attempt to compose herself, wiping her red eyes with a tissue, and her friend put a comforting arm around her. He marvelled the power Eleanor still had to move people like this, some three months after her death.

As they moved forwards and paused to kneel and say a prayer, they both felt moved; the trees swayed gently in the breeze, and the little stream was gurgling in the background.

"What a beautiful spot for a resting place," remarked Zoe.

As they stood up, Alan glanced towards the gate where the police were holding back the crowd, which was still huge, and allowing just a few to enter at a time, and join the rest filing past. By the gate he spotted Peter Grant. He was cowering at the side, looking decidedly uncomfortable.

Peter wanted to go to the church so much to say goodbye to Eleanor, just paying his respects at her grave with no one around. But he realised with a high profile star like Eleanor, there would always be someone around. One of his biggest fears was crowds, he didn't like being touched, which was why he was thankful that he spent most of his working life at home. Being squashed against other people on the tube was not for him. Ever since he was a small child he had recoiled against contact. His mother had understood. He had always tolerated being touched by her, and he had felt certain that if he could have become close to Eleanor, his goddess, he would have been able to touch her.

It had taken all his courage to come out today, because even several hours after the funeral, the streets were still full of mourners. At the church, police were still in attendance, keeping order amongst the throng of people. Peter gritted his teeth, and made his way towards the gate, he felt dizzy as he could feel the breath of others around him; it was too close, he needed his own space! He could feel panic building up inside him, it was like being slowly strangled, and a feeling of claustrophobia swept through him.

Through his panic he recognised the figure of DCI Alan Clarke with a young lady, and he grabbed the gatepost, breathing hard, as they came over.

"Good evening, Peter. So many people here today, all paying their respects. How are you?"

His voice was kindly, and Peter could feel his empathy. It made the experience seem a little less daunting. Peter always remembered people who showed him empathy, as most people didn't get him. That WPC Wendy had been the best of all. She had really understood because she had a brother with Asperger's, and he had always felt comfortable in her company.

"I don't like being pushed!" he said curtly.

Zoe could see he was struggling with being surrounded by people. In the hospital she had known patients who just couldn't cope with being in a ward with others. It could make them ill, physically sick sometimes. So without even thinking, she spoke to reassure him.

"I know how you feel. The only way I can cope with it is to remind myself that all these people really cared about Eleanor, just like we do, and if she could see the amount of support she has, she would be very happy."

Alan broke in. . . "So sorry Peter, I haven't introduced you to Zoe, my partner. Zoe, this is Peter Grant. Zoe is a nurse, and she knows about these sort of situations."

"I think I have met you before, Peter. You were at home about

134

five years ago, when I came round to ask your mother to shorten a dress for me. I was so sorry to hear that Mary died, she was such a nice person."

Peter gulped, but it was comforting to hear his mother mentioned, he was trying so hard to cope with all these crowds, and seeing the familiar faces was helping him.

"There is a gap here," said Alan, taking advantage of a space. "We have already filed past and said goodbye to her, but we can wait until you have if it helps."

Peter felt gratitude sweep through him, even though he was unable to express it. He could feel that these two were not judging him. He thought he remembered Zoe coming to see his mother a few years ago. She would have been younger, but that ready smile and those bubbly curls reminded him of Eleanor, and gave him peace.

He nodded, and moved forward, trying to walk far enough away not to touch anyone. The policeman was ensuring that the queue moved slowly and with dignity, which he approved of. His beautiful goddess was being respected, and her resting place was beautiful. The rippling of the stream, and swishing of the branches moving very gently in the breeze, gave him a feeling of serenity. He glanced at the headstone as he filed past. It was a poignant moment, as he felt sadness sweep through him that she had died at thirty-five. It was true, the saying: 'Only the good die young'.

"We had better wait for him, and make sure he gets on his way safely," whispered Zoe. And Alan felt a wave of love shoot through him at her kindness. Zoe was so understanding.

After Peter had filed past and reached the gate, he was relieved to see they were still there. They walked with him until he reached the bus stop. He got on the bus after thanking them rather abruptly for their help. Words never came easily to him.

When they were in the car travelling home, Alan rested his hand on Zoe's arm, and spoke huskily.

"You made him feel comfortable, thanks for that."

"No problem. It was a brave thing to do, facing all those crowds when he has Asperger's."

"Can you believe that one of my PCs actually arrested him for the murder of Eleanor simply because he didn't like him, in view of him being different? He had no evidence, the poor bloke was terrified. It's a wonder he trusts anyone in the police."

"He can sense you are kind."

"Well, Wendy was the person who stood up for him. She worked with the idiot that arrested him, and she has her own brother with Asperger's, so she understood him completely."

"Thank goodness she was there as well as you, and he had someone fighting his corner. We see a lot of people at the hospital with Asperger's. Very clever people, but they struggle in other ways."

Whilst they were travelling home, Alan had many different feelings inside him. Relief that Eleanor had finally been laid to rest, and he knew it had been a huge comfort to Isabel and the rest of the family. Guilt because, although the case remained open, they still had no idea who had killed her. Emotion, because someone he had looked up to and admired ever since he was a teenager had gone. Eleanor had left a huge legacy of love behind her, she would never be forgotten. But her death left a huge chasm that could never be filled. It was the end of an era.

He parked the car, and they entered the flat. He could feel some reassurance that they were getting back to normality. It had been quite a traumatic day. Alan put the kettle on; it was time for a cup of tea.

Chapter Seventeen

Wendy had also come to pay her respects to Eleanor, as it just seemed the right thing to do. The only person that hadn't was Ross, and he seemed conspicuous by his absence. On her way to the church she had seen Peter getting on a bus, and spotted Alan with a girl she assumed was his girlfriend, saying goodbye to Peter. The girl was in a nursing uniform, wearing a fleece over the top. She remembered hearing that Alan's partner was a nurse, and she couldn't help wondering if they were still questioning Peter about the murder. But then she reasoned with herself, Alan had stated at the meeting that Peter had been eliminated from the enquiries because he had never been to Eleanor's apartment.

She had found Alan to be a fair man. Hard when he needed to be, but also full of empathy. He had treated Peter with respect, so wasn't it more likely that he was just being kind? As probably the crowds would have disturbed Peter, and maybe he was just seeing he got safely onto the bus.

Visiting Eleanor's grave brought it all back to her. Like so many others, she felt the tragedy of such a lovely woman dying so young. Whether you were a fan or not, that didn't matter, no one deserved to lose their life at such a young age, and in such horrific circumstances. If only the police could find the killer, because there was a big possibility they could strike again. She shivered inside at the thought of it.

Glancing at all the people around her, she wondered if one of them held the secret, or could it be a member of the family? They all seemed very respectable, with sound alibis, but there was something about this case that made her want to keep probing, especially as Peter had suffered because of it. It was continually on her mind, and she knew it would be until justice was done. Three months after, she still felt as though it had only just happened.

Later that night, she tossed and turned. Visions of the grave were rising up at her, and she could see Eleanor floating in a white dress. She could also hear Ross's voice, jeering, saying Peter was the murderer, or Matthew, and Eleanor turned and smiled that beautiful smile that made her whole face light up. She looked at Ross's face, and it was all twisted with spite, and his eyes were blazing with anger, she could see some sort of flames coming out of his eyes. . . then she woke up! Her heart was thudding, her whole body was sweating with fear, because it suddenly flashed through her mind. What if Ross was the murderer? A crooked policeman. It had happened before, and could happen again. Obviously she could not share this with anyone else. If she were wrong it could cause a lot of trouble, but she made up her mind she would go into work, and do her own bit of private investigating.

Ever since he had wrongfully arrested Peter she had found it hard to work alongside Ross. He made no attempt to hide his contempt of her, his partner, who had dared to cross him. You couldn't choose who you were paired with at work, and in the beginning, she had been totally overwhelmed by Ross's arrogance and belief that he was right about everything. But he had proved that he wasn't right, and incurred the displeasure of DCI Alan Clarke, and once she had plucked up the courage to stand up to him, their relationship could never be the same again.

Since then he had treated her with disdain, and didn't share much with her, so it was difficult to work with him. So she attended the team briefings, made her own notes, and only went out into the community with him when she had to.

When she came in on this particular morning he had been consigned to another case. Officers wanted backup, and Ross had been part of that. She didn't mind at all, as it meant she had the office to herself, and could carry out her own investigations. The very first thing she did was check the records about him. It didn't tell her very much; he had been with the force for two years, was now aged twenty-one, and that was about it. His address was shown as Chelsea, not far from where Matthew Roberts had lived. There was no record of how long he had lived there, and no mention of any family, so it seemed like he lived alone.

Wendy felt disappointed. She was hoping to find something more about him, some sort of lead on the idea that was growing more and more inside her. When she thought about it, his behaviour had been odd. He had never spoken about Eleanor; it was as though she didn't exist, even though she had been in a period production just before her death. So Wendy had thought Eleanor was of no interest to him, but then, during the team briefing, he had been quite vitriolic about her. Not long after that she had found a photograph of Eleanor, torn in half in their waste paper basket. Of course, someone else could have put it in there, but it was highly unlikely, as most visitors to their office simply popped in and out very quickly. He had torn that up in a fit of anger, and why would he be angry with Eleanor? Nothing made any sense?

Finding nothing to work on only made her even more convinced that Ross had something to hide. She had to get to his flat and search it. As mad as that idea sounded, it would be a good way to see if he was hiding something. But she didn't have a key to his flat, so how could she get in? She knew exactly where that complex was at Chelsea, and she could probably bluff her way through the communal door, but that would not get her into Ross's flat. Neither did she have anything concrete to share with anyone so she could not get a warrant. Just having a hunch was not enough.

There was a feeling deep inside her driving her on, even though she didn't have a clue how she would get in. She was going there anyway. So she went out to the desk where the duty constable was.

"I don't feel at all well. I need to go home. My partner is helping with a consignment, so he won't need me today."

The duty officer surveyed her. Nothing much was happening today, even the public were not coming in with their usual complaints, or to report crimes. He was finding it a long day already. This young lady had dark circles under her eyes, and she didn't look that well.

"OK Wendy, just put it in writing on the form that you have gone. Are you due in tomorrow?"

Wendy gulped, she wasn't good with deception, but this time

she felt it was in a good cause. She couldn't share it with anyone until she had discovered some evidence.

"Yes, but if I go home and get some sleep, I am sure I will be fine tomorrow."

She quickly filled in the form he gave her and escaped. Being in the police force was all about forms; even a form when you go home sick!

She had written the address and post code on a piece of paper, but she felt she already knew where that particular complex was. It had an underground car park, so she figured if she made her way to that, it would be easier to get inside the corridor. Then she had to hunt for number nine, and try to get inside.

The first part of her plan went well. When she arrived outside the complex, she headed down the ramp to the car park. She tried not to be conspicuous, aware that CCTV would be in operation. After a couple of minutes, a young man pulled in, driving a sports car. He jumped out, and as she moved towards him, hoping she could follow him in, he spoke to her.

"Sorry to trouble you. My watch has stopped, can you tell me the time?"

Wendy fell into step beside him, hoping the cameras would think they were together. As they rounded the corner, out of view, she stopped, pulled up her sleeve to expose her watch, and said:

"Yes, of course, my watch is very accurate. It's eleven o'clock."

"Thank you so much," he said, as he put in a code and pressed the button to the intercommunicating door.

"No worries," said Wendy, smiling, and slipping through the door with him.

She pretended to adjust her shoe, taking it off and complaining she had a stone in it, but waving away any help from him. She was glad she had changed out of her police uniform. It was in the holdall she was carrying, as she often changed when she went straight out after work. There was nothing flattering about her uniform or the heavy lace-up shoes she had to wear with it. But this time she hadn't changed because of vanity, it was to conceal her identity until such time when Ross would find out it was her who had rumbled him.

Wendy looked at the apartment numbers as she walked along the corridor. The man she had spoken to had now gone, and number nine was at the far end on the left. Well, she had got this far, and she had no plan about what to do next. She stared at the brown wooden door with the figure nine emblazoned on it; she was so near, and yet so far.

As she stood there a middle-aged woman wearing jeans and trainers opened the door. She was trying to hold a bucket with dusters and cloths in, so she was obviously the cleaner. But her phone was ringing at the same time, and in an effort to answer it, everything fell to the floor. Wendy went to help her, retrieving the phone, and as the woman silently thanked her, and went to answer it, she turned the other way briefly. Wendy took the opportunity to gently click the catch of the door, but close it, to look as if it was shut.

The cleaner was busy with her conversation. It sounded like an emergency, as she was promising to go and get someone right away. She glanced back at the door. It looked closed, and Wendy held her breath, hoping she wouldn't check it. But she had other things on her mind, so she put the key safely away in her pocket, and picked up her bucket and cloths. "Thanks for helping me pick them up," she said, and Wendy smiled, watching her speed away as quickly as she could.

Wendy could not believe her luck. It was as if someone was watching over her and helping her. This must be the right thing to do. She glanced up and down the corridor, but there was no one, so she quickly pushed the door open and went inside.

It felt weird being inside his home. In the hall there was a mirror, and the floors were all wooden, so she tried to tread as quietly as she could. On one side there was a cloakroom, but it was the lounge she was interested in, as it had a bureau with a flap that came down and had drawers in it.

The drawers were a mess; bills and receipts had been bundled in them, it would take forever to go through all that stuff. But when she pulled the bureau flap it came down. She spotted a passport, so she picked it up and opened the first page. There was a picture of Ross looking very serious, but what caught her eye was the name, Roger Weston. There was no doubt in her mind that this was Ross. The passport had run out last year, so he couldn't use it now, but was Roger Weston his real name, or an assumed one? This was an exciting discovery, as a fake passport, or a fake name, was usually because someone had something to hide. She couldn't wait to go back to the station and check it out, but sadly she would have to wait until tomorrow, only then could she make her rapid recovery.

When she left the flat, she unlatched the door and banged it shut, so no one would even know she had been. She could have searched for longer, but she felt unsafe in there because someone could come in at any time, even Ross could call in there on his way back to the office. The fake passport was something to start off with, and who knows what else would be uncovered?

She spent another sleepless night, mainly because she couldn't get it off her mind. It didn't prove Ross had murdered anyone, but she couldn't wait to get to work and check out Roger Weston.

In the morning, her mother commented on her pale face, and tired eyes, and Wendy would have loved to share her find with her, but she knew she couldn't, not yet anyway.

"Why don't you take a day off, dear, and get some sleep, you look really peaky."

Wendy smiled, whenever her or her brother were under the weather, her mother always referred to them as 'peaky'.

"I am OK Mum, you mustn't worry. I just have to get through today, then I have the weekend to lie in."

Her mother didn't look convinced, but Wendy's mission now was to check out Roger Weston, and then go and speak to Alan Clarke about him. She felt that he would be the best person to share it with. Let Ross explain to him why he had two different names.

When she got to work she remembered that Ross would be in the office today, so she couldn't check anything out. He kept tabs on everything she did. But Wendy would not be thwarted from her purpose, she decided to take a chance and go to Alan's office. Obviously she would get a rollicking for illegally entering Ross's flat, but if it helped with the investigation, then she would be forgiven. She booked in first and then went to their office. Ross was in usual fine form, telling another WPC just how much the operation yesterday had relied on him. Wendy had heard it all before, so she left him bragging and made her way to Alan's office, and then tapped gently on the door.

"Come in." It was Sarah who spoke, and when Wendy entered the room, she was disappointed to see that Alan was not in.

"I am sorry to bother you. I was looking for the governor."

"I am afraid he's not in today. But we are partners, so if there is anything I can do to help, just ask."

Wendy hesitated, unsure of what to do. To someone as meek and mild as she was, tall and strident Sarah felt a little intimidating. To say she didn't like her was not correct. She had heard nothing but good about the work Sarah did, and how well she supported Alan, but right now it was Alan she wanted to share her discovery with. Her mind whirled, trying to think of something to say.

"It's nothing much really, it's just Ross. Since I stood up for Peter, he hasn't forgiven me, and he is rather frosty towards me."

Sarah sighed sympathetically. "Yes, we all know what Ross is like. When the guv comes back tomorrow I will mention what you said to him. Will that help?"

"Thank you."

Wendy smiled as she closed the door, but she could feel the passport as if it was burning a hole in her pocket. Maybe she could have shared her find with Sarah, and they could have checked it out together. If only Alan had been there to take charge. She had a computer at home, but it was the police records she needed to check, just to see if she could find out anything about Roger Weston. Maybe she could bluff her way in there. She could say she was doing further checks on suspects, which in her mind was absolutely true.

She went downstairs to where all the rows of dusty files were kept. It was usually DCIs that did this, unless they had instructed people such as herself to get the information. But, to her relief, the officer there barely gave her a glance when she asked to check some files.

He nodded. "Help yourself," and then disappeared to the back of the room to put the kettle on.

Wendy drew a trembling breath. She could feel her hands shaking with anticipation, which she did her best to hide. She searched the shelf amongst the Ws. Such a lot of Weavers, Watkins, ah here was Weston. No! Kathleen Weston had been convicted of child cruelty in 2003, her children Roger and Marion had been removed from her care and sent to foster homes after she had attempted to kill them by setting light to their home.

Wendy felt sick inside at what she was now uncovering. Was this the same man? It must be. But there was nothing else on the file, no police record about Roger Weston, only his sister. What a terrible start he had in life, but it didn't make him a murderer. Marion Weston, on the other hand, had been convicted at the age of sixteen in 2012 of criminal assault, having attacked another girl named Vicky Lowe. The photograph of Kathleen showed a tall dark haired woman with penetrating eyes. She had a haunted look. Obviously she was suffering from mental illness to do such a thing. It was hard not to feel a great pity for this family.

Something about this woman reminded Wendy of someone, but who was it? The children were very young in the photograph. The spiky haired little boy with the arresting eyes could have grown up to be Ross, and the girl, who was two or three years older, looked like a younger version of her mother.

"Can I make a copy of a file?" she asked boldly. Nothing was going to stand in her way now.

"Feel free," said the officer, waving her towards a photocopier on the other side of the room. He watched her idly as he drank his tea, one day this lot might be stored on a computer database for anyone to access, but right now, they were kept in this room, and he was glad, as it was his job on the line if they changed anything.

Wendy, now equipped with this new knowledge was wondering how she could keep it to herself until tomorrow. It looked like she had got away with visiting Ross's flat. He was acting his usual obnoxious self this morning, and obviously hadn't checked the bureau, and discovered that his passport was missing. But it wouldn't be long before he did, and with Alan not in today to share it with, she was surely at risk? If Ross, or Roger as he truly was, got wind of what she knew, he would have no qualms about silencing her. She gave a shiver when she thought about Eleanor. Fear gripped her; if only Alan was in. Well, she couldn't sit back and wait, she would have to go back in the office and share it with Sarah.

Sarah looked up with surprise when Wendy re-appeared, she looked distressed, her eyes had fear in them.

"Is there something wrong Wendy?"

Wendy's voice was shaking with uncertainty as she showed her the passport and the file, peering behind herself to make sure no one else was coming in.

"Ross has a fake passport, or a fake identity, not sure which, and these records show his mother Kathleen Weston tried to kill her two children. It seems his real name is Weston, and he has a sister called Marion."

Sarah studied the photo and read the file carefully. Then she opened the passport, and studied that. It was a few minutes before she spoke, but Wendy felt relief that she had at last shared this bombshell with someone.

"Very good work, Wendy. This is all very interesting."

"Do you think Ross has inherited his mother's madness?"

"Maybe, but I think we should wait until the guv is back before we do anything. By the way, how did you get his passport?"

Wendy felt her cheeks redden. "I got into his flat, and found it in a bureau."

"Desperate measures, eh? Without a key, too."

"Well, I was lucky. As I arrived the cleaner was coming out. She dropped her bucket, and her mobile rang. She thought she had closed the door."

"You do know that what you did was illegal?" said Sarah severely.

"Yes."

"Well the guv can take over tomorrow. You can leave the passport safely with me."

Wendy didn't really want to part with the passport. She had wanted to give it to Alan herself, but after telling Sarah everything, she could hardly refuse, so she left everything with Sarah, all the paperwork too.

"Thanks, he can have a good look through it all tomorrow."

To Wendy it felt like the conversation was over for now. She had to go back to the office with Ross and carry on as normal, and that would be so hard. She voiced her concern.

"No, I will give you something else to do, and I will email him and tell him you are working for me this afternoon."

Wendy looked at her gratefully, Sarah did understand. Her only worry now was tonight. Even living at home with her mother and brother as she did, was she safe? She was going to make sure all the doors were bolted when she went to bed. Maybe she was being a bit paranoid. Her imagination was running riot at the moment, but Sarah seemed very calm about it all.

"You'll be OK," said Sarah, reassuringly.

And Wendy started to feel a bit calmer. Tomorrow was the day it would all be sorted. No wonder Ross had wanted Peter blamed,

g

he had probably planted the bronze horse on Peter himself. It was all beginning to fit nicely together now.

Chapter Eighteen

Ross knew as soon as he entered the door that his flat had been invaded. There was a very strong smell of perfume in the hall and lounge. It didn't belong to his cleaner, she was rather masculine both in dress and ways, and had never left a lingering aroma like this behind her. It certainly wasn't a robbery, as everything was tidy and neat, and nothing had been stolen.

He didn't check the bureau immediately, but when he did, and discovered the passport missing, fear and anger rose inside him. He had spent years getting away from that surname. It had been such a curse, and now he had been discovered. Two years ago he had left Manchester to come to London, and had landed this job. He was determined to better himself. He had visions of being a DCI one day, and he had been jogging along quite happily until Eleanor had died.

And now it seemed someone was snooping on him, maybe to blame him for Eleanor's murder, and expose him as the son of poor mad Kathleen Weston, who had tried to burn down her own house with her kids inside. She had been locked away for years, and, by all accounts, didn't even know what day it was.

Ross had been separated from his sister for many years. He was four years old when it happened, and social services had not kept them together, so he just had to tough it out. He had been fostered by a kind family, who had stopped him from becoming a juvenile delinquent, and they had been proud when he joined the police force. But he had to cut the ties and move to London so he could change his name to Ross Green. Being alone made him feel vulnerable, so he developed a thick coat of confidence and arrogance to survive.

Now it looked like it was all going to come tumbling down on him, because his new life was rumbled, but who by? Once they checked his name out, and they would, they would find out about his mother, and then assume he had inherited her madness. Fear coursed through him, as he realised that now he might be arrested for Eleanor's murder.

He had tried so hard to push the blame on Peter or Matthew. Either of them would have done, but it hadn't worked, and although she had now been buried, the case remained open. This probably meant he would have to move on somewhere else, but in the meantime he would have to turn up today and act normally, and he might even be able to find out who had come round.

As soon as she entered the office he knew. That pungent smell of perfume; it was Wendy, and he had to act fast before she opened her mouth and ruined his life. She was all nervous and jittery today, saying she hadn't slept very well.

He watched her movements. It was just as he thought. She went downstairs to check the police records, and then, luckily for him, Clarke was off today, but it didn't stop her going to Clarke's office and offloading it all onto Sarah. He broke out in a sweat when he thought about it, she had to be stopped.

It was already dark when Wendy left for home. She lived fairly close to the station, so it was just a short bus ride. She was in a high state of nerves when she left the building. The net was closing in on Ross, but had he realised she had been snooping at his flat? Had his cleaner told him about bumping into her, and then described her? She had no idea of the answers, and she couldn't wait for Alan Clarke to come and take charge of it all.

As she stood at the bus stop, she was glad that there were others, it made her feel safer. She glanced all around her, but she could not see anyone suspicious. Everyone seemed intent on getting home as quickly as possible.

At last the bus came along. So she joined the queue, fumbling in her bag for her bus pass. There were no seats left, so she stood clutching the rail as the bus lurched its way towards her home.

When she got off, she glanced nervously behind her, then breathed a sigh of relief, as no one was following her.

She told herself sternly to stop being so imaginative. Everything was fine. She only had to walk down a couple of streets to get to the front door. She set off, and there were other people in the street, so she wasn't alone. She strode purposefully along, then crossed the road and rounded the corner. She was in her own road now. The house was in sight, and safety. She turned again as she reached the gate and opened it, nobody in the street was anywhere near her. Relief flooded through her.

Suddenly a tall hooded figure sprang out from behind a bush. In that split second, as Wendy saw the shadow of a raised hand holding a hard object, she made a futile attempt to escape. And then blackness descended on her, and she knew no more.

The figure picked her up as if she was a baby; small slight Wendy was being carried like a child. She was put in the open boot of a car, then it was closed, and the vehicle sped away. This all happened within a few seconds and the car roared down the quiet street and was gone.

Wendy's mum Karen was feeling a bit anxious about her daughter. She felt she worked too hard. When she first professed a desire to be a policewoman, Karen had been horrified. She had seen on the news, police men and women dying whilst doing their duty. It wasn't a safe world out there any more. But such was Wendy's desire to do her bit to try and make the streets a safer place, in the end her mother had no choice but to agree.

Ever since her husband Gerald had walked out on them when it was discovered that Leo had autism, Karen had protected her children as a lioness protects her cubs. Leo had been given extra help at school. An understanding teacher had been very patient in coping with his needs, and then Leo had been assessed. He had high functioning autism, known as Asperger's syndrome. He was interested in maths and the sciences, and passed his exams without any problems. Now he was at University and wanted to be an engineer after he graduated, and Karen was immensely proud of what he had achieved.

She had kept Gerald away from either of the children, as he wanted to stay in touch with Wendy, but Karen wasn't having that. Her son was not going to be ostracised by his father simply because he was a bit different. So all ties had been cut, and she now had no idea where he was, nor did she care. Her pain of his rejection of his own son was always there, but she felt it had knit them closer together. Her children were her life.

Wendy was such a good daughter, and she too loved Leo, and understood that he had difficulties in his social life. He found it difficult to interact or speak to strangers. Sometimes people thought he was rude, but Karen and Wendy both knew it was simply the way he was made.

When Wendy didn't arrive home at six o'clock, Karen just assumed she had gone out for a drink after work with her colleagues. It had happened before, sometimes when they were discussing work, or even to celebrate the conclusion of a difficult case. But it was unusual that she hadn't texted to say she would be late. She repeatedly rang Wendy's mobile, but it just rang out, then a recorded message invited her to leave a message, which she did several times.

When it got to eight o'clock and there was no reply, she did start to worry. Even though Wendy was now twenty-four years old, she was still her daughter, and bad things can happen to anyone of any age. She rang the station to see if Wendy was still there, but the duty officer checked and said she had signed out at five o'clock, and to the best of his knowledge nobody was going for an after work drink.

This was even more worrying for Karen, as it was completely out of character for Wendy not to contact her. She could feel the cold fingers of fear clutching at her. Surely the one thing she had always dreaded had not happened ?

Karen was aware that Wendy had found working with Ross difficult. Her daughter didn't complain much, but she had shared with her mother the incident when Wendy had defended Peter, after he had been wrongfully arrested. Karen, with her own son also affected by Asperger's, was shocked and horrified that Peter had been bullied in this way. She could imagine if Leo was in the same circumstances, it would have been hard for him to defend himself. What a cruel world it was for those who were a little different! Karen didn't have a very nice opinion of Ross after that, and she blamed her daughter's recent dark circles and peakiness on the strain of working with such a man. She would have

150

suggested to her that she applied for a transfer, but as quiet as Wendy usually was, she was still her own person, and Karen knew she would tell her that no matter where she worked, there would be some people she liked, and some she didn't, because that was life.

So at nine o'clock, and because she had his mobile phone number written on the kitchen notice board in case of an emergency such as this, in case Wendy's phone didn't work, and they usually worked together, she rang Ross. Keeping her voice as polite as she could, she explained that Wendy had not arrived home from work, and she had rung the office, and they had confirmed that Wendy had signed out at five o'clock.

Ross was surprisingly normal, with no trace of his usual arrogance that Wendy had told her about. "I am really sorry to hear that. Wendy wasn't in the office with me this afternoon, she was working elsewhere, but I am sure she will turn up. I expect you have tried contacting her?"

"Yes, it just goes into answer phone, and I have left several messages. It's not like her at all."

"Maybe she has a new boyfriend, and it could be that her phone isn't working, modern technology often lets us down," he said encouragingly.

"Maybe, but I feel I must report her missing. She is a young woman in a very unsafe world out there. Look at poor Eleanor Harrison, and what happened to her."

"That was in broad daylight, in her own home. Clearly she had upset someone, but, of course, it was such a tragedy. Why don't you wait until the morning, and give Wendy a chance to contact you. I am sure she will. She might feel you are being over protective. . . but of course you are not," he added hastily.

Karen considered his words. He sounded really kind and caring, not at all what she would have expected; so the man did have a heart. She knew she was a little overprotective of both her children, it was her way of keeping them safe without a father to lean on. Wendy had told her off before about it. "OK, thanks Ross, I will leave it until the morning then. Thanks for your help."

151

Chapter Nineteen

With the funeral now behind him, Alan was able to take a day off. Zoe had also wanted to take the day off, but all she could get was the afternoon. She was working from eight o'clock until midday, a very short shift today, all because one of her friends had agreed to come in and cover the rest of her day.

Alan had booked lunch in a nice restaurant, fairly close to the hospital. If they could get in there before twelve-thirty, it wouldn't be so crowded. He had asked her if she wanted to go somewhere nice in the afternoon, shopping, or whatever, but Zoe had said that coming home and having a relaxing afternoon would be perfect, as she still had to get into work early tomorrow to make up the hours. Alan didn't mind that at all, and he didn't imagine them sitting on the sofa relaxing today. Their love life had taken a back seat lately because of the hours they both worked, but this afternoon was theirs, and he made up his mind nothing was going to spoil it.

He usually kept his phone on all the time, but there was a polite notice in the restaurant asking customers to refrain from using their phones at the table so as not to spoil the enjoyment of others. So Alan thought, what the hell, he didn't just mute it, he turned it off, and gave Zoe his full attention.

She had changed out of her uniform, as she never liked to be seen in public in it, and was wearing a turquoise dress, which made her eyes look bluer and even bigger than usual. He had always loved her eyes, so full of expression, and her tousled curls made him want to ruffle her hair. She looked very beautiful today, even though a little tired. He was such a lucky man to have her, and he hoped he never took her for granted. His life without Zoe would be nothing!

"So much to choose from. Are you having a starter?" she enquired. Her smile was infectious. Alan buried his sombre mood and smiled back. She wasn't going anywhere, they were very happy.

"I think I will have some soup. How about you?"

"Yes, tomato sounds good. But after I am going for scampi; it's only light, I can't eat as much as you."

Alan studied the menu, he loved a meat pie, and there were various fillings. It was a standard joke between him and Zoe, that he could eat a big meal, and never put on an ounce, because he was built like a greyhound. Whereas she, being not very tall, had to keep her portions small, or else she might find her waist and hips spreading. But looking at her trim little waist he doubted it. She was just right, and even if she did put on weight, he would still love every inch of her. But he didn't say that, it sounded a bit sloppy, and he might embarrass her. He just squeezed her hand gently.

"I think I will go for the steak pie."

"Yes, I thought you would."

As they left the restaurant to head for home, it was beginning to fill up, so he was glad they had got there early. It was difficult to find anywhere in London to have some peace and quiet. He was so looking forward to some quality time together. The last three months had made him more aware that he had someone special in his life. He had not planned to marry for many years, believing that his career was all that mattered. How wrong he had been. Zoe was so lovely to come home to after a traumatic day at work, and soon he was going to ask her to marry him. He wanted to spend the rest of his life with her. He only hoped she felt the same.

When they got home, he switched his phone back on and was relieved that he had no texts or phone messages. Everyone was respecting it was his day off. Good. They sat down on the sofa, and he kissed her gently, stroking a stray curl out of her eyes. Zoe responded by kissing him back very passionately. It had been a while, and she needed his love very much.

Alan didn't need a second invitation. He picked her up and carried her into the bedroom.

"You saucy little minx, it's only two o'clock," he said as she stripped her clothes off.

"Come here you sexy man," she said, quickly, her eyes sparkling with fun.

He followed suit. He loved it when she took the initiative. Then they spent the afternoon making love. The release for both of them was immense. With such stressful jobs that they both had, the joy of lovemaking was even more precious. They finally tumbled out of bed at six o'clock, having fallen asleep after a particularly energetic bout of lovemaking. They both felt sated, so put on their dressing gowns whilst Zoe made a cup of tea. Alan glanced idly at his phone, which he had left on the sofa earlier, he had a voicemail.

He tossed up whether to ignore it, as all he felt like now was a shower, something to eat, and a cosy evening with Zoe. He certainly didn't want to cope with any emergencies. The message was from Sarah.

Zoe put his tea down in front of him. "There you go, two sugars to restore your energy!"

"I need that, you made sure of it!" he said meaningly, kissing her cheek. Zoe was enjoying this private moment, but it was soon to be shattered.

"I have a voicemail from Sarah. What should I do?"

She could feel annoyance sweeping over her that Sarah couldn't let him have just one day to himself. She felt like Sarah was intruding on their life together, and she couldn't help wondering if it was deliberate. That torch Sarah held for Alan was shining very brightly. But then commonsense kicked in. Sarah was his partner at work, and Alan had agreed always to be on call. She had no choice really than to accept it, it would always be like this, and their love could only survive if she was supportive towards him.

"You best see what she wants," she said calmly, squashing down all her forebodings, and smiling gently at him.

Alan looked admiringly at her. This hadn't been the case with Kate, his previous girlfriend, with her his work ethic had cost him the relationship. Not that he cared now, as he realised he had not loved her, nor anyone else until Zoe came along. He couldn't change the way he was, and only Zoe understood.

Alan listened to the message. Sarah was telling him that

154

Wendy had come to the office to see him today. When Sarah asked if she could help, she had said that it was difficult working with Ross since she had defended Peter, and apparently she was coming back to see Alan again tomorrow. Sarah also explained that she had given Wendy work to do away from Ross for that day until Alan returned and could sort the situation out. He put his phone down and turned to Zoe.

"I don't know why it couldn't have waited until tomorrow. Nobody died, just Wendy the young WPC is finding it hard to work with PC Green, and I guess wants to move."

Zoe remembered him mentioning Ross Green. Since she had moved in he was sharing more of his working life with her, and she liked it. That way Sarah couldn't shut her out. She had a pretty good idea why Sarah had phoned him on his day off, she just couldn't leave him alone, but she said nothing because Alan wouldn't get it. He didn't understand the workings of the mind of a devious woman.

"Well, you are the man to fix it."

"Yes, and I am not going to ring her back. It's not that important."

They sat there in a companionable silence sipping their tea. For once Alan was not thinking about work, his thoughts were full of Zoe. Each day she was becoming more and more important to him. He wondered if she would accept him if he proposed, but she wasn't expecting him to, and he couldn't bear it if she said no. Maybe he should wait a little longer, they had only been living together for three months.

Zoe finally broke the silence. "I am going up to take a shower. Do you fancy joining me?"

"Yes please!" laughed Alan, "I can't get enough of you!"

They both threw off their towelling robes and ran to the bathroom, giggling like a couple of naughty children. For once in her life, Zoe felt that she had won that round with Sarah. Alan was so wrapped up in her, and their life. Even if it was only for today, it was very precious. Sarah needed to find herself a boyfriend, because Alan was off the market, and the sooner she realised that the better.

Later they finally tumbled into bed, physically exhausted. Zoe felt positively glowing with love. Happiness like this was so uplifting, she felt she could take on the world. She turned to say goodnight to him, but Alan was already asleep. His face had such a peaceful expression. She kissed him gently on the cheek, and he stirred slightly.

"I love you," she said, and within seconds she was also asleep.

The next morning it was back to reality for both of them. Work loomed. Zoe left first, as her shift started at eight. Whilst she was on the tube, pressed up against other people, all intent on getting to work, she was still basking in the afterglow of the previous day. When the train came to a grinding stop, she joined the throng of people all hurrying to their destinations.

The hospital was not far from the tube, and she was thankful that it was dry, as she had to walk across a park to the entrance. She didn't particularly notice the car which was parked on the rough ground at the entrance, nor the hooded figure that sprang out as she came level with the tree. For a split second, Zoe was hidden from view, and the figure took advantage of it, by hitting her from behind. Taken unawares, she crumpled up and fell to the ground. Thinking it was a mugging, she threw her purse at the figure; she just wanted to live. Then she felt the thick curtain of unconsciousness descend on her. She was dragged into the boot of the car, then the car sped away from the park, and was soon amongst the heavy and slow moving London traffic.

Alan had time for a leisurely cup of tea and some toast before he reported in at nine. But when he got to his office, chaos reigned. Sarah had not yet arrived, and the duty officer was in there with a lady who was wringing her hands together, and clearly very distressed.

"Boss, this is Karen Stuart, Wendy's mother. She is very concerned because Wendy didn't come home last night."

"Yes, I want to report her missing!"

Alan studied her. She was small and slight like Wendy, but her hair was grey. Just an ordinary looking lady, except for the desperation in her eyes. He remembered hearing that she was a single mother, and that Wendy had a brother with Asperger's syndrome.

"Good morning, Karen. I am sorry to hear that, could she have stayed the night with a friend?"

"She always rings or texts me. I have left her voice mails, and there is no reply. I know my girl, and I know something is wrong."

"OK, we'll check her number out too."

Alan gave her number to the duty officer, who went to check it out. All the while his mind was whirling; was it his fault? Maybe he should have taken the message from Sarah more seriously. Could Green have upset Wendy enough to make her leave home and her job? But surely not, policewomen and men were tough people, they had to be to do the job. All he needed to do was put Wendy with someone less arrogant than Green.

The duty office returned, confirming that he had rung the number several times and it just went onto answer phone. Karen was by now pacing up and down and begging them to find her daughter.

"What do you think has happened to Wendy? She left home happily yesterday for work, did she?"

"She was finding it hard working with Ross, but apart from that she was happy. What I am anxious about is that the murder of Eleanor has not been solved. There is someone dangerous out there, free, and I am worried that he might have my daughter, he might kill her too," and with that she covered her face with her hands and sobbed loud heaving sobs.

He sent the officer to get Karen a cup of tea, and then invited her to sit down. There was a box of tissues on the side, so he handed one to her.

"Do we know where Sarah's got to?" he asked awkwardly. She was always better with hysterical women, and she usually took charge at these times.

"Yes, her washing machine is leaking everywhere. She was waiting for the repair man to come. He just has, so she hopes to be here soon."

Alan knew that Sarah lived in an old house, which she rented. She was always complaining that everything inside was like the house; out of date, and he could imagine her frustration at having water gushing out everywhere. It was so unusual for Sarah to be late, so he knew it would be a good reason.

The tea seemed to calm Karen a little, and Alan assured her that they would start searching for Wendy immediately, and leave no stone unturned. She gave him the contact details for two of

Wendy's friends, and he sent a PC and his partner to check them out and find out when they had last seen Wendy.

The telephone on his desk sprang to attention, ringing imperiously, so he picked up the handset. It was a representative from the geriatric ward, asking him if Zoe was ill, as she had not come in today.

"But she left at seven-thirty, she must be there by now!"

"No, she has not booked in anywhere, we checked."

Alan could feel fear inside him. First Wendy, now Zoe. Oh, not his beautiful Zoe! Surely Eleanor's murderer hadn't struck again, and in broad daylight! What did they want with Wendy and Zoe, they were just two innocent victims in all this? His heart was banging inside his chest, and he could feel nausea inside him.

"I want everyone in my office now, and as much publicity as possible; tell the press and other media. We need to find these two young women, and find them quickly!"

Ross had been worrying ever since he realised that Wendy had rumbled him. He felt as if his life was over. He would be locked up forever, as they would think his mother's madness had rubbed off on him. His DNA was at Eleanor's and at Peter's homes, but that was because he was part of the investigation, and had reason to be there. They needed someone to blame for this murder, and he could not prove he was innocent.

Well, he couldn't face going into work today. Alan Clarke was back and Wendy would tell him of her findings. He had no choice but to move on, but where? They were bound to put out a description of him, so he wasn't safe anywhere. His only hope was to go somewhere like Australia, a long way away. He almost wished he could go back to being Roger Weston again, just to get out of the country. Ross Green was known, and he knew his name would be circulated.

He tried to book himself a ticket online, but there were none available for that day. He was trying to think clearly, but panic was spreading through him. With shaky hands he lifted down his suitcase from on top of the wardrobe. There wasn't a minute to waste, he had to get going.

Ross flung his clothes into the case, then telephoned the airlines. But that was even worse, he was in a queue, and there were five people in front of him. Why was it so hard to leave England? Maybe he should sling everything in the car, then drive to a remote part of Scotland and stay there for a while. He had been on holiday recently, and the village where he had stayed had been about a century behind the times, with no TV, running water or electricity, it was the land that time forgot.

He switched on the TV to check on the weather. There could be snow there, even in late October, but he knew it wouldn't be hard to find a cottage to rent. It was all so simple there, no bank accounts, cash sales, and very little communication with other villagers.

The local news was on, and up flashed the face of Karen, Wendy's mother, and then DCI Alan Clarke came on saying that his girlfriend Zoe was also missing, so if anyone had any information, could they please get in touch. He had never seen Alan look distraught before, but then this was personal. At that moment Ross knew he couldn't do it, he couldn't go away. However scared he was he needed to go and tell Alan what he knew.

When Karen had spoken to him last night about Wendy, he had not been that concerned, thinking her just an over anxious mother. But for a long time now, he had suspected that Eleanor might have been killed by his sister Marion. He wasn't close to Marion, they had been split up whilst very young, and his over-riding memory of her was an elder sister who bullied him, then laughed with a strange mocking laugh. She reminded him a lot of their mother. She had the same laugh, was tall and commanding, and very angry and spiteful if she thought she had been crossed. He had never expected to see her again after twelve years. But three years ago, he had moved to London, and their paths had crossed. They had both changed their names to get away from anything connected with Kathleen. He was fine with that, but he could see she hadn't lost that wild streak, although she was good at hiding it from others.

So he didn't keep company with her. She made him feel uneasy, but she was still his flesh and blood. He had suspected Marion of Eleanor's murder from the beginning, so he had arrested Peter in the hope he would make a confession. Because if they discovered it was Marion, it would be traced back to him, and the connection would be made. His conscience had still felt the need to protect his sister. But not any more. With both Wendy and Zoe missing, they were in huge danger. Marion hated her own sex, and he believed she would unleash her madness and kill them, just like he believed she had killed Eleanor.

Chapter Twenty

Wendy woke up confused. She couldn't see anything and she couldn't move. Where was she? She tried to bring her muddled brain into action. Then she realised she had a blindfold over her eyes. She hadn't gone blind, and she felt relief. Rope was biting into her hands and feet, and she seemed to be in an upright position, so she guessed she was probably tied to a chair. The back of her head was throbbing. And then she remembered: someone had hit her. But why?

She was aware of someone beside her, and she heard an eerie mocking laugh.

"You couldn't stop poking your nose in could you? You left me no choice, you're going to die!"

The voice was muffled, as though being spoken through a tin can. It didn't sound like Ross, it sounded almost like a computer, but Wendy could feel the movements of the person, and their breath was on her face. So he had been the murderer all along, and now he was going to silence her. She had no doubt that he would carry out his word.

Fear and anger vied for supremacy inside Wendy. Terror for her own life, but anger at what he had done, and then tried to blame others. Would nobody ever know just how evil he was? She thought wildly of how she might escape. How could she fool him? She made gurgling noises from behind the gag over her mouth.

Marion Weston surveyed the trussed up figure beside her. She had the power, and this lowly WPC was nothing! The voices had told her she was all important and she must rid herself of this pathetic creature. There was no holding back now, and tonight, when it was dark and quiet, she would do the deed. She knew she was not just a woman, she had the determination and the strength of a man, and tonight this creature would die. Killing was easy. This time she would have to dispose of the body, whereas she had left them all to find Eleanor Harrison. But nobody came into this garage, or even past it. The lane was too bumpy for most cars to negotiate, and it only led to her house, so it would be easy to dispose of Wendy's body.

"What are you gurgling about?" Marion asked crossly. She didn't want Wendy to die just yet, she liked wielding her power. She undid the mouth gag, but kept the one over Wendy's eyes, and Wendy took a deep breath.

"Please, I need the toilet."

That mocking laugh again. Ross was truly mad. She had never heard him laugh like that before.

"I'm not going to fall for that one. Do you think I am stupid? Pee in your knickers for all I care!"

Wendy winced at his crudeness. Well that hadn't worked. She could feel his restlessness. He was pacing about, but the evil bastard was enjoying every minute of it. She wasn't going to give him the satisfaction of knowing that she was petrified.

"You are disgusting, Ross!" she said angrily. And Marion laughed again. She actually thought it was Ross, how funny was that!

"Well you can sit and stew in your own juice, but remember I have had my instructions; you die tonight!"

Wendy heard the footsteps dying away. He really was going. How could she escape before he returned? She could feel the coldness of concrete under her feet, so she guessed she was either in a garage or a cellar, or some sort of warehouse. She tried to move her hands, in the hope that the knot might be loose, but the rope was cutting into her flesh, and felt immovable. It was the same with her feet. All this effort had exhausted her. She remembered thinking she didn't just want to stay here and wait for death. She wanted to fight back, but the knock on her head had made her dizzy, and she lost consciousness again.

*   *   *   *

Marion had hated Eleanor Harrison with an all consuming hatred. She was the most well known and talked about British celebrity that had ever been. She hated her beauty and the fact that everyone loved her. Nobody had ever loved Marion, not even her kid brother. She had been told by the voices she was not worthy of anyone's love, so she didn't need to be nice to anyone.

Marion remembered her mother, a tall dark haired woman, with a broad Northern Irish accent, and a temper that was best never unleashed. She didn't remember ever having a father. He had taken off when he found out how wild Kathleen was. He could not control her, no one could. She never showed any love towards her children, they were just an encumbrance, and Marion could still remember that night, the heat and the flames, when they had rescued herself and Roger from the burning house.

She was split up from her brother and fostered in various homes, but no one could cope with her. She felt angry at the world, and she was guided by the voices because she had no one else. When she was a teenager, she developed a passion for a boy the same age, but so did another girl, and he seemed to like the other girl more. It was a rejection that Marion couldn't take, so she attacked the other girl with a knife. The girl survived, but Marion had to spend some time in a mental hospital having treatment, and it was three years before she was allowed to leave.

Being in there taught her one thing to survive; she had to have another side to her character, even if it was a made up one, just to fool people and try and make them like you. So she had come to London with a new name, and an ambition to do well in life, earn good money, have a nice home, and hopefully one day meet the man who could understand her. And she had met him, and she was madly in love with him, but there were still some obstacles to overcome before they could be a couple. She hadn't dreamt that her path would cross with Ross. After all these years, she didn't feel any bonds towards him. He had always been a tiresome little brother who had to be kept in line, and the only one out of the two of them that their mother had shown a glimmer of love towards.

It was amusing that Wendy thought she was Ross, and that he had done the murder. That wimp, he wouldn't have it in him. He was all bluff and arrogance. It just proved how well she had covered her tracks and kept the whole police force guessing. She

163

loved the power that had given her, the knowledge that she had outwitted them all.

She had found killing Eleanor very satisfying. It had been so quick. She had gone down, and her whole face was smashed in because Marion wasn't sure that one blow would be enough, so she kept going. Planting the horse at Peter's had been easy, but her only regret was that he had escaped being charged. Matthew committing suicide had been helpful, as it had put him in the frame. But the case was still open. However, nobody knew about her, except her brother, and nobody suspected her. Her brother would say nothing, just in case it incriminated him.

She left Wendy, she could spend all day knowing it was her last, and Marion felt exultant about that. Wendy would wish she had never poked her nose in; it had cost her her life. Back at the house she put herself on some toast and switched on the radio. She just had time to listen to the news. Nothing yet about Wendy being missing. She had done well. They might think Wendy had done a runner. And it was at that moment she decided that Zoe had to die too, and she would carry out her plan to capture her. She started salivating at the thought that tonight she was going to kill two women. Could life get any better?

Alan had lost his usual cool and calm demeanour. He couldn't be detached from this; his beautiful Zoe was missing too! He tried her mobile frantically, but it didn't respond, it was switched off. It wouldn't have been quite so bad if Sarah had been there to keep him calm. All his colleagues were trying to soothe him, and suggesting maybe he should go home, as he was too personally involved with this case now. Were they mad? He couldn't go anywhere, he had to find Zoe before any harm came to her!

His mobile clicked and a message came through. The name flashed up: Ross Green. PLEASE MEET ME IN THE COFFEE SHOP NEXT DOOR. DON'T TELL ANYONE. I THINK I CAN HELP YOU TO FIND ZOE.

Alan's heart thudded with apprehension. Wasn't Ross Green in his office? He had assumed the man was in.

"Is any of my group absent besides Sarah today?" he asked, feeling confused.

"Yes, Green hasn't shown up. But Sarah is on her way now, her washing machine is fixed."

"OK, thanks. I am going out for a few minutes. Just step up everything, and find these women!"

He hurried to the coffee shop, not even stopping to buy a drink when he entered, then saw Ross sitting in the corner. He wasn't in uniform, and was wearing jeans and a hooded fleece jacket. Alan sat opposite him, wondering what he could possibly know.

"What's going on then?" he demanded.

Ross could see what a state he was in, and there wasn't time for long explanations now, so he kept it short.

"My sister's name is Marion Weston. She is mentally ill, and I believe she may have killed Eleanor, and I also believe she may have kidnapped Wendy and Zoe."

"But why? How are they connected with Eleanor? I don't understand?"

"It's a long story, and we have to move fast. I have done stuff I am not proud of, but I want to make amends. I know where my sister lives. I think we should go there."

This was a completely different Ross Green than the one that Alan was used to. Gone was the arrogance and he seemed genuinely concerned.

"OK, but I will need backup."

"I hope you didn't tell anyone you are here with me."

"No, I just slipped out like you said."

"We need to go to the house first, then call backup. You have to trust me on this."

Alan was totally bewildered. But his instincts told him that Ross was being honest with him, so he came to a quick decision.

"OK, here are the keys to my car, go and sit in it discreetly. I will go back to the office and say I am going home, as it's already been suggested. I won't tell anyone what we are doing."

Ross nodded, took the keys and then pulled up the hood of his fleece so that he wasn't easily recognisable. He knew where Alan parked his car, so he made his way out of the coffee shop.

When Alan arrived back in the office, Sarah had arrived at last.

"Sorry boss, I was flooded out," she explained. "I can't believe that so much has happened since yesterday." She touched his arm gently. "So sorry to hear about Zoe. We must find her!"

Alan was grateful for her no nonsense approach. Now she was

here he felt calmer already. He was very tempted to tell her quickly what was going on with him, but the team were around him, and there was no privacy. It was true Ross had said tell no one, but Sarah was his partner, and she shared everything with him. Still, there would be time later when he called for backup, and in the meantime he wasn't the only person who was upset.

"Thank you, Sarah. Can you act as liaison officer with Wendy's mother, Karen Stuart. She is in the interview room and in great distress. Maybe you could arrange for her to do an appeal for Wendy's safe return. It can be televised, also mention Zoe, and after that someone can take Karen home until such time as we have news for her."

"Certainly boss, I am on that!" said Sarah, bustling away.

Alan turned to his team. "I am going home. It's been suggested that I should not cover this case because of my connection with Zoe, and maybe that is true, but it mustn't stop all of you doing your utmost to find out what is going on and bringing these two innocent women back to safety."

There was a murmur of agreement, and one of the men spoke up.

"We will do everything we can, guv. We already have officers out searching and interviewing, and we will let you know as soon as they are safe."

Just then the duty officer came in with a mobile in his hand. It was still on, but the battery was almost flat. "This has been found by a bush in the garden of the house where Wendy lives."

"Take it to Sarah, she is with Wendy's mother. We can then be sure that the mobile belongs to Wendy."

Alan took his leave then, before he became more involved, and with the knowledge that Ross was sitting in the car waiting for him. But his mind was whirling all the time. There could be two reasons why that mobile was in the garden. Firstly, Wendy might have dropped it, which was highly unlikely, as women hung onto their mobiles for dear life, or secondly, she had been kidnapped in her own front garden, which was unbelievable. Only a very confident kidnapper, or a mad one, would take such a risk, and he couldn't imagine another woman doing that. What sort of woman was Marion Weston?

*   *   *   *

166

Zoe sat up. Her whole body was aching, and it felt like she had been thrown down a flight of stairs. Pain screamed at her from everywhere. She had some sort of blindfold on, and when she tried to move, she could feel bars around herself, holding her arms tightly behind her. Was she in prison? She felt like she was going mad. She wondered if it was day or night, and how long had she been here? All these questions tumbled through her brain, and more? Who was doing this to her, and why? She tried to call out, but her voice sounded very feeble.

"Where am I, and what do you want with me?"

She heard a movement behind her, and then a weary voice spoke.

"Thank god I am not alone. I'm Wendy Stuart, a WPC, and I believe we are being kept captive by PC Ross Green, and he's very dangerous. We need to get out of here. Who are you?"

The effort of speaking had exhausted Wendy. Without anything to eat or drink since the day before, her voice was no more than a croak, but she was desperate to make contact with someone.

Zoe responded. "I'm Zoe, girlfriend of DCI Alan Clarke, but what does Ross Green have against us to imprison us this way?"

"I found out he has an assumed name, and I was about to tell Alan. I think he killed Eleanor. That is why I am here, but I don't know why you are?"

Fear coursed through Zoe. She didn't know what she had done to be there, but it sounded like Green was a desperate man. What would he do to them when he came back?

"I can't move. My arms and legs are tied."

"Well, I seem to be in a cage. I can't believe it, he's put me in a cage like some animal!" Anger coursed through Zoe, and with it a new determination to get out of this predicament. She felt around behind her and found the catch, it was a bit wobbly. She put all her weight behind it and pushed, she could feel it moving, but the door still held firm.

"Are you OK?" asked Wendy.

"Yes, but I can't move the door of this cage!" Zoe banged herself against it again and again, heedless of the fact that her body was hurting all over. Despair and desperation lent power to her weary limbs, and suddenly the door crashed open, and she fell to the concrete floor. Scrambling up, and now with her arms free, she pulled the blindfold from her eyes, trying to look around her.

When her eyes became accustomed to the gloom, she realised it was a large garage. The voice she had heard was obviously that of a young woman she could see tied to a chair, and also blindfolded. The cage she had just escaped from was a very large dog's crate. Only a crazy man could pull a stunt like that!

She ran towards Wendy, intent on freeing her, but then they both heard footsteps, and she froze to the spot.

"Don't worry about me, just get help," whispered Wendy.

The footsteps became louder. He must be outside, so Zoe hid at the side of the car which was parked in the garage. It was black, and not that easy to spot, and as she peeped out she saw the hooded figure enter at the other side. Her first instinct was to run, as it would only be a few seconds before he realised that she had escaped, and she had to get away and get some help.

"Help, I feel ill," came from Wendy, and the figure turned angrily towards her.

"Shut your mouth. Can't believe I left your gag off!"

In the few seconds that the figure was distracted and walking towards Wendy, Zoe ran out the of the garage. But she hadn't run far, when she heard the roar of anger. She had no idea where she was, or which way to go. The garage seemed to be in the middle of nowhere, along an unmade road. Further along was an old house, but it wasn't far enough away to go for help. Her gut feeling told her that it might be where Ross lived, so there would be no help there. And to make it all so much worse, darkness was descending, and there were no street lights. She ran into the blackness, praying that he couldn't see her. She knew she just had to keep going until she found people, lights and safety.

Marion was filled with rage when she realised that Zoe had escaped. Nobody was allowed to outwit her, especially that empty headed bimbo! How had she done it? She hadn't expected her to get out of that crate.

She ran out into the darkness, knowing she had to find her. Once she found someone to blab her mouth off to, all her plans would be scuppered! Marion had been looking forward all day to her mission tonight, and now the voices were angry with her. She had failed in her duty to them. Wendy was just an irritating annoyance, but Zoe was the main prize. She would get the greatest satisfaction out of killing her.

But it was fruitless. She had no idea which way Zoe had gone.

She would have to take the car. With the headlights on she would be bound to find her. If Zoe was out in the scrub, she could strangle her there and then, and dump her body in the river.

She ran back into the garage. The car had been standing for a while, as she normally took the train to work. The keys were in a drawer in the garage. She found them, whilst yelling at Wendy to "Button it!" The car eventually spluttered into action. She left the engine running and ran over to where Wendy was trussed up. There was a gag laying on the floor. She picked it up and rammed it into Wendy's mouth, making sure she couldn't take it off. Jumping back into the car, she drove wildly out of the garage, completely ignoring the choking noises that Wendy was making. Let her choke to death, she really didn't care. Zoe was the prize!

h

Chapter Twenty-one

Ross tried to fill in Alan about Marion as they were driving towards her home. It was a few miles outside London, in the leafy suburbs. He had never been there, but he had noted it on her file. In fact, when their paths crossed, neither of them had acknowledged each other. But he knew, it might be twelve years, and they had both changed a lot, and grown up from being young children, but it was definitely Marion. So they had kept out of each other's way, and both got on with their lives.

Alan could feel pity for Ross. With a mother who was insane, and had tried to kill her children, and no father, what sort of start had he had in life? This morning there was no trace of his usual arrogance, he was humble and apologetic, and infinitely more likeable.

"You should have told me about your mother, and why you needed to change your name. I would not have judged you."

"Yes, I have made it worse. And don't ask me why, but deep inside me I still have a glimmer of loyalty towards Marion, because she is my sister, but I truly regret trying to blame Peter."

Alan drove faster as he was talking, knowing that time was of the essence here. There was so much about all this that was puzzling.

"So she must have known Eleanor, if Eleanor let her into the flat. But how does she know Wendy and Zoe? I just don't get it."

"Well the connection is. . . " Ross's voice tailed off, and Alan wasn't listening, because as they rounded the bend, coming towards them on their side of the road was a van. It looked like the steering was gone, as it careered backwards and forwards across the road. Alan did his best to steer clear of it, trying to judge where it was safe, but suddenly it was right in their path, heading towards them. He made one last frantic attempt to turn the wheel, but so did the other driver, and the van hit them head on, causing the car to spin round, then it turned upside down. . . and then there was silence.

Ross came to quite quickly, but he could see Alan slumped over the wheel, blood was trickling down his face, and his eyes were closed. He tried to rouse him by shaking him, but there was no response. It seemed he was unconscious. His own face felt bruised, and when he put his hand to his cheek, there was blood on his fingers.

Panic swept through him. Surely Alan was alive. He touched Alan's limp hand and he could feel a very faint pulse in his wrist. Being upside down made it even harder. He tried to open the car door, yelling for help at the same time.

Everything became a blur after that; people talking to him, telling him he would be alright, they would get them out one way or another. He could hear ambulance and police car sirens, and lights were flashing, but still he remained trapped inside the car next to the unconscious Alan. He thought fleetingly of how their mission had failed. Those two young women might be doomed, and a tear of frustration trickled down his face.

Then there were firemen there, explaining that the car door was all twisted, so they would need to cut them out. His cheek was throbbing, and he felt disorientated from it all. He prayed that they would both get out of this car alive. Then he felt a fog descending over him. He tried to fight it, there was so much he needed to say. Someone had to rescue those two women, but once again he passed out.

When he woke up later, he found himself in a hospital bed. He had a drip attached to his arm, and a nurse was bustling around with some pills in her hand.

"Oh, you are awake, thank goodness. How do you feel?"

"My cheek hurts, and I feel dizzy."

"You had a lucky escape. Your car had turned right over. We just need to run some tests, and you will probably have to stay in overnight. But all being well, we are looking at sending you home tomorrow."

"What about Alan? He was driving the car, and I couldn't wake him up."

"I will go and find out for you," she said smiling, as she bustled out.

Ross tried to sit up, gingerly putting his hand on his cheek. It felt tender, so maybe it was bruised. He wondered what had happened to make the van drive straight into them. That driver had been all over the road. Had his steering gone, was he drunk, or on drugs? Whatever it was, he needed to know.

Nausea swept over him. He was willing himself to be able to leave this hospital and get backup, but the effort of sitting up in bed was enough, and he knew he wouldn't be able to stand up.

The nurse came bustling back in. Her face showed her concern, and she spoke gently to him.

"I am afraid Alan is more injured than you. He is unconscious at the moment, as he hit his head on the steering wheel and has concussion. We are doing tests and scans, as we believe he may have internal injuries, but one thing is for sure, he won't be able to go home tomorrow."

"We are police officers, and we were on our way to interview a murder suspect. If we don't move fast, innocent people may be murdered."

The young nurse looked at him in amazement, wondering if the medication they had given him was causing hallucinations. He was dressed in a hospital gown, and he felt feverishly in the pocket.

"If you are looking for your clothes, they are in the locker."

He had come in plain clothes today, as he had got no further than the coffee shop, and Alan had also been wearing plain clothes. No wonder she was looking amazed. She silently handed him his trousers, and he felt in his pocket for his ID, which he then flourished in front of her.

"I see, and you say you were on your way somewhere to interview a suspect? Some of your colleagues are outside, waiting to speak to you, so if you feel fit enough to see them, you can let them know."

"I am well enough to see them!"

Ross spoke firmly. It was himself he was trying to convince. There was no way he could languish in hospital whilst his mad sister was on the loose. With Alan now laid up, he had to impress

172

on the others how important it was to find Wendy and Zoe before Marion did her worst.

The nurse, whose name was Lisa, helped him to sit upright with a pillow propped behind him, then she went to get him a cup of tea. When she returned, she was accompanied by two officers. But they were not from the station, and Ross had never seen them before. One was a DCI, aged about thirty-five, named John, with dark hair and in uniform, and he was accompanied by a WPC named Carla, who had auburn hair pulled back under her hat, also in uniform. There was sympathy in their eyes for his plight, and Ross left them in no doubt as to just how serious the situation was.

"DCI Alan Clarke and I were on our way to the house of my sister, Marion Weston, as I believe she is holding captive, my WPC partner Wendy Stuart and Alan's girlfriend Zoe."

"I see. Why would she be doing that?"

"Because she is mad, she needs help. I think she is responsible for the death of Eleanor Harrison. She hates women. She sees them as a threat to herself."

"Well I suggest you give us the address and postcode of the premises, and we'll get round there quickly, with backup of course."

"I need to come with you!" said Ross, trying to get out of bed. But his head was swimming and his cheek was hurting. He gritted his teeth, trying to ignore the pain. They had already wasted so much time, it might even be too late.

John was quick to see how weak Alan still was. There was no way he could come with them.

"You've had quite a shock, and we will need to talk about the accident later, but right now we need to go and finish off what you and DCI Clarke were hoping to do. We can't have these women at risk."

Ross knew he was right. The shock of the impact had shaken him up, and his whole body was aching. But he was alive, that was what mattered. Carla produced a pad and pen, and he gave her his sister's address and postcode.

"Oh, that is right out of London," she remarked.

"Yes," he agreed.

"There's no street lights out there."

"Why, what time is it?"

"Six o'clock and it's pitch dark, but we do have torches in the car."

Ross was amazed. So they had wasted a whole day. He must have blacked out for longer than he had realised. All he could do now was to stay here until he felt stronger, and pray that it wasn't too late. Fate had dealt himself and Alan a cruel blow today.

He watched as they hurried off, and nurse Lisa came in with a tray of sandwiches and soup.

"You will feel better when you have eaten this," Lisa commented.

Ross was trying to remember what had happened in the accident. He thought that there had been a van careering madly towards them, and after that he couldn't remember much more.

"Was the van driver injured badly?" he asked.

"He has broken ribs, and concussion, but all three of you were so lucky, it could have been so much worse."

"Yes, of course. So the officers that I just saw were here to question us all about the accident, and decide who was at fault?"

"They were here to question you, yes, but now they have gone, and it's not really my business. I am just doing my job helping you to recover from the accident, and making sure you feel fit enough to go home tomorrow. If the doctor says your results are clear of any problems, then you will go."

"Can I see Alan when he wakes up? I have something to tell him."

Lisa sighed. "You men can never let go, can you? Work will still be there when you leave hospital. I guess you can as long as you don't give him stress."

Ross sighed quietly to himself. She just didn't get how time was of the essence. But as she said, her job was to make him feel better, and his working life was of no interest to her. He wanted to make sure when Alan woke up, that he realised that someone had gone to try and rescue Wendy and Zoe. He ate the soup she put in front of him, and immediately felt stronger. When he thought about it, no wonder he had felt weak and dizzy, he had not eaten since this morning, and that was many hours ago. The sandwiches were sliced chicken breast, and then he had a cup of coffee afterwards. His cheek was not hurting so much, and he felt almost normal again. If only he had eaten before the officers had turned up, he might have been OK to go with them.

He must have drifted off to sleep again after that, and he was dreaming that they were chasing after Marion. It was so vivid, he could feel himself panting, and the sweat was pouring off him. And then suddenly she disappeared, and there was a big hole in front of him. He tried to stop himself from falling down it but he couldn't, then bump. . . He woke up to find Lisa standing by his bed.

"Are you OK?" she said soothingly. "You were talking in your sleep."

"Oh, I am sorry."

"No need to be," she said lightly. "The drugs you have had probably caused it."

"Oh, of course, I never thought of that."

Relief flooded through him, the dream had been so vivid. Although he didn't really have an emotional attachment to Marion, because of the circumstances, he had hoped, if he could have been there when she was captured, that he might persuade her to accept mental help. She might not realise she was mad, but he did. She might well be locked up for many years, but with treatment, she might be helped. He didn't know much about mental illness, and certainly murder was the worst crime anyone could commit, but in the case of someone mentally ill, it was a bit easier to understand that they were not responsible for their own actions.

He would never forget the cruel start in life that they had, and how young they were and, even though she bullied him, the pain of being separated from his sister. That wild look that his mother often had in her eyes came back to him. She always seemed to be angry. He remembered how, as a little boy, he used to hide under the tablecloth when she was angry, and one day he saw her hitting Marion with the handle of a broom. Marion was trying to protect her face with her hands, and begging their mother to stop, but she kept whacking Marion with the stick until she fainted on the floor in front of her, then she kicked her body and walked away.

When they had been rescued from the burning house, they were taken to social services, and split up. Ross had been fostered by a kind family, and he had managed to put the past behind him. He would never forget it, but neither would he allow it to dominate his life. Marion had shown many of the signs of inheriting her mother's instability, and he guessed that she had probably been passed around foster parents and homes because no one could cope with her. Nobody had got her any help for her mental troubles, they had probably just assumed she had been born a bad person. Maybe it was too late to speculate now, but he felt sad for her because she had been let down. Until they crossed paths in London, he had never heard of her again. Even then they didn't mention the past. They barely acknowledged one another, but they both knew they were siblings, it was almost like a sixth sense.

Lisa interrupted his thoughts. "Alan is awake now. You can go in and see him just for a few minutes."

"Oh, thanks. What time is it?"

"Eight o'clock, that's why it can only be a few minutes. You are not walking. I am taking you in a wheelchair."

Ross thanked her, reluctantly getting into the wheelchair she had brought in. Lisa put a blanket over him, and Ross smiled to himself. It was about one hundred degrees in the hospital, no way would he get cold, but her caring attitude was like a breath of spring, maybe it was because after everything that had happened, he had dropped his arrogant manner. He realised now he must have been getting under the skin of lots of people, including Wendy, and he did so hope he would see her again so he could make it up to her.

Lisa was a tiny petite nurse, whereas he was tall, but she expertly manoeuvred the wheelchair along the corridor. She was a pretty girl, with her brown hair and hazel eyes, and he guessed she was about nineteen years old. She seemed so willing, as if nothing was a chore.

"What time do you finish?" he enquired, as they made progress along the corridor.

"It's ten o'clock tonight."

"That is a long day."

"Yes, but it passes quickly when we are so busy."

By then they had reached another ward, and she wheeled him in to where Alan was in bed, resting against his pillows.

"I have brought someone to see you Alan," she said cheerfully. "I have to go to another ward, but I will pick you up on the way back in a few minutes."

"OK, and thanks very much," said Ross.

Alan looked at him in despair. "Well, I messed up our trip to rescue the girls good and proper, didn't I?"

176

"No, it wasn't your fault. The van drove into us."

"I know that. The driver admitted that his steering packed up. But that won't save the girls. Who knows what has happened now, and we are stuck here, useless!"

"Calm down, the police that came to question us about the accident were briefed by me, and they have gone, with backup, to the house."

"When was that?"

Ross tried to remember. His brain seemed to be a bit tired, but then he remembered the remark about taking torches.

"They went at six o'clock. The WPC knew the area, said they had torches as there were no street lamps."

"But she's had all day to do her worst," said Alan, not convinced.

Just at that moment they saw a senior nurse, flanked by two policemen. She was trying to stop them from coming in. Their voices could be heard, insisting it was of paramount importance.

She ushered them over to the bed, telling them they only had a few minutes. She looked stern and forbidding, prohibiting the bravest of men to argue with her. Alan was pleased to recognise Ted, a sergeant from the team.

"Sorry to see you in here sir, and you too, Green." He inclined his head to include them both. "You couldn't have crashed at a worse time. But never mind, the van driver has accepted the blame. His steering went."

"I know that," said Alan irritably. His thoughts were solely with Wendy and Zoe right now.

"We've just had news that Wendy was found bound and gagged, but otherwise unharmed in a remote garage."

"Oh great!"

They both sighed with relief, but then Alan cut in.

"But what about my Zoe. Was she there too?"

"According to Wendy she escaped. Zoe had been put in a dog crate. And this is the strange part Ross, she thinks you did it, and you went after Zoe. But obviously with you being first with guv, then in here, we know that isn't right."

Ross coloured up. "It's because Wendy discovered I had changed my name, so she assumed it was for a bad purpose. I am sure the person who imprisoned them both is my sister, and she is mentally ill."

"Yes," agreed Alan. "We can explain about the name change later, what matters is finding Zoe, because who knows what Marion will do to her?"

He felt positively sick inside. His beloved Zoe was being pursued by that mad woman. He had such fear and dread in his heart, and he made an effort to get out of his bed.

"Where are my clothes? I need to find her before it's too late!"

But then the senior nurse was there, her ample frame obliterating the two policemen who stood nervously back.

"Don't even think about getting out of bed!" she boomed, her expression forbidding any argument.

"Nurse, come here and make sure your patient realises just how dangerous it is to get out of bed when he has just suffered a bad accident only a few hours earlier!"

Alan felt hopeless. The two policemen were going now. He was marooned in this bed, surrounded by bossy women, and his heart was breaking because he had let Zoe down. Lisa's voice cut into his thoughts.

"Come on, Ross, I am taking you back. You two can catch up tomorrow."

He watched as she wheeled Ross away, feeling hopeless and helpless. It was night time now, so very dark out there. His car was a write-off, so he didn't even have any transport, and he didn't know where they had put his clothes. Commonsense had to prevail. No matter what they said, he was going tomorrow regardless of their tests and scans. Zoe came first, and he had to try and rescue her if it wasn't too late, and he couldn't bear the thought of that.

He obediently took the pills that the nurse gave him with some water, trusting that they would make him feel better. They did relax him, and soon he could feel weariness invading his eyelids, they felt so heavy, but it wouldn't be right to fall asleep when his beloved Zoe was out there somewhere in the dark being pursued. They needed to get their act together, the police force, and find Zoe!

But now the sleeping pill he had been given was doing its work. He tried to fight off the thick curtain of sleep that was wrapping itself around him. He had so much to do, but his weary body argued back. His mind was willing, but his body was not. His eyes closed, and he drifted off into a troubled sleep.

Chapter Twenty-two

Zoe kept running. Terror added speed to her legs, and then she heard the car engine start up. It was inky black everywhere, and she had no idea where she was. But when the car swung into action, she would be picked up in the headlights. She couldn't let that happen. She knew now she was fighting for her life, Ross was a madman.

She felt grass under her feet, and touched a stile. If she took this footpath, maybe the car couldn't reach her, it was her only hope. She tore her uniform as she clambered over the stile, but she didn't care about that. She could hear the car skidding over the rough ground. He was driving like a madman, and then the headlights were sweeping round as he tried to find her, but she ducked behind the bushes at the side and held her breath.

Her heart was beating so fast she was sure he must be able to hear it. She sat tight for what seemed an eternity, and then the sound of the car gradually faded away. She clambered up. There was no choice but to follow this path to wherever it led. Eventually, surely, she must come to a house or a road, and then she could ask for help.

Progress was slow, as she couldn't even see her hand in front of her face. The wind was howling, and then she felt raindrops on her. She kept going, battering against the elements, determined to survive. But then she caught her foot in something that she couldn't see, and fell heavily to the ground. Her ankle was giving her great pain as she struggled to stand up, and then failed. Tears of frustration poured down her face, she couldn't let this evil man

179

win, so she made a supreme effort to haul herself up. Once upon her feet, she ignored the pain that was shooting through her ankle, and made very slow progress onwards. So intent was she on escaping, that she was oblivious of the rain, which had soaked her hair and was invading her nursing uniform, making her shiver.

She had no idea how long that journey took. It was the will to live that spurred her on, until finally, in the distance, she could make out a farmhouse with bright lights ahead of her. She staggered towards it, trying to make out the door. It was a big heavy oak door, and it had a heavy metal knocker, so she knocked on it with the last bit of energy she could muster before crumpling up on the doorstep.

Norman Foster and his wife Betty heard the knock at the door. Living out in the country as they did, with the nearest house some five miles away, they were used to people knocking on their door. Sometimes it was cars that had broken down, or people who had lost their way, especially as there were no street lights, but because of their lonely situation, they were always careful to see who they let into their house. They were both in their sixties; almost time to retire. But with a couple of hired hands, Norman still ran the farm, and Betty spent a lot of her time baking and cooking amazing meals in the flagstoned 17th century kitchen.

"I'll check it out. You stay in the kitchen," said Norman.

When he peered through the window and saw the figure huddled on the doorstep, he immediately opened the door and called to Betty.

"Quickly, someone has collapsed on the doorstep!"

"I am coming. Make sure they are alone."

"It's a young woman. She is in nurses' uniform."

Norman picked Zoe up, and carried her in. She was a tiny slightly built girl. He saw that her uniform was torn and her hair was soaking wet. In fact, all her clothes were wet and sticking to her.

"Go and get me a big towel," said Betty.

Norman returned with a bath sheet, and then went to put the kettle on to fill a hot water bottle.

Betty wrapped the towel round the shivering body. This woman needed to get out of those wet clothes, but she was barely aware of what was going on. Her teeth were chattering, and Betty wondered whether they should ring for an ambulance. Norman returned with the hot water bottle, which she placed at the side of her, so she could feel it through the towel.

Eventually Zoe stopped shivering. Her eyes opened, and there was a glimmer of a smile.

"Thank you, I feel warmer now."

"What are you doing out here in the wet on a night like this?"

With a voice that was scarcely more than a whisper, Zoe explained about Ross, the crooked policeman. How he had captured herself and WPC Wendy Stuart, who had been tied up, while she had been put in a large dog's crate. She then went on to explain that she had escaped from the crate and run away from Ross.

Norman and Betty looked at each other. This was serious stuff, and they needed to let someone know that Zoe was safe. But it was late, past eleven o'clock, whatever should they do? Zoe's next words left them in no doubt.

"My parents need to know I am safe. They will come and get me. And my boyfriend Alan, he will be really worried."

They didn't possess a mobile phone or a computer. Norman and Betty were quite happy with their life the way it was, but they did obviously have a landline. Betty picked up the phone intending to ring Alan's mobile but, to her great consternation, the line was dead.

"Norman, the phone is out of order!" she said desperately.

"Well, that will be the storm," he reminded her.

Betty turned towards Zoe. She looked so vulnerable, sitting there with a towel wrapped round her. She realised with a sinking heart that there was nothing they could do right now to help her.

"I think you should get some sleep," suggested Betty. "You look really pale, and we can try the phone again in the morning. It might be working again after the storm subsides. I have a spare bed made up in case of visitors."

Zoe felt so weary, she didn't feel like protesting. They were being so kind to her, and the old farmhouse had a fire glowing in the grate, and was very welcoming. In the morning all would be well, but in the meantime she felt safe here. Ross couldn't harm her.

"Thank you so much. I am tired, and I need to sleep," she said.

After Betty had made sure she was comfortable, she discussed with Norman what they should do. There had been something on the local news earlier about someone called Wendy Stuart, a WPC, being missing, and then she remembered a bit about Zoe the nurse. It was a bizarre situation, but the poor girl was exhausted, she needed to sleep. So in the morning, when the police station was open, they would telephone and explain that she was safe with them.

It had not been a good day for Sarah. She prided herself on always being on time for work, so that when Alan arrived she was there for him, to share whatever was set before them to do that day. But circumstances had got in the way, and when she arrived the station was full of the news that both Wendy and Zoe were missing, and the police station was in chaos.

Sarah had always been good at calming people. This is why she was the family liaison officer. She was proud of the fact that Alan trusted her with distressed relatives. She had calmed Wendy's mother, and assured her they would find her soon, and then she had been asked to visit Zoe's parents. They were even more distressed, especially as news had now come through that Alan and Ross had crashed on the way to try and find the two girls.

She hadn't realised that Alan was going to look for the girls. She thought he was going home, and it hurt her to think he hadn't told her, and then to find out that Ross had gone with him. Now that was two people she had imagined would never get on. But all her anger soon dimmed when she got a call on her mobile from the station to say that there had been an accident, and both Alan and Ross were in hospital.

If only she had been able to visit him, and make sure he was OK. But she couldn't be sure that Ross wouldn't make trouble for her, and she didn't want that. She had also been told that Wendy had been found tied, bound and gagged at a disused garage, not far from where she lived, but Zoe had escaped. Apparently Wendy was convinced that Ross had been the man who had kidnapped her, although she hadn't seen him. But knowing that Ross had been with Alan, and was now in hospital, it seemed that everyone knew Wendy was mistaken. Ross had told the police who visited him that he believed his sister had been the kidnapper. Sarah found all this fascinating news, and she wondered where Zoe was now. So she had to go to bed that night knowing it had not been a good day, for her or for Alan. She felt sure tomorrow would be better. It must have been fate that had prevented Alan from finding Zoe, and as far as Sarah was concerned, Zoe being out of his life didn't bother her at all.

She had always hoped that one day he would realise that the woman he was meant to be with was sharing his working life. He had always said they had a good partnership. But that was only at work, and Sarah's dearest wish was that partnership would extend to their life as a couple, because she knew she would always love Alan, and no one else even came close!

When Norman and Betty woke up in the morning, they were hoping that they could make contact, and let people know that Zoe was with them and safe. They kept trying the local police station, but the lines were engaged.

"You do it next time!" said Norman, after failing to get through.

"I know. Do your remember that nice WPC, I think her name was Sarah, the tall one with the dark hair? She gave me her mobile telephone number when we joined the neighbourhood watch, just in case we ever needed her."

"I don't like mobile phones!" grumbled Norman. "Yes, I think I know who you mean."

"Don't worry dear," said Betty soothingly. "I will dial her. But I hope I don't have to leave a message, it always seems strange talking to a recording machine."

She dialled Sarah's number. Although some five miles away, she was their nearest neighbour, and Betty had always found her very helpful. It only rang twice before she answered:

"Sarah Stevens here."

"Good morning, Sarah. It's Betty from Hewitt's farm here. Do you remember me?"

"Of course. How are you Betty?" Sarah's voice came crisply over the line. She was wondering what Betty wanted.

"I am OK dear, but we have a predicament. A young lady called Zoe, a nurse, collapsed on our doorstep last night. She told us she had been kidnapped and held hostage by a PC called Ross. She was really frightened, and last night she was very cold, so we put her up. She is much better this morning, and now she wants to go home."

"Well done, Betty. I did hear about Zoe being kidnapped. It sounds like you and Norman have looked after her very well."

"We tried, but we can't seem to get through to the police station to tell them, and last night we couldn't get through to her parents. Our telephone line was down, but it is working now. Her family must be so worried."

Sarah spoke soothingly to her. "It's OK Betty. How about I contact the station and Zoe's parents, then they won't worry any more. I can easily pop round and run Zoe home, it's no problem."

"Oh, how wonderful. It's Norman, you see, he's a bit deaf now, and doesn't like using the phone."

"No worries," laughed Sarah. "I will be round shortly."

She smiled happily as she put her mobile into her pocket. Zoe was safe. Today had already started well. It was going to be a much better day than yesterday.

The doctor had seen Ross, and he had been pronounced fit to go home. He felt relieved, but what about Alan? They had said he would take longer to recover. He had ordered himself a taxi, which was now waiting, so he made his way to the ward Alan was in to check on him.

Alan was out of bed and sitting in a chair.

"I can go now. How are you feeling?" said Ross

"I am fine, but Zoe may not be. I can't wait for the doctor, I have to come with you now!"

Ross could tell by the urgency of his voice, that Alan meant business. Zoe was clearly very dear to him, and it was only natural that he wanted to go and look for her.

Just then Alan's mobile rang. It was the duty sergeant. "Good morning sir, how are you and PC Green today."

"Yes, we are both good," he said a little impatiently. "What has happened?"

"Quite a lot actually. The officers who went to find Wendy last night succeeded. She was found bound to a chair and gagged in a disused garage. She was unharmed, but has this idea in her head that Green was her captor. Of course, we know she is confused, as he has been in hospital with you all this time."

"We were told all that last night, and we know that Zoe escaped. Hasn't she been found yet?"

184

"Zoe ran off into the night. We have no idea where she went, but we hope she is safe."

Alan exploded with anger. "Not good enough! The whole world should be out there looking for her. She is very precious to me. Tell everyone to make it a priority!"

"Yes sir. Are you leaving hospital today?"

"Yes, right now!" he said.

Ross looked at him doubtfully. Alan hadn't seen the doctor yet. And he was short tempered, which was unlike Alan. He was usually a very calm man.

Alan snapped his mobile shut, and Ross could see determination written all over his face.

"Get my clothes out the locker. I am getting dressed and coming with you."

"Are you sure?"

"I have never been surer!"

Ross glanced guiltily around him while Alan feverishly dressed himself. Nothing was going to stop him, Ross knew that, and he was worried that someone might come in. But everyone seemed busy, luckily for Alan, and so they managed to slip out unheeded to the waiting taxi.

Alan reiterated about Wendy being found in the disused garage. "God knows where it is, any ideas?"

"Yes, it's near to my sister's house. I haven't been to her house or the garage, but the postcode is very close."

"Where do you want me to take you?" asked the taxi driver.

"Here is the postcode of the house. Take us there please?"

The man nodded his thanks, and the taxi moved away. Alan was so worried. He was feeling quite nauseous at the thought of Zoe still being missing. Was she still alive? He had no idea, but they had to check out the area.

Ross drew a trembling breath. He had to tell Alan something that would devastate him, this was finally his opportunity, and he needed to get it over and done with.

"Sir, my sister Marion, she changed her name to Sarah Stevens. She is your working partner."

Alan opened his mouth to say something. This was mind blowing news. It couldn't be true! Not Sarah, his partner. He trusted her with his life. She wasn't mad, she was a calm caring woman, it couldn't be right! But even as his mind was refusing to

185

accept this revelation, he remembered that at times when he had come to pick Sarah up, this had been the route. He had only ever sat outside her house waiting for her, but he recognised the road. The house looked empty, and Ross insisted he stayed in the car whilst he checked it out. For once in his life Alan did as he was told. The shock of this news had drained him completely, but he had his phone ready in case Ross did not come out.

However, after a few minutes Ross reappeared, confirming that the house was empty, although it looked as if his sister had slept there last night.

"The garage is about a mile that way I think," he told the taxi driver, who by now had realised they were looking for someone.

"Why would Sarah want to murder Eleanor, and capture Wendy and Zoe, I don't understand any of this?" said Alan brokenly. He felt nothing made sense any more.

"Sir, I know it's a huge shock for you, but my sister seems to have inherited our mother's madness. I have never spoken to her since I saw her working with you. We have never admitted our blood ties to each other, but she looks so like my mother, with her tall frame, her hair and eyes, and like you I was fooled at the start. She was such a good WPC. She cared about people, she worked with grieving families, and she always seemed so calm. I thought maybe she might have had treatment for her problems, and I saw her as a different person. Neither of us wanted to acknowledge our past. However, just before Eleanor's murder, I heard Sarah on her mobile, arranging to go and see Eleanor. Eleanor had reported having a ring stolen from her dressing room at the theatre, and Sarah said she would come to her apartment on her way to work in the morning, as she had to pass that way."

"My God!"

"Yes, and it was that morning that Eleanor died. Sarah came in later. I noted that she had said she was at the dentist, and you both went out to the murder scene towards midday. She even had time to remove the bronze horse and plant it at Peter Grant's flat, because she went back with the warrant to search it the day after I brought him in. I did a really bad thing by pushing the blame onto Grant and arresting him. I was trying to stop our past from coming out, and also, we were siblings, even though we didn't get on, I felt a sort of loyalty, but not any more!" he said fiercely.

"But why did she kill Eleanor?"

186

"My sister hates women, and she sees them all as a threat. Eleanor was too perfect. She was everything that Sarah wanted to be, and, most of all, she was so loved. I don't think Sarah has ever felt loved, and so she wanted to get rid of the person who made her feel even more unworthy."

"And Wendy and Zoe?"

"I am only guessing, but Wendy didn't like me after I arrested Grant, and our partnership became very awkward. I believe she came to my house and discovered my original passport with my true name on. In fact, she left a strong aroma of perfume behind, which she was wearing when she came into work the next day. She then put two and two together, and got eight, which is why she thinks I kidnapped her. She may well have voiced her concerns to Sarah. This is all supposition, but it would give Sarah a reason to silence her."

"But what about my Zoe?"

"Well, Alan, I can see it in Sarah's eyes when she is with you. She is obsessed with you, and obviously you haven't realised. She wants you, and Zoe stands between you and her. In her crazy head she imagines if nothing stands in her way she will get you."

Alan was trying to digest all this information. The shock of finding out that Sarah wasn't the person he had thought she was, but an insane murderer, was difficult to accept. But more important than ever was the knowledge that every second counted. As Zoe had escaped, she might still be alive, or had Sarah got her somewhere?

They had arrived at the garage, so they both jumped out of the taxi and went to look around. The garage was empty. Alan spotted the large dog crate, and he felt sick to think his beloved Zoe had been put in there like some wild animal. When they came out, the taxi driver was still waiting. Alan didn't care how much it was going to cost, he had to find her.

As they walked away from the garage, Alan noticed a field with a stile and a footpath, and then he spotted a piece of Zoe's uniform. It was hanging from the stile, flapping in the breeze. His heart almost stood still. Were they going to find her body in the field? He had a great fear coursing through his inside, but an overwhelming need to find out.

Chapter Twenty-three

Sarah was feeling exultant. She finally had Zoe in her power. She could rid herself of the one person that stood between herself and Alan. Of course, he would grieve for Zoe, but she, Sarah, would be there to pick up the pieces for him to lean on, then he would finally realise how much he needed her. They made such a good team. They worked together, and they could have a wonderful life together. She would finally get the love she had craved for all of her life.

She had thought about Ross very carefully. He wouldn't have the guts to tell Alan about her, because it would destroy his own life and reputation as well. He had an alibi. He couldn't have kidnapped either of them, so they wouldn't know who had done it. If he did accuse her of being his sister, she would deny it. Alan would never believe something as outrageous as that. She had built herself a good reputation since working with Alan. She was known for being efficient, caring and calm, just what every family in a crisis needed. When she was at work, she didn't hear the voices. Being with Alan was good for her, but at home alone, they plagued her, and she had never forgotten how much her own mother hated her and her little brother. Even though she had shown Ross a glimmer of love sometimes, she had still set fire to the house with them inside, wanting to kill them.

Those voices dominated her when she felt the depression sweeping over her. It was easy to adopt a different persona at work, because she really felt that people did like her there. She was aware that she had a forceful personality, but Alan understood her, and he didn't mind. As a woman, she had incredible strength. Even though she was tall and slim, she had the strength of a man. She had played a lot of sport at school, and always kept herself fit, so capturing the two girls had been so easy for her. She was proud of her strength. It was going to be that strength she used to kill Zoe. Poor unsuspecting Zoe. My, this was going to be fun!

She had phoned in to say she was sick today, with a bad stomach bug. The duty sergeant had said he hoped she would be better soon. She wanted to enquire about Alan, but then decided to ring his mobile. Let him tell her how he was. So she rang him before she went to pick up Zoe from Norman and Betty's farmhouse. She dialled his number whilst she was sitting in the car, and her heart lifted when she heard his voice.

"Good morning, sir. I heard about your accident. How are you now?"

"Oh, I don't feel at all great. But never mind me, Zoe must be found. There's a dangerous woman on the loose!"

Sarah could hardly contain her mirth, and she had to restrain herself from laughing.

"A dangerous woman, what do you mean?"

Alan explained how helpless he felt. He was sitting in a chair by his bed, waiting for a doctor to sign him off, and Ross had told him that he believed his mad sister had kidnapped Zoe.

So Ross had told him. But still she found it funny, and believed she could slide out of this by denying they were related. Nobody could force her to have any DNA tests.

"So Ross has a mad sister. Let's hope they are not in league together."

"No, actually he's a good bloke, now I have got to know him, but he's had a rough life."

That remark really angered Sarah. So her cowardly brother was going around making people feel sorry for him! She had also had a rough life, but it had toughened her up. She kept her voice calm. It was good Alan wasn't coming out of hospital yet, so she could rid the world of that creature, and dispose of her body. Alan might even think she had left him; that would be even better.

"Look after yourself. I am at home with a stomach bug today. Hope to see you soon."

As she got herself ready to go and collect Zoe, Sarah could feel her excitement growing. But she knew she had to curb it. She must lull them all into a false sense of security, then once she had got Zoe away from the farmhouse she could put her plan into action. There would be nothing more satisfying than ridding the world, and Alan, of practically perfect Zoe!

Her car was more willing to start today. But she couldn't blame her failure to track down Zoe last night on the car. She had driven around the area, cruising down lots of unmade roads, but now she realised how Zoe had fooled her. She hadn't gone along any road, she had cut across the fields and that is why she had ended up at the farmhouse. Going by car was a longer way round, but even across the fields, it was about five miles.

The journey was soon over, and as she approached the front door, it opened to show Betty standing there, anxiously flanked by Norman, who was muttering something about his dislike of phones.

"Good morning, Sarah. Zoe is eating some porridge. She seems much better today, but maybe a doctor should check her over when she gets home."

"No need to worry, Betty. You and Norman did an excellent job, and now I am here to make sure Zoe gets home safely."

As Sarah entered the farmhouse kitchen, Zoe was seated at the pine table. She was eating a bowl of porridge, and there was a glass of orange juice half drunk. Sarah exalted when she saw Zoe's look of relief. Well, it was just like Goldilocks and the three bears, and it wouldn't be long before that look of relief would turn to terror. She felt a thrill inside at the thought of it. Those voices kept reminding her that she had a job to do, and she could never ignore them. They would plague her until she had done their bidding.

"Hi Zoe. How are you today? You've been through quite a lot of trauma I hear."

Zoe tried to hide her disappointment that Alan wasn't with Sarah. He must surely be worried about her disappearance. And what about Ross? Wendy had said it was him, so had they captured him? There was so much she didn't understand.

"I am feeling much better today, but I did think Alan would come with you. I lost my phone when I was kidnapped, so I haven't been able to contact him, or my parents. . ." her voice trailed off. Suddenly she felt really tired and depressed. None of

190

the people she loved were here, only Sarah, and she could tell by her body language, that Sarah was acting a part. She didn't really care that much about her.

"Brighten up," said Sarah cheerfully, mainly for Betty's benefit. "We are off to meet Alan now. He's on a really important case, but he's driving out to meet us."

"Course he is," said Betty soothingly. "He wants to know that you are safe."

Zoe felt a bit more heartened by that. She had missed Alan, and couldn't wait to tell him about her ordeal. She thanked Betty and Norman for their hospitality. Betty had washed her uniform and lent her one of her own skirts, but it hung on Zoe's tiny frame, and the sleeves of the blouse were as loose as the rest of it. She couldn't wait to get home and change into something of her own.

Sarah reiterated her thanks to Betty and Norman, and as they left to get in the car, Betty watched them, then turned and remarked to Norman:

"Well, she's safe now. That Sarah is such a caring policewoman, she'll make sure Zoe's all right."

Zoe sat in silence. She couldn't wait to see Alan, and to feel his arms around her. He would keep her safe. But she was aware that Sarah liked him too, so she didn't make any comment. The car continued its progress along leafy lanes, and she guessed they were the other side of the river in a suburban area. They had left Chelsea behind them. This was not an area that she knew at all.

"Where are we meeting him?" she asked curiously.

Sarah smirked to herself. It didn't matter if she told her, as she wouldn't live to share it with anyone else. She had remembered the disused country church with the river winding nearby; a perfect place to put the body, and then when she was found they would think it was either suicide or an accident. Then the voices reminded her that Wendy would tell the police that Zoe had been captured too, and they would all realise that it couldn't be Ross because he had been in hospital that day. Ross would blame his sister, but she didn't care. Her eyes flashed with fury. She had outwitted everyone for so long now. She was all powerful, she could make anyone believe anything, she was invincible!

"We are in the suburbs near to Tooting, a few miles away from London."

Zoe glanced at her in surprise. She hadn't realised that Alan would be meeting them this side of the River Thames. As a nurse she was used to dealing with patients with all sorts of problems, and there was something about Sarah that disturbed her. There was a look in Sarah's eyes that unnerved her, and she started to feel uncomfortable.

Sarah spotted the old church in the distance. It had not been used for many years, but it still stood proud against the skyline, with the bell tower above. The graveyard had many inhabitants from centuries past and, in her opinion, this was just the right setting to do the deed. She drove onto the rough area outside the church. The grounds overlooked fields. It was a very pretty country setting and, as always, there was no one about.

Sarah jumped eagerly out of the car, and Zoe followed, presuming Alan was inside the deserted church, but it was certainly a strange place to meet up. Sarah was marching past the graves to the back of the grounds which led to the riverbank, but Zoe pushed at the solid oak door of the church, which creaked open.

"This way. He will be on the riverbank," called Sarah impatiently. She hadn't expected Zoe to head for the door. But Zoe was now curious to see inside the church. There was a musty smell, and it was very dusty and neglected inside, slowly falling into disrepair. But nothing could dim the splendour of the stained glass windows. Zoe stood studying them, feeling the atmosphere of the place. It was centuries old, and she thought it a shame that it was no longer used. She turned to see Sarah standing in the doorway.

"He's not coming in here!"

Sarah was angry, she had planned to hit her with a piece of rock, there were plenty of pieces by the river, and then dump the body there. Instead of that, she was hanging about in here, this dusty old ruin, which made it all harder. Zoe was only tiny, she was taller and stronger, maybe she could overpower Zoe, then with her hands round her throat, she could strangle her. But she would have to take the body across the churchyard, out to the field at the back to dump it in the river. Of course, she was strong enough, but there was always the risk that someone might drive by and see.

Zoe was hoping that Alan would come soon. There was something about Sarah. Her body language seemed aggressive, her tone was angry, and there was a strange look in her eyes. She shivered.

"Can you text Alan and see where he is?" she suggested.

Sarah could sense her fear, and that made her feel all powerful. She thought about Alan in his hospital ward, and this silly bimbo had no idea. She gave a cackle of laughter.

Zoe stiffened. That laugh, she had heard it before, and fear coursed through her when she remembered where. It was yesterday, when she was in the dog crate. It suddenly hit her. Could Sarah be the person who had been there? And maybe she was working with Ross.

Sarah saw her look of fear. She was rumbled, but she didn't care. Zoe wouldn't live to tell the tale.

"You have finally got it. It's me. I murdered Eleanor, she was just too perfect to live!"

"She wasn't perfect. She was human, just like us all, with good and bad things about her. Nobody's perfect!"

Zoe's response threw Sarah. She was supposed to be scared of her, but feisty Zoe did not appear to be. She was too busy defending Eleanor.

Sarah shouted menacingly, her eyes alight with passion:

"It's your turn now, Zoe. Alan and I are good together. We make a great team, but you are standing in the way, so you have to be removed!"

At that moment, Zoe finally realised that Sarah was completely mad. Fear gripped her, knowing that her life was now in danger. This woman was a murderer, and she was next on the list! Physically Sarah was taller and stronger than Zoe, but being wiry was an advantage, and she was certainly going to fight for her life, she wasn't just going to lie down and accept death!

She tried to remember some of the training that had helped her at work. Maybe talking might help, keeping her calm. Surely someone would come and rescue her soon.

As Sarah moved towards her, Zoe knew she would have to give the performance of her life, and show no signs of fear. It was a tough call, but otherwise this mad woman, whose eyes were positively glittering with hate, would attack and kill her. She was glad Sarah couldn't see her hammering heart, and she cleared her throat and spoke in a low voice that she tried to make sound as soothing as possible.

193

j

"Sarah, you honestly don't have to kill me. No man is worth that, not even Alan!"

Sarah stopped dead in her tracks, as she was about to spring like a panther and attack. Now what did she mean by that? Alan was worth the moon, the stars, everything! She glared at Zoe. What was so disconcerting was instead of showing fear or rage, Zoe seemed calm and in control. She had been for counselling to a woman who was calm like this after she had attacked that woman, and for a while it had helped, until the voices came back. She had expected the voices to be egging her on right now, but they were silent.

"You are with Alan, aren't you?" Confusion was written all over Sarah's face.

"Well, he's not here is he? And he wasn't coming either. And he didn't come and look for me when I was kidnapped."

Zoe's heart jolted with pain for having to say that, because she was sure there was some sort of explanation, and if she ever saw him again, she would be told.

Sarah realised that Zoe, because of being locked up, didn't know that Alan had had an accident on the way to try and find her. It sounded like she thought he had failed her, and that is just what Sarah wanted. It flashed through her mind, that if Zoe didn't want him, he might turn to her for comfort.

"You still have to die. I told you I killed Eleanor."

Zoe knew she had distracted her a little, so she carried on. "I am planning to go away from here Sarah, so I wouldn't be around to tell anyone about that. I will pretend that I never heard it, as I always believed it was Ross anyway, and maybe you are saying that to impress me."

Now Sarah didn't know what to do. The thought of nothing changing was tempting. To be able to go on working with Alan, to turn her back on those voices, and to be the person he wanted and needed was overwhelming. But how did she know she could trust Zoe. Her experience of women always led back to her mother, who should have kept both of her children safe, but didn't.

Whilst her mind was whirling she heard footsteps on the pathway outside, and the door was pushed open, creaking and squeaking. Into the church came Ross and Alan.

Chapter Twenty-four

Having seen the material hanging from the stile, Alan's first instinct was to run into the field and follow the footpath, but the taxi driver was sitting waiting patiently in his cab. Ross had the presence of mind to ask him where the footpath led, so he got out his map and they studied it together. It was clear that the path led to Hewitt's Farmhouse, some five miles away, so now it was time to call for backup so the fields could be combed by police and dogs.

Ross called Alan over and explained exactly where they were.

"How about you call for backup? And in the meantime, our driver will take us to the farm to check if Zoe is there."

Alan was so grateful for Ross's commonsense. Normally the calmest of police officers, because it was Zoe they were searching for, his emotions were all over the place. He was praying inside that they could find her before it was too late. He had sent Sarah several text messages asking her where she was, but had not received a reply. He wasn't going to risk telling her that he knew she was Marion. Zoe would have no idea that Sarah was dangerous. Thank God she had escaped, he just hoped that Sarah had not caught up with her. He remembered her phone call earlier. She wasn't off work with a stomach bug, she was hunting for Zoe!

The taxi driver took them over to Hewitt's Farm, then Alan paid him off. He was grateful for Ross's support and strength at this time. There was no trace of his former arrogance, just a humane and caring young man. Alan called for backup, so the taxi left, and they walked up to the front door with the heavy metal knocker.

It didn't take Betty long to open the door, and she looked at them, wondering what was wrong.

"Hello, we are police officers, checking if you have seen this young lady." Alan flourished his warrant at her, and then showed Betty a picture of Zoe on his phone.

"Oh yes, Zoe. She collapsed on our doorstep last night in the storm, so we took her in, warmed her up, and then she stayed the night. This morning our neighbour Sarah came and picked her up to take her home. I am surprised that you didn't know."

Alan swallowed hard, this was the one thing that he had dreaded.

"Did she say she was taking her home, and how long ago?"

"Yes, and she was going to contact you and her parents to stop you worrying. Probably about half an hour gone."

They didn't have time to explain it all to Betty, and luckily backup had arrived, so they thanked her, and sent an officer in to take all the details.

"We have to go in the patrol car, and check everywhere!" said Alan desperately.

Ross jumped into the car with Alan. Someone else was in the driving seat, so Ross suggested they drive back towards the country area, guessing that if Sarah did have bad intentions, she would stay away from main roads and civilisation.

As the car progressed along the country lanes, they both kept their eyes trained in all directions, in case they saw something. It was Alan that spotted the country church in the middle of nowhere, and the black car parked outside, which he recognised immediately as belonging to Sarah.

"Quick, over there. You need to pull over. And after we go in, get everyone here!"

Ross jumped out quickly. Voices could be heard from inside, and his heart lifted, Zoe might still be alive. They nodded at each other, and crept silently down the path. When they pushed the door, it reluctantly creaked open. Sarah had her back to them, but she turned at the noise, eyes blazing with fury. Zoe was facing them, but in one swift movement, Sarah grabbed her from behind and twisted her arm.

"So you conned me, you bitch. You didn't lose your phone!"

Zoe gasped with pain. She couldn't move, and once again Sarah's voice rang out.

"Don't either of you try any heroics, or I will strangle her!"

Alan's heart was pounding with anxiety for the predicament, and relief that Zoe was alive. His natural instinct was to run forward and rescue Zoe, but judging by the look in Sarah's eyes, it was not an option.

"Let me try?" whispered Ross. He blamed himself for not making the effort to reunite with his sister. Regardless of what had gone on when they were young, he should have admitted to her verbally about the connection. Her life had been more troubled than his. He should have got her the help she needed. It was not her fault if she had inherited their mother's madness, but it was his fault that she had not had any medical help. She had already killed Eleanor, nothing could undo that, but he had to stop her from doing the same to Zoe.

He adopted a soft soothing tone to his voice. Staying calm was the most important thing in this sort of situation.

"Please listen to me, sis. I am so sorry that I didn't reunite with you when I first saw you working with Alan. I knew it was you, but, because of my own cowardly nature, I couldn't bear to revisit the past."

Sarah had been expecting anger and recriminations, and was totally taken aback by Ross's gentle tone. She tightened her grip on Zoe. She wasn't going to be fooled by this, she couldn't afford to show any weakness.

"Don't try and pretend you care!" she said bitterly.

"But I do, we all do, and if you let Zoe free, then maybe we can get you the help you need. Did Eleanor provoke you into killing her?"

Sarah laughed that cackling laugh again, and Zoe flinched, as it echoed through her ears. She saw the agony on Alan's face. He was near and yet so far from her, but Sarah was so unpredictable.

"Only by being herself. She made such a fuss about a stolen ring. As if it mattered, all the money she had!"

"But that is no reason to kill anyone!" said Alan.

"She acted so perfect, but she wasn't. Everyone loved her!"

"None of us are perfect. We are all human beings with faults and failings," said Ross, taking a step towards her. "Take you, Sarah, you have worked with Alan, and helped so many families in the last few years, and at work many people have a great respect for you, but you also have this other side to your character. With the right help, the nice Sarah will defeat the other Sarah that is Marion."

"But the voices won't let me rest. They are telling me what to do."

She gave a sob, and Ross took another step towards her. She momentarily loosened her grip on Zoe, who flung herself forward into Ross's arms.

Alan moved forward and put his arms around Zoe's trembling body, all else forgotten, and at that moment Sarah realised she had nothing left to bargain with. She ran to the back of the church where the rickety stairs led up to the bell tower, and Ross ran after her, imploring her to stop.

"It's OK baby, you are safe now," said Alan, wrapping Zoe tightly in his arms, and several more police officers ran into the church to help. Zoe and Alan were both crying with relief, and it was at that moment Alan knew, without any doubt at all, he had to marry her. Because after nearly losing her, she had become even more precious to him and he wanted to spend the rest of his life with her.

The backup officers followed after Ross, only to find Sarah poised on the parapet at the top of the building. Her eyes were shining with an unnatural look, and Ross shivered when he remembered that self-same look in his mother's eyes.

He tried to talk her down, but Sarah had now gone, and Marion stood up there, declaring her unrequited love for Alan, and her hatred for all women, because they had all let her down. She declared there was a better life than a lifetime in prison, and her friends were reaching out their hands to receive her. She blew him a kiss, then gave that eerie laugh again, and suddenly she spread out her arms, as if to embrace someone, then she jumped off. There was a pregnant pause, and a sickening thud as she hit the ground, and they all knew that she had come to a sad end.

Ross was the first person out there, and when he saw her crumpled body on the ground, he wept. But as he looked at her face, there was a look of peace, the wildness had gone from her eyes, and he tried to comfort himself with the thought, that in death, she had found the peace that she hadn't ever managed to find in life.

Chapter Twenty-five

Six months later
After declaring their intentions towards one another on that day which would be impossible for either of them to forget, Alan and Zoe made a mutual decision to wait a few months before they got married.

Eleanor would always remain in the hearts of her fans. Her memory would continue to inspire young women to follow in her footsteps, as talent will always shine through. It had been a huge loss for the nation to lose such a talented icon at that age, but she had left a legacy of films and appearances on recordings, so her fans could remember her exactly as she was at the height of her career.

The sad death of Sarah affected everyone at work. Because she had been liked, and was popular, nobody there had ever guessed there was a troubled side to her. The case was now closed with her admission that she killed Eleanor. Even though his heart grieved at what he had done, Ross had had the presence of mind to record her words on his phone. As much as he hated it, he had exposed her as the killer, but it felt the right thing to do. He was glad that she hadn't known, as she would have felt deserted by everyone, and especially by him.

He would always have a conscience about her. She had been his only relative left, and he had really hoped he could get her some help for her mental condition. However, she had taken matters into her own hands, and jumped.

After all the drama had died away, and Sarah had been laid to rest, he went back to work. Wendy had realised she had misjudged him, and was sorry. She was impressed at just how much he had supported Alan. It had earned him new respect, and when they worked together now, it was much more harmonious, and he had dropped his arrogant manner. She actually found she quite liked him now, and looked forward to working with him as his partner. But then she found out he was being promoted, and she felt disappointed.

Alan had totally changed his opinion of Ross, too. He had given him such loyalty and support when his feelings for Zoe had impacted on his ability to deal with the case, and he realised that thanks to Ross, and his gentle persuasion towards his sister, he had caught her off-guard, and Zoe had been able to break free. In view of all this, Alan had put in a recommendation that Ross be promoted, because he had done an admirable job. When the news came through that Ross would be promoted, Alan went into his office to tell him and Wendy the good news.

"Congratulations Ross. In recognition of what you did that day, you are being promoted!"

Ross looked up, his face breaking into a wide grin. It was great news.

"Thanks boss. I know it was due to you."

"Oh, I wouldn't say that, but now you have to choose a partner from the WPCs."

Wendy tried not to look downcast, but to be happy for him. It was Ross's day today.

"Oh, that's easy. We work well together, don't we Wendy?" he said smiling, and was rewarded by the look of happiness on her face.

"Yes we do!" she said.

"That's good," said Alan. "I am going home early tonight. I'm getting married tomorrow, and I hope you guys are coming."

"Of course," they both said in unison, as he closed the door.

Alan jumped into his car smiling. What a lucky man he was. Tomorrow he would be married to the girl of his dreams.